GUARDED DESIRES

HEART OF FAME, BOOK THREE

LEXXIE COUPER

guarded *desires*

LEXXIE COUPER

DEDICATION

For Sami Lee. For believing in Chris's story and helping me find it.

For Jambrea Jo Jones. For holding my hand and showing me the path.

For Susan McGrath Romito. For pointing out the stepping stones and walking with me to the end.

GUARDED DESIRES

CHAPTER ONE

Chris Huntley's reaction to the tall man in the dark sunglasses scared the shit out of him.

Standing on the balcony of the harbour-side mansion the studio had rented for this trip, Chris watched the imposing Australian stride along the mansion's private jetty away from the yacht that had delivered him. Faded blue-denim jeans barely contained thighs that were long and muscular. A broad, sculpted chest and powerful shoulders strained against a snug white T-shirt, as did biceps that spoke of impressive strength.

Aslin had said the guy was built, but damn, he hadn't mentioned *like a goddamn wrestler*.

Liev Reynolds moved with the confidence and potency of a man threatened by nothing. Chris knew the attitude well. Aslin Rhodes, his brother-in-law, moved the same way. A menacing calm that said loud and clear you would get hurt and hurt badly if you tried to mess with him. Chris had always assumed it came from being an ex-soldier, but as he watched the Australian approach the mansion, he knew it had nothing to do with military training. For starters, Liev Reynolds had no military background at all.

Chris gripped the stainless-steel balcony railing harder.

His entire life, he'd cast himself in the role of sexy, funny ladies' man. His reputation—hell, his career—was built around that role. The guy that made women laugh with his sharp wit even as he made them want to strip off their clothes and beg him to have sex with them. Just about every time he left the comfort of his home in Beverly Hills and went out in public without Aslin and his sister, more than one woman would do that very thing.

He'd made millions of dollars thanks to his sex appeal. The studio that produced his sitcom milked his sex appeal for every advertising penny. The studio of his first action film had capitalized on it in their pre- and post-release marketing. The critics of the film had noted it. The preproduction media buzz of his next film, a comedy horror, was already talking about.

He was, for want of a better word, a mega sex symbol. Up there with the best of them, with the sexiest men alive. Linked to almost every delectable woman the gossip mags and celebrity sites could name. If there was a single, sensual, eligible actress out there, Chris had apparently slept with her.

He didn't fight the reputation. In fact, he welcomed it. True, he didn't have a girlfriend. Nor even a steady fuck-buddy, but when it came to the media important facts didn't matter.

Chris could live with that. He'd learned to live with it. It was part of his life now. He was a sex symbol, women wanted to sleep with him and he slept with women. That was the way it was.

Which explained why he was petrified watching the Australian bodyguard his brother-in-law had arranged to protect him while back in Oz draw closer. Because he'd never ever had his dick harden at the sight of a man. Harden, for fuck's sake.

His gut churned. A vise-like invisible band wrapped his chest. His breath grew shallow. Rapid.

With every step Reynolds took closer to the mansion, an unmistakable tension stirred in Chris's cock.

The kind Chris only experienced in the presence of a beautiful woman.

What the fuck?

Since when was he attracted to men?

Since never, that's when.

He stared hard at the Australian, his heart beat a rapid triphammer. It had to be something else. Something *not* Liev Reynolds.

Chris searched his brain, trying to remember what he'd been thinking about before the privately chartered motor yacht had delivered Reynolds to the mansion.

Bethany. Asleep on your shoulder. Her hair tickling your face.

Chris snapped straight, clicking his fingers. "That was it," he muttered. He'd been thinking about the flight over and how his new personal assistant had fallen asleep on his shoulder. The first non-professional thing the young woman had done since his sister and Aslin employed her six months ago.

He'd been thinking how nice her hair had smelt, like coconut and some exotic flower. He'd been thinking about the warmth of her cheek seeping through the cotton of his shirt. He'd been thinking how disapproving his sister would be. How Rowan had been adamant his new P.A. stay as emotionally detached from him as possible.

He'd been thinking about how much fun he was going to have telling Rowie about the flight.

That had to be it. He was thinking about an attractive young woman now in his employ and his cock had taken the messages from his jet-lagged, sleep-deprived brain and mixed them up into something else. And those messages just happen to reach his cock when his gaze fell on Liev Reynolds climbing from the motor yacht.

Simple.

He chuckled out a shaky breath. Simple. Sort of. He didn't think he was sexually attracted to his new P.A. Fuck, that would complicate things a tad, but he *was* sure as shit that was less complicated than being sexually attracted to the Australian bodyguard currently striding along the jetty. Being sexually attracted to a man would complicate the shit out of things. And confuse the shit out of Chris as well.

But he wasn't. So there was nothing to worry about.

He gripped the balcony's railing and dropped his stare to the man in question.

And bit back a groan as a thick spasm claimed his cock.

Chris's mouth went dry. Jesus, what the hell was going on?

Think of Bethany. Think of Bethany.

Closing his eyes, he turned his thoughts to his P.A.

His cock didn't spasm.

He opened his eyes and looked down at the Australian drawing even closer to the mansion.

His groin throbbed. His balls grew heavy.

Chris stepped back from the railing. He ground his teeth. Bunched his fists. Fuck.

Looking down at his crotch, he choked back another groan.

In a few minutes time, he was meant to be discussing with Liev Reynolds the expectations of being his bodyguard during the *Dead Even* press junket in Australia. How the *hell* was he to do that with the goddamn obvious makings of a goddamn erection?

Exhaling a slow breath through his nostrils, he slumped against the railing and watched Reynolds disappear from his line of sight beneath the balcony's overhang.

Fuck. Maybe he should reschedule the meeting? Maybe he should have a shower and fix the unsettling erection with his hand? Maybe he should ask Bethany to join him, just to be sure that's what the stupid erection was all about in the first place?

Maybe he should—

The soft chime of the mansion's doorbell ended the

unnerving question. He jerked around, his heart slamming fast into his throat.

A petite young woman with wild strawberry-blonde ringlets tumbling about her freckle-dusted face looked up from where she sat on a leather sofa situated in the middle of the living area. "I think Mr. Reynolds is here, Mr. Huntley. Shall I let him in?"

Chris drew in a slow breath, forcing his heart rate to slow as he counted to ten. It was a meditation technique Aslin had encouraged him to use during the filming of *Dead Even*, the action blockbuster on which he'd met his brother-in-law, the very film he was back in Australia to promote with a press junket and red-carpet screening. He hadn't needed to meditate since filming ended. His sitcom was on hiatus while he was in Australia and life was pretty damn stress free at the moment.

"Mr. Huntley?"

Chris flinched at Bethany's voice. She was only six months into the job and already better at it than his last personal assistant. She was proficient, friendly but detached and utterly professional. And so far it didn't seem like she was planning to kill everyone important to him like the last nut job that had been his P.A.

He smiled at the young woman, letting the tension melt from his shoulders. "Sorry, Bethany. I was wool gathering. Let him in please."

Bethany Sloan smiled back and nodded, rising to her feet as she did so. "As you wish, sir."

She placed the iPad on which she'd been busy arranging his schedule for the next seven days onto the coffee table in front of the sofa. Straightening the simple linen pantsuit she wore with an efficient brush of her palms, she walked from the room.

Chris watched her go. Efficient, affable and professional. Not ditzy or quirky or a closet psycho. Selected by his sister and Aslin for those specific attributes, along with the fact her security background check was spotless.

When it came to looking out for Chris's wellbeing, his sister was thorough.

Letting out a sigh, he turned back to the stunning view of the harbour and gripped the stainless steel rail.

It made sense the arriving Australian bodyguard wasn't responsible for his unexpected arousal. He *was* jet-lagged. He'd only arrived in the country three hours ago, and the flight attendant in the first-class section on the flight over had flirted with him the whole fourteen hours, even while Bethany slept on his shoulder, enamored enough with Chris to suggest—in a not-so subtle way—a threesome. Perhaps his arousal was a delayed reaction to that? He'd never had sex with two women at once. Maybe after Reynolds left he'd ask Bethany to locate the flight attendant, invite her to the mansion and suggest she bring a friend.

A wry snort sounded in the back of his throat at the thought of asking Bethany to do such a thing. His off-handed suggestion they both have a glass of wine when first arriving at their new home for the next seven days had been met with a frown and disapproval.

Come to think of it, the *more* he thought about Bethany the more he realised his hard-on—now currently deflating, thank fucking God—had to be a sleep-deprived reaction to her untamed hair, her freckles, her super efficiency and her complete and utter lack of adoration toward him.

Yeah, that had to be it. He was used to women of all ages throwing themselves at him, flirting with him. It stood to reason he'd be turned on by one that didn't, right? He'd also found a challenge appealing, hence his move from award-winning sitcom star to action-film movie star. His agent hadn't approved of the move, nor had his manager. The only one that had thought that particular challenge a good idea was his sister, and Rowan was currently on the other side of the world about to give birth, Aslin no doubt hovering over her like the proud, protective British mountain of muscle soon-to-be father he was.

If only Rowan and Aslin knew what they'd done by employing Bethany. Chris's stupefying physical reaction to the sight of Liev Reynolds striding along the jetty had nothing to do with the man and everything to do with the young woman's complete lack of interest in—

"Mr. Huntley?" Bethany's clipped voice with its New York accent sounded behind him, and he started. "Mr. Reynolds is ready for you."

For some stupid reason, Chris's heart smashed up into his throat again.

With one final look at the sweeping harbour view before him, he sucked in a deep breath and turned to face his P.A. and the Australian bodyguard recommended to him by his brother-in-law.

He had to bite back a soft groan when his gaze fell on the man.

There were a lot of similarities in Liev Reynolds's physique to Aslin Rhodes'. Both were tall, menacing and powerfully built. However, that was where the similarities ended. For starters, Chris hadn't got a wholly disturbing stirring in his groin when he'd first met the Brit who eventually married his sister.

Reynolds was taller than he'd appeared from a distance. Taller. Broader. Stronger. Laugh lines fanned out from the corners of his eyes, eyes a brilliant blue and framed by thick dark-blond lashes. His square jaw was clean shaven, his neck a muscular column, his shoulders wide. Under the snug white T-shirt, his chest was well sculpted and muscular. As were his deltoids, biceps and triceps. A six-pack set of abs was hinted at in the shadows of the white cotton. His hips were low and narrow, and faded blue jeans did, in fact, hug thighs that were muscular and corded, just as Chris had suspected from his first view of the man. Liev Reynolds was, to put it bluntly, the epitome of male potency.

Chris's stomach lurched.

Jesus, what was going on with him?

The Australian bodyguard took a step forward and extended his hand. "G'day, Mr. Huntley. Liev Reynolds."

Chris looked at the offered greeting, one socially accepted between men throughout the western world. His mouth grew dry.

The Australian chuckled. "I'm not into fist bumps. Sorry."

Chris blinked, the realization he hadn't shaken Reynolds's hand hitting him with sinking horror. "Sorry," he blurted, snatching the man's hand just as Reynolds was retracting it. Hot licks of tension shot through him at the hasty contact, spearing into his groin. His cock throbbed. "Sorry," he repeated, ignoring the unnerving sensation as he shook Reynolds's hand with an up-and-down motion he knew was borderline frantic. "I'm jet-lagged."

Beside the Australian, Bethany raised one straight red eyebrow.

Reynolds laughed, returning Chris's shake with a firm, steady grip. "No worries, mate. I can only imagine what it's like flying halfway 'round the world. Rhodes told me to go easy on you."

Chris's gut clenched. He gazed up at the taller man, wishing to fuck Aslin was here right now so Chris could beat the shit out of him.

Goddamn it, thanks to the Brit, he was about to spend the next seven days in the constant company of a sexy woman who wasn't interested in him and a…a…fuck, there was no other way to describe Liev Reynolds but sexy as well.

Sexy.

Jesus, what the hell was going on?

CHAPTER TWO

The day that Liev Reynolds told his older brother Ian he was bi-sexual, he'd lost almost everything that was important to him. Ian, older by three years and his only sibling, had told Liev he was sick. Told him he needed help. Told him their parents would be disgusted and thanked bloody God they were dead and not here now to be embarrassed by their youngest son.

From that day, Ian refused to see him or talk to him. The only contact Liev now had with his family was with his brother's teenage daughter. She didn't care her uncle slept with both men and women because he took her to the concerts her parents refused to take her to, picked her up from the inner city clubs when she and her friends couldn't get a taxi, and—in her words—was, "awesome and wonderful and smart and naughty".

Liev still wasn't sure what the *naughty* part meant, but he suspected it had something to do with the fact that deep inside, his dux-of-the-school niece wanted to rebel against her parents' strict, no-nonsense upbringing. The closest she got to that rebellion was defying her dad's demands she not interact with her *sick* uncle.

When all was said and done, Liev didn't give a rat's arse what Ian thought, as long as he got to spend time with Caitlin. If his brother cut him off from the only living relative that cared for him…well, then Ian would see just how angry his *sick* brother could get.

Liev's sexuality hadn't stopped him being a highly awarded firefighter. Nor had it stopped him protecting not only the country's leading politicians but the world's biggest rock star as well. Acting as one of Nick Blackthorne's bodyguards whenever he toured Australia was the highlight of Liev's professional-protector career and more than once he wished he could share the achievement with Ian. They'd both been Blackthorne fans. But the last time Liev had worked alongside Aslin Rhodes in guarding the performer, Ian had hung up before Liev could even say g'day.

Which meant there wasn't a hope in hell he was going to call his brother and tell him he was now going to be the personal bodyguard of, according to Caitlyn, Ian's favourite sitcom star. Not a bloody hope in hell.

Nor was he going to tell his brother the American actor was so bloody good-looking it was a wonder Liev's cock didn't burst free of his jeans. Fuck, he'd hoped this wasn't going to happen again. Seems like he'd hoped in vain.

He'd never told Aslin Rhodes he'd been sexually aroused by Chris when Rhodes had asked him to watch over Chris when the actor had been in Australia last year. There hadn't been a need. He hadn't met Chris, just guarded him from a distance, as instructed by Rhodes. Rhodes trusted him. They'd worked side by side numerous times. Rhodes knew he was bi and didn't care.

What would his friend say if he knew Liev was now standing in the actor's living room, doing his best to appear nonchalant when he was really wondering what the man's cock would feel like in his hands? In his mouth?

What it would feel like to penetrate the actor's arse and fuck him senseless?

Bloody hell, this was a first for Liev. Men turned him on, just as much as women, but never ones who were famous for their scorching heterosexuality. And when it came to heterosexuality, Chris Huntley was as scorching as they came.

Fuck it.

"How long have you known Aslin for?"

Chris's question yanked Liev out of his disquieting contemplation. Slipping his hands into his jeans' front pockets, he smiled at the actor. "Eight years. We both worked out at the same gym whenever he was in Sydney. One day, the support bodyguard Rhodes used when Nick Blackthorne was in the country was unavailable and Rhodes asked if I'd be interested."

"So you are used to guarding celebrities then?" a familiar female voice asked.

Liev turned to face the little bundle of fiery-red efficiency beside him. He'd shared numerous conversations with Chris Huntley's personal assistant since Rhodes recommended him for this job. Bethany Sloan was clipped, precise and efficient. And nothing like he'd expected her to look. She looked like she belonged in a fantasy book about fairies and sprites. If fairies and sprites carried smartphones and iPads and moved with economical poise and determination, that was. There was a tightly contained sensuality about her Liev found intriguing. "I am." He offered the P.A. a reassuring smile. "Groupies and fans don't worry me much. I've also already spent some time guarding Mr. Huntley."

"You have?"

Liev swung back to the actor, steadying himself against the churning heat in his gut looking at the American caused. "When you were here last year filming *Dead Even*. Rhodes asked me to watch over you while he was trying to find the person responsible for the attempts on your sister's life." He grinned. "From a distance, mind you. He was very adamant about that. No one was to know I was there."

The actor ran a slow inspection over him, from head to toe and back again. Liev resisted the urge to shift his feet. The scrutiny was ambiguous but unsettling all the same. If Liev wasn't careful his bloody dick would give away *how* unsettling. "Well, you did a good job," Chris said, narrowing his eyes as he studied Liev's face. "I don't recognize you at all. And I know I'd —" He stopped. "And I don't forget a face."

Liev accepted the compliment with a nod of his head. The actor had intended to say something else, but what? "Thanks, mate."

"So you think you're the right man for the job?"

Bethany's calm question sent an unexpected finger of tight anticipation down Liev's spine. Whether it was because of his sexual attraction to her boss or the fact she had a thoroughly sexy American accent, he wasn't sure. With the way his body was behaving, he was beginning to think this job wasn't a good idea after all. The pay was phenomenal for seven days' work. But was it worth walking around with a semi for the duration?

It would be so much easier if he were in some kind of steady, committed relationship. But he didn't do steady, committed relationships.

Giving Bethany a wide grin, he nodded again. "I'm the man for the job. Aslin Rhodes wouldn't have recommended me if I wasn't."

"That's true," Chris said. "When it comes to protecting those he loves, Rhodes is almost manic." The actor pulled a face. "That sounded much more impressive and far less weird in my head."

Liev laughed.

Chris grinned.

Liev wished he hadn't. The man's smile was everything Liev liked in the expression. It showed off Chris's white, even teeth. It formed tiny laugh lines at the edges of his brilliant-blue eyes.

It hinted at a shallow dimple in his left cheek. It was relaxed, cheeky and infectious, and Liev knew he was going to have a hard bloody time not picturing it later that night in the shower.

And in bed.

Yeah, taking this job probably wasn't a good idea at all.

"May I get you a coffee, Mr. Reynolds?"

Liev dragged his gaze from Chris's face to focus on Bethany again. She was studying him with an ambiguous expression, her eyes slightly narrowed.

"Or a beer? A drink?" she went on. "The bar is fully stocked and I am quite proficient at mixing any drink you'd like."

"Bethany is quite proficient at everything," Chris said, dropping into the sofa. He rested his calf on his knee, stretching his arms along the back of the piece of furniture. "She has my days planned down to the last second." He tossed his personal assistant a quick smirk. Liev couldn't miss the warm affection in the look. "When am I going to the bathroom next, Bethany?"

Bethany flicked the slim gold watch on her wrist a look. "In two hours and fifty-four minutes, Mr. Huntley."

Chris grinned at Liev again. "See?"

"That drink, Mr. Reynolds?"

Liev shook his head. "Thanks, but no. A coffee will be fine. I'm a teetotaler."

"Really?"

Liev returned his focus to Chris, his chest squeezing a little at the actor's relaxed sensuality. "My parents were killed by a drunk driver when I was young. It had a profound effect on me."

Chris's expression turned dark. "I know what it's like to lose your mom and dad. It sucks."

Liev nodded. "It does."

A strained silence stretched across the room, made all the

more tight by the way Chris's stare held Liev's. Liev knew about the murder of Chris's parents twenty years ago. Aslin had filled him in on the situation in preparing him for the job. It was one of the reasons Chris didn't like being swarmed by fans, one of the reasons he preferred to remain out of the public whenever possible. The guy may be one of the funniest men on television, but when it came to his personal life he was a homebody.

Liev liked that.

What's that mean? You sizing him up for something more than just being your boss? Ha. You're deluded, dickhead.

"How do you take your coffee, Mr. Reynolds?"

Liev started at Bethany's calm question. He drew in a slow breath, forcing his heartbeat to slow down. Being this on edge wasn't going to cut it. He'd be jumping at shadows after a day if he kept this up. Not the ideal state for a bodyguard to be in. "Black is fine." He smiled at the tiny bundle of constrained efficiency. "Espresso if that's possible? And it's Liev, not Mr. Reynolds. Please."

Bethany's pink-glossed lips twisted as she digested his requests. For the first time, Liev noticed just how full her lips were.

Christ, mate. Stop looking at everyone in here with your dick, will you?

"Take a seat, Liev…" she indicated the armchair opposite Chris, "…while I get your espresso."

Chris chuckled. "She likes you, dude. I've been asking her to call me Chris since my sister and Rhodes employed her."

Lowering himself into the plush leather chair directly across from Chris, Liev scoped out the immediate layout of the room. The harbour-facing wall was made entirely of four glass concertina doors—now open to allow the breeze from the water to flow into the living area. The balcony had no ground access, something Liev had noted as he walked the jetty on arriving. The architecturally impressive home was three stories. On the top floor were the three bedrooms, the master bedroom facing the harbour with glass concertina doors and a smaller balcony. The first floor comprised the living areas, kitchen, laundry and office. The ground floor was the entry foyer, a guest bedroom, fully kitted-out gym and a massive, completely sound-insulated hundred-seat home cinema. Liev had pulled some strings with city-council—thanks to his contacts as a volunteer firefighter—and procured the plans of the building before arriving, studying them until he knew every square inch. He knew where all the windows and doors were, the easiest ones to gain access with the aid of a ladder and those the sensors of the built-in security system didn't detect.

He also knew, thanks to a quick phone call, some fast-talking and a little flirting, the security system's deactivation code. How easy it was to gain those four numbers still made his gut clench. He'd already had a rather terse conversation with the manager of the security firm, pointing out how exposed their clients were if their staff gave out vital numbers to anyone who could spin a convincing story. The last thing Liev would do before leaving today was change the number to something else.

If he could procure it with a bullshit tale of being a visiting relative who wanted to surprise the owner, any of Chris's more determined fans could as well.

Better to be safe than sorry.

"So," Chris's voice drew Liev's attention back from the details of the job, "tell me about yourself. All Rhodes said about you was, and I quote, *I'd trust him with my life, he's a scary sod when he needs to be and more powerful than he looks.*" The actor snorted, his gaze roaming over Liev with such intensity Liev had to suppress the urge to squirm in the seat. "Which means you must be stronger than the Hulk 'cause you look goddamn invincible."

The compliment lashed over Liev like a hot caress. He ground his teeth, willing the tight throb in his groin to go away. "Rhodes has a way with words."

Chris chuckled. "Damn straight. Last week he told me I was a big girl's blouse when I needed to take a break during training." He frowned. "I still don't really know what that means."

"It means you didn't *need* to take a break." Bethany appeared at Liev's side to hand him a small brushed-steel cup on a matching saucer. "That you could have trained harder and longer."

Chris raised his eyebrows. "How do you know that, Bethany?"

She gave her boss a steady look. "I know everything."

Without a word, she turned and walked away, but not before Liev noticed a tiny smile pull at the edges of her mouth.

His gut clenched. Little Miss Efficiency had a naughty streak. Crap, he didn't need to know that.

"She does, it seems." Chris let out a melodramatic sigh. "And I suspect she reports to my sister on the hour. Which means Rowie knows everything as well. And here I was thinking I'd get to run amuck in Australia this time. Party hard. Maybe even get laid."

Liev choked on his espresso.

Chris laughed. "Sorry. Didn't mean to do that to you. And I'm not planning on getting laid. Haven't got time for that, do I, Bethany?"

Bethany reappeared at Liev's side, placing a platter piled high with fresh fruit, cheese and water crackers on the coffee table. "It's not in your schedule, Mr. Huntley."

"See?" Chris slumped back in the sofa, his face a mask of dramatic dismay. "No time for fun. Guess it's just the three of us for the next seven days. Can you deal with that, Liev?"

A hot lump filled Liev's throat. He shifted in the armchair, the crotch of his jeans uncomfortably tight. His stupid brain was presenting all sorts of options for the three of them for the next seven days. None of them remotely professional. "I can deal with that."

"Good." Chris reached forward and snagged a hunk of brie from the platter between them. Liev couldn't help but notice the way the muscles in his arm and shoulder coiled and flexed with the movement. Rhodes had told Liev the actor was working out hard. It was obvious. Bloody obvious.

"Four, Mr. Huntley."

Liev blinked at Bethany's obscure statement.

Chris frowned. "Four what?"

"There will be four of us," Bethany corrected. "Jeff Coulter arrives tomorrow."

Chris smacked his palm to his forehead. "Shit, that's right." He pulled a face. "Damn, don't let Jeff know I forgot him."

Bethany's lips twisted into another ambiguous smile. "Not at all, sir. Would you like me to retrieve your overnight bag from the yacht, Liev?"

It was Liev's turn to frown. "Overnight bag?"

"You do realize part of your role as Mr. Huntley's personal bodyguard while he is here in Australia requires you to stay in his presence twenty-four seven?"

Liev swallowed. "Umm."

Bethany cocked a straight auburn eyebrow. "Is this a problem?"

Liev's gut knotted. "No. I just…wasn't…"

The actor's personal assistant frowned. "I'm sorry. I think this may be my fault. I'm sure I mentioned it to you when we last spoke on the telephone."

"No." Liev shook his head. "It's news to me. But not a problem."

"Are you sure?" Bethany flicked a quick look at her boss. "I'm certain another bodyguard could be—"

"No," Liev interrupted, shaking his head again. "It's all good. I'll just whip home and grab some stuff."

"Excellent." Bethany's answering smile was stunning. If Liev wasn't already so unsettled by his sexual attraction to the American actor sitting opposite him, he'd be floored by the young woman standing beside him. Come to think it, his horny bloody brain had already tried to create a debauched fantasy involving all three of them.

"I shall arrange a taxi to meet you at Circular Key to drive you home. Is that okay?"

"Perfect." It would be easier for the taxi to collect him from where he was now, but Liev didn't want too many people knowing the location. And with Chris being in town, the paparazzi were out in force. Images of Chris arriving at the airport had appeared online already. Liev had scanned the celebrity gossip sites during the yacht trip across the harbour, noting more than one image of the actor in the airport terminal was attributed to the infamous Australian paparazzo, Carl Holston. Rhodes had pre-warned him Holston would be a nuisance.

Paparazzi weren't something Liev had had to deal with guarding politicians. It was only the odd job he had taken protecting Nick Blackthorne with Aslin that had exposed him to their particular kind of scum. And in Australia, Holston was the king shit of them—

"Chris!"

The scream came from beyond the open doors. High, wild and female.

"We love you Chris!"

Liev was on his feet before the shout finished. He crossed to the balcony, Bethany in tow.

Outside, bobbing up and down on the water at the end of the jetty was a water-taxi. Standing at the stern, dressed in little bikini-tops and miniskirts, were four young women.

All four squealed as Liev stepped out of the living area, one of them waving a sign with a mobile phone number scrawled in what looked like pink lipstick beneath the words *Call me, Chris. I'm yours.*

"So it's begun," Bethany murmured at his elbow.

Liev cast her a sideways glance. A scowl pulled at her lips and eyebrows as she fixed her stare on the giggling women.

Swinging back to the water-taxi, Liev withdrew his mobile from his back pocket and dialed a number.

The woman with the sign let out a screech. She gaped at her friends. Her friends gaped back. The one closest to her snatched the sign from her hand and said something to her. All four of them stared at Liev and Bethany as the woman pulled a mobile from the small purse hanging over her shoulder and raised it to her ear. "Hi? Chris?"

"G'day, love," Liev said, watching the woman's face. "I suggest you tell the driver of the taxi to take you as far away from here as he can. Now. Before I—"

The woman hung up. Liev saw her do it before he heard the connection between them cut.

"*Boo,*" one of the women called across the distance.

"Spoil sport," another shouted.

However the young woman whose number he'd called had scurried off the stern and was now talking to the driver of the water-taxi.

There was a delay—no longer than a few seconds—and then the small motorboat pulled away from the end of the jetty, taking the booing, giggling, waving young women with it.

Liev dialed another number on his mobile, watching the small watercraft as it skimmed across the calm waves.

"Skippy's Water Taxi," a voice said.

"G'day, mate," Liev answered. "Can I speak to the boss, please?"

Forty-five minutes later, Liev tucked his mobile back into his jeans' pocket. Every water-taxi service in Sydney had been notified no fares to Chris's location were to be accepted without approval of Liev Reynolds or Bethany Sloan. It had cost Liev a small percentage of his income for the job to grease the palms of all the owners, but it was worth it. At least that was one thing crossed off the list. While in a phoning mood, he called the water police and negotiated a five-hundred metre no-go-zone around the jetty. After that, he called his contacts in the local police command base, letting them know he was Chris Huntley's official bodyguard during the actor's stay in Australia. One asked Liev to get his daughter Chris's autograph. The other laughed and told Liev he was a lucky bastard and did he want to swap jobs for seven days.

He was still grinning about the question when he turned back to the living area to find Bethany and Chris looking at him.

He froze.

Oh boy.

Bethany—the bundle of poised control and efficiency— was studying him with open approval, her arms folded across her breasts, her lips twisted in that same smile she'd worn earlier. If Liev didn't know any better, he'd think there was a gleam of interest in her eyes. But he *did* know better. Rhodes had filled him in on Bethany Sloan. She was utterly professional, utterly no-nonsense and completely straight-laced.

Which made it safe for him to include her in his sexual fantasies with Chris.

Chris.

An invisible clamp wrapped around Liev's chest. His breath grew thick.

He slid his stare to the actor standing at Bethany's side, one-hundred percent certain what he'd first thought he'd seen on Chris's face when turning back to the living room wouldn't be there.

It couldn't be.

It was just a trick of the light. It had to be.

Looking at the actor, Liev bit back a strangled groan.

Because it *was* still there. On the American's face. Subtle and almost masked by the relaxed grin Chris was famous for. Almost but not quite.

Desire.

Curious, confused desire.

Liev's stomach lurched. His groin grew tight.

Crap. What was meant to be an easy seven-day job looked like it was well on its way to becoming something else altogether. Something far more bloody conflicted and complicated.

Liev didn't do conflicted and complicated.

Liev did simple.

But there was nothing simple about the way Chris Huntley was looking at him. Nothing.

And there was nothing simple about the way Liev's body was responding to that look.

Nothing at all.

Crap. Crap. Crap.

CHAPTER THREE

The man was naked and dripping wet. Chris knew this for a fact because he'd heard Reynolds start the shower attached to the third bedroom only a few minutes ago.

He bunched his jaw, wriggled deeper into the sofa and switched on the large flat-screen television mounted on the wall beside him. He needed a distraction.

Of all things, an episode of *Twice Too Many* came on. The one from the first season where Will Abbott, the OCD lawyer Chris portrayed, lost a bet to his best friend and had to do a pole dancing routine at the *America's Got Talent* auditions.

He studied the screen, watching his younger self slide up and down the pole with hopeless hilarity to the sounds of canned laughter.

It wasn't working. No matter how he tried, he couldn't keep his mind on the ridiculous situation the writers of the episode had concocted. It kept wandering back to the Australian currently naked a mere forty or so feet away.

Chris had hoped the three and a half hours Liev Reynolds had taken to retrieve an overnight bag from his home would be enough time for his strange reaction to the man to disappear.

It hadn't.

When Liev arrived back at the waterfront mansion, an overnight bag in hand, Chris had found himself just as unsettled and disturbed as before.

He didn't understand it.

Added to that was the way Bethany kept looking at him, her gaze contemplative. He'd wanted to ask what she was thinking about, but for some stupid reason he didn't dare.

Which also made no sense.

Goddamn it, maybe he needed to jump on the next flight back to L.A.? He didn't have any of these problems back home. The worst he had to deal with was his sister watching his diet like a hawk and Aslin making him work out every day at six a.m., whether he wanted to or not. None of this why-am-I-thinking-about-a-guy-naked confusion. None of this damn-my-P.A.-is-hot crap either.

Pointing the remote control at the television, he flicked through the channels, done with his oil-slicked, scenery-chewing self on the screen. Nothing caught his attention and finally he gave up, killing the power to the device and tossing the remote aside.

He shoved himself from the sofa and wandered out onto the balcony, the cool breeze blowing up from the harbour playing with his hair as he leant on the railing.

Perhaps he'd always been this way? He'd never really had any kind of long-term relationship with a woman. He enjoyed sleeping with them. Hell, he loved boobs. He could play with a woman's boobs for hours on end if allowed, but he never really felt connected with any of the women he'd dated on an emotional level. Rowan had put it down to the fact he'd only dated other actresses and celebrities since finding fame. She'd encouraged him to try branching out, had even tried to set him up once with a young woman she'd taught karate. Then, when Aslin had come along, his sister and brother-in-law had taken it in turns introducing him to all sorts of women from different walks of life.

None had piqued his interest. They'd all been lovely and friendly and down-to-earth, a trait Rowan deemed vital for any future sister-in-law it seemed, but none…grabbed him.

Like the way Liev Reynolds grabbed you?

Chris's stomach rolled and, before he could stop himself, he cast a quick look over his shoulder in the direction of the third bedroom and its en suite.

The closest he'd ever come to being *grabbed* that way by a guy was the time he and his co-star had been working out together in preparation for their film, *Dead Even*. Chris hadn't been able to stop watching the other actor's pecs as he performed a set of dips. The way the famous action star's muscles coiled and flexed had been almost hypnotic.

Perhaps that had been the beginning of it all?

But that didn't explain the absence of a steady girlfriend throughout high school. Or the way his balls throbbed whenever he thought of Liev in the shower. Watching a fellow actor work out was one thing. Thinking about a virtual stranger's naked body in the shower and how much he'd like to see that naked body slicked with water was another thing entirely.

Chris's cell phone rang.

He flinched, banging his shin on the steel rung running the length of the railing.

"Shit," he muttered, rubbing at the ache as he dug in his back pocket for his cell.

"Are you okay, Mr. Huntley?" Bethany called from the kitchen where, as far as he knew, she was preparing a post-dinner cheese and fruit platter. She had a thing for cheese and fruit platters he'd noticed. It was the third she'd made since they'd arrived in Australia.

"I'm fine," he called back, yanking his still-ringing cell free of his jeans. "Just trying to break the railing with my leg."

"Please don't do that." Her stern voice floated back to him

from the mansion's interior. "Clumsiness isn't covered in the property insurance."

Snorting, he tossed the kitchen a disgruntled look and rammed his cell to his ear. "Speak to me."

"Congratulations, Chris," Aslin Rhode's deeply-British voice rumbled through the connection. "You're now a proud uncle."

"Booyah!" Chris punched the air. "Way to go, Rhodes. Details, dude. I need details."

His brother-in-law chuckled down the phone. "Baby girl. Eight pound six. Came out fighting already. She kicked the obstetrician in the throat as he was helping her out."

Chris laughed. "Just like her mom. Awesome. What's her name? Tell me you named her Christine. *Tell* me you named her Christine."

"We did not name her Christine," Rowan's faint voice called across the line and Chris burst out laughing again.

"Tess Emily Rhodes," Aslin said, pride and love threading through each vowel and syllable.

Chris's heart clenched at the name and he smiled, leaning his butt against the railing before sliding down to sit on the balcony. "Tess Emily Rhodes," he tried the name out, loving the way it sounded on his tongue. His niece. Holy shit, he had a niece. "It's beautiful."

"She is," Aslin answered. "I'm sending you a picture now."

Chris's phone bleeped in his ear and he pulled the cell away to gaze at the image on the screen. Rowan smiled up at him, her face red and puffy, her hair a scraggly mess, her eyes tired and shining with so much joy his throat squeezed tight. His sister had never looked so beautiful. Almost as beautiful as the tiny pink baby with a shock of black hair wrapped in a fluffy pink blanket in her arms.

Grinning, he put the phone back to his ear. "Thank God she got her dad's looks."

"I heard that," Rowan said, her indignant protest faint.

"I'm hanging up now," Aslin said "Just wanted to let you know what we did." Once again, Chris couldn't help but smile at the pride in his taciturn brother-in-law's voice.

"You did very well, Rhodes," Chris replied. "Very well indeed. Give my sister a hug for me."

"I will. Oh, before I go, how is Reynolds going for you?"

Bam. Just like that, Chris's gut clenched. His heart jumped into his throat. His breath joined it. "Good," he answered, squeezing his eyes shut—a stupid move, given that the second he did an image of Reynolds popped into his head.

There was a pause on the other end of the line. "Good? What's going on, Chris?"

Chris shook his head. Another stupid move, given Aslin was on the other side of the world. "Nothing."

"I don't believe you."

He pulled a face, scraping the fingers of his free hand through his hair. "You're starting to sound like Rowie."

"No, I sound like a suspicious sod, which I am. Tell me what *good* means?"

For a crushing second, Chris contemplated telling his brother-in-law what was going on. He trusted Aslin with his life. The Brit was the most honest, real person Chris knew. The words were there, on his tongue. And then he swallowed them. Forced them down.

Aslin was real and honest, but he was also more a…a… *man* than any other Chris knew. How would his British ex-SAS commando-cum-bodyguard-cum-brother-in-law react to the possibility Chris found one of his colleagues arousing?

How would Rowie deal with it?

Jesus, how was *he* dealing with it?

"Good means we're still figuring each other out," Chris finally answered, opening his eyes to stare with blank focus into the living area. Movement inside told him Bethany had finished with the platter creation in the kitchen. There was still no sight of Reynolds.

"Do you not feel safe?"

Aslin's blunt question made Chris groan. Safe? No, he didn't feel safe. Not from his body's response to the guy.

Goddamn it, where was his psycho ex-personal assistant when he needed her? At least all Tilly had attempted to do was kill everyone who tried get in her way of looking after him. That was a cakewalk compared to this.

With a snort, he raked at his hair again. "I feel safe. Just getting used to the accent. It's only been half a day. Ask me tomorrow."

He could almost see Aslin digesting his words. If Rhodes decided there was an issue, Chris had no doubt Liev Reynolds would be replaced immediately. Aslin may be on the other side of the world, but he still protected Chris no matter what.

Did Chris want Reynolds gone? That would solve one problem, wouldn't it?

Without Liev Reynolds around, Chris could go back to his simple life, right?

"Do you want me to find a different guard, Chris?"

Chris pulled a face at Aslin's astute perception. He thought about the man in the shower causing him so much grief, the man who was going to be living under the same roof as him, shadowing him for the next seven days. "No," he said. "It's all good. Honest." He forced a smile into his voice. "Now fuck off and go take care of my niece. And I've changed my mind on hugging Rowie. Punch her in the arm for me instead. I'm still wounded she didn't insist on naming my niece Christine."

"Never going to happen, squirt," Rowan called out, the soft gurgles of a newborn babe's cry punctuating her reply.

"Screw you, sis," Chris said, hiding the lump in his throat with a choked chuckle. "Call me tomorrow, Aslin. Oh, and send more photos."

He killed the connection before his brother-in-law could interrogate him more. Closing his eyes, he pulled in a slow breath and slid to the floor, leaning his back against the railing.

Why had he said no? It had been a perfect opportunity to remove the Australian from his life. To remove the confusion before it became something…inconvenient.

"Like another fucking hard-on?" he muttered.

"You okay, mate?"

With a strangled yelp, Chris snapped open his eyes.

Reynolds stood before him. A curious frown furrowed his forehead.

Oh Christ, help me.

The man radiated confident strength, even with his dark blond hair a tousled mess of damp strands. A black polo shirt covered his torso, emphasizing his muscular frame with a subtle perfection Chris had never noticed on another man before. Black denim jeans hugged his long legs, and if it wasn't for the fact Chris couldn't stop his gaze lingering at the rather impressive bulge at Reynolds's crotch, he would have made some wise-ass comment about the fact the bodyguard wasn't wearing shoes.

But his gaze *did* linger on Reynolds's groin. Long enough for the man to clear his throat.

Chris's gut knotted. Heat flooded his face. Holy fuck. Holy fuck, he'd just been staring at another man's package.

"Mr. Huntley?"

He jolted to his feet, unable to meet Reynolds's eyes. "Sorry, I didn't…geez, I…" Clearing his own throat, he scraped his hands through his hair and forced his stare to Liev's. "I didn't mean to, y'know…look…*there*. It was just at eye level."

Reynolds's laugh surprised him. "No worries, mate. I'm used to it."

Chris raised his eyebrows. "You're used to guys looking at your junk?"

"Well, when you put it like that, no. But I've been in the state firefighting charity calendar four years running. When you spend a month on someone's wall dressed in nothing but a half-unzipped pair of loose work trousers you get used to being checked out. Especially when you make appearances at events to sell those calendars."

The ball of tension in Chris's gut didn't loosen at Liev's answer. It only made it worse. He'd known the man was a firefighter when he wasn't working as a bodyguard, but now all Chris could do was picture him half-undressed, glistening with sweat, his hands wrapped around a freaking massive hose jutting out from the region of his groin. Subtlety, it seemed, was not one of Chris's newly confused brain's strong points.

Nor was remaining impassive to the thought of Liev. At least, Chris's *cock* wasn't remaining impassive. The stiffening heat in his trousers was enough to make him want to groan.

Damn it, he needed to get laid. By a woman. Fast.

"Want to hit a bar?" The question burst from him before he could stop it.

Liev narrowed his eyes.

Chris puffed out a ragged breath. "I've just become an uncle. I need to loosen up."

A muscle in Liev's jaw twitched. "Loosen up?"

"Ah, shit," Chris held out a hand, "no drugs. Honest. My sister would kill me. Hell, Rhodes would kill me. No, I just need to blow off some tension. Do you know a place? Somewhere noisy?"

"I do." Liev crossed his arms. "But I wouldn't be doing my job if I took you there. Too accessible to the public. Too easy for you to be swarmed. And then Rhodes would kill *me*."

"And I don't want to lose my new bodyguard before I break him in, right?"

The quip was meant to be just that. A quip. It was what Chris did best—make jokes when things were tense. And things were tense. At least, for Chris they were. But Reynolds didn't laugh.

He stood motionless, his blue stare holding Chris's, his jaw clenched. "No. You don't."

A lump filled Chris's throat. His breath choked him. He couldn't move.

Every fibre in his body strained for the man in front of him. Every nerve-ending sparked with a carnal need he couldn't understand. His palms itched. His mind told him exactly how smooth and perfect Liev's muscled arms would feel to touch, how hard his chest would be, how sculpted his abs.

How thick and heavy Liev's cock would feel in his hand.

Chris stared at him. Into his eyes. Eyes that only a short while ago were unknown to him.

Eyes that revealed nothing.

And yet, the tension hung on the air between them. Chris wasn't completely naïve. He'd seduced his fair share of women. He knew exactly what sexual tension was. He mastered it on screen. He'd mastered it in the bedroom.

What this was, right now, was sexual tension. *Real* sexual tension. This was explosive. This was tearing him apart.

This was…this was…fuck, this couldn't be.

It couldn't—

Liev's nostrils flared. He swayed forward, barely. An almost imperceptible movement.

It was enough. Enough to jerk Chris out of his frozen state. He stumbled back a step, forcing a weak chuckle from his constricted throat, through his dry lips. "Damn, I think…" He stopped. Swallowed. Raked his hands through his hair. Scrubbed at the back of his neck. "I think jet-lag has finally hit me." He flicked his gaze up to Liev's face, unable to look at him for more than a second. "I'm going to call it a night."

Ducking his head, he hurried past the Australian. "I think Bethany wants to go over tomorrow's events with you," he all but stammered over his shoulder as he scurried from the balcony. Yes, scurried. God, he was pathetic. "She's…" He swiped at his mouth, catching a glance at Reynolds's bemused expression. "She's made a cheese platter."

And with that, he turned completely away from his body-guard and bolted for his bedroom.

Yes, bolted.

Because he really *was* that pathetic.

CHAPTER FOUR

L iev gripped the balcony rail and stared hard at the dark water before him. Sydney Harbour never slept. Boats and yachts moved over its calm surface even at two in the morning.

He scanned the marine craft closest to the jetty. Since contacting the water-taxi companies and water police a few hours ago there had been no more ecstatic women in bikinis squealing for Chris's attention. That didn't mean the water way was safe. It wouldn't be long before a group of resourceful fans decided to charter a boat of some sort and try to gain access to their object of adoration that way.

As it was, more than one privately owned yacht had elected to anchor just offshore of the mansion's jetty in the last four hours. The water police moved them on quickly, but Liev didn't think it was a co-incidence. To be safe, he'd taken the identification of all the craft, along with a snapshot of each boat. His contact in Sydney City Police Command was checking each one out.

Liev had never been a boy scout, but he firmly believed in being prepared. He wanted to know who owned each and every boat posing a possible risk, just in case.

Behind him, the luxurious home was silent. Bethany had

retired to her bedroom an hour ago after drilling him on Chris's appointments, appearances and events for the coming days and enquiring how he intended to keep the actor safe.

He let out a ragged breath. The personal assistant was a conundrum. Her aloof proficiency was just as arousing as her wild fairy-like appearance. Both stroked the side of his libido attracted to women. Throughout their conversation about their boss's routine, he'd hoped to see the interest he was sure he'd witnessed earlier in her eyes appear again. It hadn't. Her voice was clipped, her manner direct and professional. He'd managed to get her to laugh a few times—mainly when he'd used some Australian colloquialism she didn't understand. Going off like a frog in a sock had her giggling so much tears had trickled from her eyes—but apart from that, she was reserved and poised.

His *other* sexual attraction was far more frustrating.

Because there wasn't a hope in hell he'd missed the sexual desire in Chris's eyes earlier that night. Hell, he'd almost acted on it. Had leant forward to capture the man's lips with his.

And then Chris had fled to the master bedroom and Liev had come close to letting out a growl of contemptuous self-disgust.

Grinding his teeth, Liev pushed himself from the balcony, cast the harbour and its boats one last look and then walked into the living area, closing the glass concertina doors behind him.

Chris Huntley's heterosexuality was famous. According to the magazines and websites Liev's niece devoured, the list of women he'd dated and slept with was legendary. In the last month alone, more than one had declared Huntley was to soon be a father. If Liev was to believe everything he read, the actor currently asleep in the master bedroom had sowed his wild oats with just about every young starlet in Hollywood.

But Liev *didn't* believe everything he read.

Chris Huntley may be Hollywood's hottest sex symbol

right now, but Liev's gut was telling him the actor's heterosexuality wasn't as indisputable as the world believed.

Liev had spent a lifetime caught between two sexual appetites. Close to thirty-three years of it. From the day he'd accepted the hard-on he was desperately trying to hide at school had nothing to do with the hot girl from History class sitting beside him and everything to do with the hot captain of the boys' soccer team running around on the field in front of him—at the sage age of thirteen—he'd known he walked a line most boys didn't.

From the first blowjob given to him by a male's mouth, a few years later by a fellow senior from a different school during an excursion to the ski-slopes—Liev knew he didn't care the line he walked was socially…shunned.

The first blowjob he'd received from a girl—six months after that, from the hot girl from History class—had been equally explosive and cemented the fact in his mind he was bi. Sex was sex, and Liev had no issues with the gender of his partner. If he or she turned him on, he was happy to oblige.

Was that the case with Chris Huntley? Was Chris bi as well?

He knew the sexual preference of actors, especially ones deemed sex symbols like Chris, was treated like a precious commodity. The more virile and desirable women found an actor, the more money his work could pull in. An actor who'd built his career on his potent heterosexuality could see said career destroyed at just the hint of homosexuality. Why else all the defamation lawsuits?

Or was he just grasping at straws? He'd been attracted to Chris from the first episode he'd watched of *Twice Too Many*. Guarding him from a distance last year had only furthered that desire. Now, being in Chris's presence, breathing in his subtle scent…fair dinkum, it was pretty damn amazing. Seeing the sharp intelligence in the actor's eyes his sitcom character didn't allow out, watching Chris's body move with latent strength, a body more honed to physical perfection thanks to his role in *Dead Even*…well, amazing didn't really come close to describing how Liev felt right now.

He let out a low groan.

He had to stop thinking about the man. Even *if* Chris Huntley was sexually interested in Liev—and it was a big bloody *if*, about the size of the country to be honest—nothing could come of it. Bodyguard's second rule. Never, ever get sexually involved with the client.

Never. It was the second rule Aslin Rhodes had taught him. It was the second rule Liev worked by.

He'd guarded more than one female politician who had suggested activities beyond his job requirement, and he'd declined every one. A bodyguard who fucked around with his client wasn't just unprofessional. He was stupid.

Liev wasn't stupid, despite what his older brother wanted to believe.

Whatever the spark he'd felt between him and Chris earlier that night—and Christ, he was one hundred percent certain he wasn't the *only* one to feel it—nothing could come of it.

Even if Chris strode out of his bedroom at this very second, took Liev's hand and wrapped it around Chris's erect, pre-come dripping cock, Liev would pull away.

It would be fucking hard, but he would do it.

Hard. Like his dick was now.

So damn hard it hurt.

Biting back a muttered curse, he killed the lights in the living area and kitchen, hurried up the stairs to the third floor and strode to his bedroom.

The room was opposite Chris's. The door to the master bedroom was closed. No light filtered from beneath the thin gap at the bottom.

Liev turned to his door.

And stopped as the door beside his, the door to Bethany's bedroom, opened.

She stood on the threshold, her exquisitely petite body barely covered by a tiny pair of black knickers and a tank top that stopped short of her navel. She studied him, one hand coming to rest on the wooden doorjamb, the other playing with the small gold pendant resting in the shallow cleavage of her breasts. "Finished protecting us for the night, Liev?"

Liev's gut clenched. He stared at her, his chest tight. There was barely an inch of fat on her frame. A belly-button ring glinted at him in the muted light, drawing his attention to a delicate tattoo beneath it. A word was inked in her flesh in an ornate script he couldn't read from where he stood. A name maybe?

His cock throbbed. On the outside, Bethany Sloan may appear straight-laced, but the navel ring and the tattoo hinted at something else. Something…wilder.

Swallowing the frantic, beating lump in his throat, he nodded. "Yep. Doors are all locked, windows too. If someone's getting in now, they're using a blowtorch or wrecking ball."

The corners of Bethany's mouth curled. "And I assume you'd stop them before they made it through the hole."

"I would."

She stopped playing with her necklace and brushed her fingertips over the swell of her right breast, her gaze direct. "What are you planning to do now?"

Liev forced a chuckle to his lips. "Go to bed."

"Alone?"

He nodded at her question.

The smile teased her lips some more. "Tell me, in your mind, who is going to be in there with you?"

Liev kept his expression relaxed. Calm. Inside…fuck a bloody duck, there was nothing calm about him. "In my mind? Jennifer Beal."

Bethany chuckled, the sound low and more husky than any he'd heard her make. "Bullshit."

"You don't like Jennifer Beal?"

Bethany ran the tip of her tongue over the edge of her teeth. "If my tastes ran that way, Jennifer Beal would very much be my sexual fantasy of choice, but I call bullshit because I think *you've* got the gender wrong."

An invisible fist smashed into Liev's gut. "Really? Who do you think I'm taking to bed then? In my mind."

Bethany laughed. "We both know who." She flicked a glance at the closed master bedroom door.

What little composure Liev was clinging to frayed at her statement. He ground his teeth, holding his body motionless.

Bethany cocked an eyebrow. "Or am I wrong? If I asked you to join me in *my* room, what would you say?"

Liev let a slow smile spread his lips. "I'd say no. Professional duty and all. Can't really protect the boss when I'm fucking his P.A., can I?"

Another one of those husky laughs slipped past Bethany's lips. "No. Good to know Mr. Huntley is well guarded then. It would seem Mr. Rhodes was right about you."

Liev couldn't stop his eyebrows shooting up. "Oh yeah? What did Rhodes say about me?"

An ambiguous smile pulled at Bethany's lips. "That you were just what Mr. Huntley needed."

And with that, she stepped back into the dark shadows of her room and closed the door.

Liev's blood roared in his ears. He stood rooted to the spot.

The irrational urge to kick her door open, to throw her on the bed and fuck her senseless surged through him. But even as the violent thought formed in his head, Bethany transformed. From a fiery redhead to a sexy blond. From a woman to a man.

From Bethany to Chris.

"Fuck," he muttered, balling his hands into fists. "Fuck, fuck, fuck."

He spun on his heel and stormed into his room.

Fuck.

Shutting the door behind him, he pressed his forehead against the wall.

Damn it. Bethany had not only suspected his desire for their boss, she'd called him on it. He had no doubt the display in the doorway had been intended to test his professionalism, but then, as she'd raked her gaze over his body, he'd seen it again. That interest he'd noticed before in her eyes. There and gone in a heartbeat.

So now here he was, hornier than he'd ever been, lusting after a man he could never have and a woman who knew how much he—

Without waiting for the frustrating thought to finish, Liev yanked open his fly, shoved his jeans down his hips and wrapped his hand around his dick.

The second his fingers pressed his engorged length raw pleasure shot through him. He groaned, lolling his head back. Closing his eyes, he pumped his fist.

His knees gave out. Stumbling backward, he dropped onto his bed, pleasure rendering his legs weak. He choked his cock, fucking his hand with punishing pressure and force.

In his mind, he saw Bethany at the door. Saw that smile on her lips, that challenging, knowing smile as she brushed her fingers over the swell of her breast.

In his mind, he saw Chris watching him. He saw Chris undress. Saw him walk toward him and lower to his knees.

He groaned, letting his fevered brain tell him it was Chris's hands on his flesh as he reached for his sac and kneaded his balls.

A searing pressure began to build in the base of his spine. Radiating through his stomach, his groin. The soles of his feet tingled. He curled his toes and pumped his cock harder, squeezing his fingers with increasing rhythm and pressure until just his hand wasn't enough.

His hips bucked. His teeth clenched.

He mauled his scrotum and fucked his hand and watched

as Chris lowered his mouth over his shaft and sucked on its rigid length.

"Fuck," he ground out, scalding need turning his blood to molten steel. He was going to come. He was going to come and he wasn't prepared.

He had nothing to prevent his seed splattering on the bed's duvet but his—

His orgasm tore from him before he could release his cock. Before he could stagger to the bathroom.

He choked out a cry, wrapping his hand around the crown of his erection, his release oozing between his tight grip even as he continued to pump his hips upward.

It lasted an eternity. A lifetime. He'd jerked off before, what red-blooded male hadn't, but never like this. Never so brutal, so punishing.

His seed continued to spurt from his dick, coating his palm, trickling down his wrist. He bit his lip, afraid if he didn't he'd call out the one name he couldn't. It was one thing to imagine Chris Huntley feasting on his climax. It was another to vocalize the fantasy, even if Bethany knew.

Especially when the man was only a few feet away. Only separated from him by a few feet of carpet and two closed doors.

Five minutes later, his heartbeat rapid, his breath shallow, Liev stared at his reflection in the bathroom mirror.

"Crap," he muttered, running cold water over his hands. "You can't do that again, dickhead."

He couldn't. It was too risky.

For starters, what would happen if someone tried to gain access to the house while he was mid-ejaculation?

He needed to control himself until after the job was done. When he was back in his own home, without the immediate demands of his job hanging over his head, then he could jerk off as much as he wanted.

Until then, he was celibate.

Seven days. Seven nights. He could control himself for that length of time.

No matter what his body was telling him, he could control himself. Worst-case scenario, he'd quickly toss one off in the shower each morning. At least then he'd be less inclined to spend the day semi-erect in Chris's company. A quick wank to take off the tension and then he could direct all his focus and energy on actually being what he was employed to be. Chris's bodyguard. Just that. Keeping the actor safe and out of harm's way from his adoring—

Downstairs, the doorbell chimed.

Charged adrenaline ripped through Liev's veins. Snapping off the tap, he ran out of the bathroom, past his crumpled bed and from his room.

The doorbell rang again.

By the time Liev was halfway down the stairs, zipping up his fly and tucking in his shirt, whoever was outside had begun to knock as well.

"Mr. Reynolds?" Bethany called behind him.

"I've got it," he threw over his shoulder.

"What's going on, Liev?"

Chris's voice came from the top of the stairs. Liev ground his teeth. "Go back in your room please, Mr. Huntley," he said without slowing down.

He strode across the living area, activated all the external lights and hurried down the stairs to the foyer. With one quick look back up to the living area to find Bethany watching him from the top step—alone, he was glad to see—he turned to the door and opened it.

The young woman from the water taxi stood on the other side, the one Liev had called thanks to her *Call Me, Chris* sign. "Shit," she whispered, stumbling back a step.

Letting out sharp breath, Liev stepped out onto the front step and pulled the door almost closed behind him. "Love," he said, giving her a hard look, "you really need to go home."

She nodded, and once again he noticed she was barely dressed. This close however, he could see she was younger than he thought. Hell, she had to be no older than his niece.

Jesus, what was a girl of seventeen doing out at two in the morning offering herself to an American celebrity? Where were her parents? Her family?

"I…I just…" She stumbled another step away and Liev had to grab her arm as her heel slipped off the top step. "Sorry," she muttered, looking everywhere but at him. "I just wanted to meet him, is all."

Liev sighed, releasing her arm. "Not at two in the morning though, love." He gave her a gentle smile. "And not dressed like that."

The young woman's bottom lip wobbled. She nodded, eyes downcast.

Liev cast the dark street behind her a steady look. "How did you get here?"

"Taxi."

He suppressed the urge to curse. Studying the top of her head, he withdrew his mobile from his back pocket and punched in a number.

Wide, terrified eyes snapped up to him. "Who are you calling?"

"Another taxi."

The girl chewed on her bottom lip, her shoulders slumping. "Okay."

"What's your name?"

"Louise Phelman."

Liev raised his mobile and pressed it to his ear, waiting for Gary Turpie, a taxi driver he knew well, to answer. "G'day, Turps, it's me, Reynolds. Sorry for ringing so late, mate. You still on duty tonight?"

Twenty minutes later, he helped Louise Phelman climb into Turps's taxi, gave his friend her address and watched them drive away.

A few lights filled the windows of the multi-million dollar houses around him. A few shadowy silhouettes darkened some of them.

Liev turned his gaze up to them, noted their location, the size of the people in each one, and then turned back to Chris's rented home.

Bethany stood on the doorstep, her black knickers and top covered by practical tracksuit pants and a *Twice Too Many* T-shirt. "That was impressive."

Liev grinned. "I'm an impressive kind of guy."

She smiled. "I'm beginning to suspect that may be true."

"Glad to see I meet your approval. Is the boss okay?"

"You do. And he is." Her smile twisted, and she folded her arms across her breasts. "Now all we have to do is get him to realize you meet *his* approval and the world will be turning the way it should."

Liev's chest squeezed. "What do you mean, get him to realize? Is he unhappy with my work so far? I haven't really had much of a chance to do the job, given that we haven't left the—"

"No, no." Bethany shook her head. "He's very happy with the way you're doing the job. The way you dealt with the water-taxi situation impressed him greatly. It's not your body-guarding skills I'm talking about."

A constricting throb pressed against Liev's temples. His throat grew thick. He studied the woman before him, eyes narrow. "What *are* you talking about then, Bethany?"

She chuckled and, without another word, turned on her heel and headed back into the luxurious house.

"Crap." Liev drove his blunt fingernails into his palms. If he didn't he'd go after her and make a scene. If she was saying what he thought she was saying…

How long had she been Chris's personal assistant for? Long enough to know the actor well?

Maybe he should call Rhodes? Just to sound his friend out.

About what? Bethany? Or Chris's sexual preference?

With a growl and one last quick scan of the surrounding area, Liev entered the house.

Bethany was nowhere to be seen. Neither was Chris.

That was good, because with the pent-up tension in his body, Liev would likely do something really stupid. Like grabbing the guy and kissing him, just to bloody well clear up the situation once and for all.

Letting out a choppy sigh, he killed the exterior lights and headed up to his room.

He needed some sleep. Chris's first appearance for the *Dead Even* junket was at eight a.m. on Australia's leading breakfast television program. Getting him there without being mobbed by adoring fans was going to be fun.

And he used the word *fun* in the same way aching for a man who may or may not ache for him in return was fun.

Yeah, this job was turning out to be a bloody pain in the arse.

CHAPTER FIVE

Four days into the job of protecting Chris, Liev had never been more on edge. His agitation was two-fold. For one thing, every bloody time he looked at the actor he wanted him more and more. Every. Bloody. Time. To make matters worse, every time they had a conversation, discussed shared likes, talked about movies and books and sports, which they did a lot given they were never apart, Liev wanted him even more. And every time Chris looked at him, Liev was sure a question shone in the actor's eyes, one Liev would have willingly answered if the bloke wasn't his boss.

For another thing, the actor's fans were tenacious. He'd spent the last four nights turning away young—and sometimes not so young—women from the harbour-side abode. At least once an hour there would be a knock on the door. And when Liev answered it, which he always did, there would be a woman barely dressed in what he assumed was meant to be attire designed to seduce Chris into falling instantly in lust with her. Every time Liev sent the deluded female away. The *offerings*, as Liev thought of them, continued way into the early hours of the morning every night. If he knew who the idiot was at the television network that ran footage of Chris eating breakfast on the balcony overlooking the water on his second day in Australia, Liev would break the bastard's jaw.

In all his time as a bodyguard, Liev had never understood the fascination of stalking a celebrity. It was one of the reasons he chose to protect politicians. Politicians didn't have to worry about crazed fans trying to crawl through the bedroom window during the middle of the night.

If the nights were peppered with uninvited guests, the days were fraught with potential hazards from over-enthusiastic fans. Chris had appeared on five television programs so far, each one filmed in the penthouse suite of the Sydney Hilton. Getting the actor into the hotel for the interviews had proved troublesome. The police had needed to control the writhing, enthusiastic crowd three times. Once again, someone had leaked the whereabouts of the interviews. Liev suspected the network that had aired Chris's residence, possibly as retaliation for having their assigned interview time taken away in response to invading Chris's privacy.

And now, approaching the restaurant in which Chris was to share lunch with a reporter from *Empire Australia*, Liev was dismayed to see the footpath outside the eatery overflowing with screaming women.

"What do you want me to do, Mr. Reynolds?" Jeff Coulter, Chris's friend and personal driver who'd arrived from the States three days ago asked, shooting Liev a quick glance from behind the steering wheel. "Is there a back entrance?"

Liev bit back a growl. There wasn't. He'd had an argument with Bethany about the lack of an alternative entry last night. The one thing he'd learned quickly about Chris's personal assistant was she was stubborn when she wanted to be. She'd studied him with those piercing green eyes of hers, folded her hands in her lap and informed him he'd just have to keep Chris close—real close—entering and exiting the restaurant.

Of course, the thought of keeping Chris *real close* made Liev's gut knot, his heart thump faster and his groin tighten.

"If he gets hurt, it's on you," he'd grumbled at her before storming from the breakfast table. A cold shower had followed. It hadn't helped. Nor had discovering Chris swimming laps in the mansion's pool a few minutes later, his muscular body slicing through the clear water with fluid ease and perfection.

"Keep him close," Bethany had murmured beside him, no doubt determined to make Liev suffer. "And he won't get hurt."

Studying the cheering horde outside the restaurant, Liev weighed up his options. He could call the cops, ask them to set up a barrier. That would be the safest option, but it would take a while to organize, and in the meantime the writer for *Empire* was waiting inside the restaurant. Liev didn't like the idea the journalist could use the delay as a means to paint Chris as a prima-donna actor in the article. Liev was familiar with the technique. It was common for political journalists to use it to discredit their subject, and as such, Liev never allowed crowds to keep his charges away from appointed meetings with the press.

He wouldn't do so now either.

Twisting in his seat, he gave the actor sitting behind him a steady look. "Are you okay with a mad dash into the restaurant, Mr. Huntley?"

Chris chuckled. "The last time I was in Australia a kangaroo tried to rape me. I think I can deal with a little crowd."

Liev blinked. "Tried to rape you?"

Beside Chris, Bethany snorted, her lips twitching.

Chris pulled a face. "I'll tell you all about it after lunch." He cast a look over Liev's shoulder through the windscreen at the crowd. "They don't look that ravenous. Do you think there'll be a problem?"

Liev shook his head. "Just stay close to me, okay?"

"He can do that," Bethany answered before Chris could say a word.

"So I'm driving closer?" Jeff asked with a grin.

Liev bit back a curse. During introductions three days ago, Chris had declared Jeff the best driver in the U.S. So far, Liev had needed to remind Coulter six times to drive on the left. Coulter was an affable bloke, but Liev suspected the crowd posed a challenge to him. He fixed the man with a level stare. "You're driving closer. But don't run anyone down, don't go over ten Ks and don't pull into the curb."

Coulter's eyebrows pulled into a quizzical frown. "Ks?"

Liev bit back a curse. "Kilometres. Just don't drive faster than a slow walk, okay?"

Behind him, Chris laughed. "I love this country."

A minute later, Coulter pulled the Audi to a halt outside the restaurant.

The squeals and screams and cheers attacked Liev the second he opened his door. Women, and quite a few men, surged around the SUV, adoration and excitement turning their faces to masks of rabid delight. Some held signs with Chris's name on them with big love hearts. All pressed forward, desperate to see the object of their affection.

Adrenaline turned Liev's blood to liquid electricity. He climbed out of the SUV, planting his feet firmly on the road to scan the ecstatic crowd. No one appeared suspicious or threatening. That didn't mean they weren't. Moving close to the Audi, he stretched out his right arm, forcing back the wall of fans trying to cram closer to the car.

More than one person pushed back. More than one tried to duck under his arm.

Clenching his jaw, he swung to face them, fixing them with a glare he knew was borderline murderous. "Unless you want to experience what a size-thirteen boot up your arse feels like, I'd suggest you back off."

It worked. The wall of hot flesh and delirious fans fell back. A step.

He stood motionless for another second, promising everyone lots of grief with his stare if they did anything stupid.

Charged tension stole through his muscles. His heart slammed faster in his chest. His balls rose up, prepared for what was to come. Every aspect of his working life survived on this mental and physical state—fight or flight. Enter a burning house to rescue someone trapped inside or run away from the flames? Stand down a furious protestor at a political campaign rally or let the politician deal with the voter's rage alone? Liev's mind, his body, chose fight every time. It was who he was. What he was born for.

He loved it.

And yet today, he was more on edge, more on guard than ever.

Because of the American man inside the SUV.

Okay, Reynolds. He steeled himself with a sharp intake of breath, wrapped the fingers of his left hand around the door handle and positioned himself so as to immediately shield Chris from the crowd. *Here we go.*

He opened the door.

The squeals were deafening. The feverish fans pressed at his back in a wave of maniacal rapture. He pressed back, holding his right arm out to protect Chris as he maneuvered on the backseat.

The actor looked up at him, his grin bemused. Their eyes connected for a second, just a second, but what Liev saw in their light-blue depths stole his breath. Slammed into him with more force than the screaming crowd trying to mow over him in an effort to see and touch their idol.

Desire.

Chris Huntley looked at him with desire.

There was no denying it.

Jesus.

"Let's go," he said, forcing his voice to sound stern as he threw the crazed crowd a threatening glare.

Chris alighted from the SUV.

The crowd squealed again. Surged forward. Pressed against Liev's back.

He braced against the pressure, curling his hand around Chris's upper arm to support him.

Protect.

Touch him.

Hot energy shot down his arm. Into his chest. His soul.

He ground his teeth. Ignoring the disturbing reaction, he pulled Chris into his body, tucking him close to his side. The subtle scent of expensive aftershave threaded into his breath and, completely indifferent to the volatile moment, a tight lick of heat stole through his groin.

Clenching his jaw harder, he turned just enough to shield Chris from the crowd and began walking, parting the shoving fans with one arm.

They protested louder but scurried backward, enough for Liev to hurry Chris toward the entrance.

And then a stark white light flash right in front of Liev's eyes.

He flinched, raising his hand to his face. Chris stumbled, his shoulder bumping into Liev's armpit. The flash fired again and a man chuckled. "Nice."

Liev caught the actor before he could trip again. But the action was enough for the crowd to sense weakness.

"Oh my God, I love you, Chris!" a female voice screeched at Liev's right.

"I love you, Chris!" a new female voice squealed.

"I love you, Chris!" another woman cried.

"I love you, Chris!"

"Chris!"

"Chris! Chris!"

The horde erupted, pressing in with greedy excitement. Hands snatched out. Fingers scraped at Liev. Chris let out a shout.

With a snarl, Liev hauled the actor hard to his side and swung out his arm, his fist bunched.

People went tumbling, falling over each other. The flash fired again, joined by others.

Madness took over. Like a feeding frenzy, the mob attacked.

Liev didn't let Chris go. Nor did he falter. Shoulder down, he barged forward.

He didn't know where Bethany was. He couldn't risk looking for her. She was smart. Smart enough to sense the crowd and not get out of the SUV. At least, he hoped to God that was the case. For now, all he could focus on was getting Chris off the street. Out of danger.

Away.

"Here!" a man shouted somewhere in front of him. "Mr. Reynolds, here!"

Liev flicked his attention upward, glaring at the screaming mob. Behind the wall of waving, grabbing people, a man in a suit pushed toward him. His face was red and covered in sweat, his hair disheveled. He grabbed at shoulders and clothes, yanking people out of his way, clearing a path for Liev and Chris. "This way," he shouted.

Without hesitation, Liev tightened his grip on Chris and charged forward.

Hands and fingers raked over his back and arms and shoulders, but he didn't slow. Behind him, growing louder every second, a police siren wailed over the noise.

"This way," the man shouted, a second before Liev reached him.

He waved Liev and Chris through the open restaurant door, muttering something Liev didn't hear.

For a split second, Liev dared to slow, to draw breath, and then the man behind him slammed into his back and he stumbled forward.

"Through the kitchen," the man shouted, just as Liev

watched the crowd surge through the door, even as the man tried to shut it. "To my office. Go!"

Without a word to Chris, Liev pulled him through the restaurant. Passed the gaping diners, passed the wait staff, through the kitchen with its busy cooks and into an office.

Releasing Chris, he spun around, slammed the door shut and rammed the locking bolt into place. "Fuck," he ground out, palms flat on the door. "That was insane." He looked over his shoulder at the panting, gasping actor. His gut churned at the stunned shock on Chris's face. "I'm sorry, Mr. Huntley. That was—"

He didn't get a chance to finish.

Chris grabbed his shoulder, yanked it hard enough to jerk Liev around and kissed him.

Liev froze.

For a heartbeat.

And then he growled into Chris's mouth, dug his fingers into the man's biceps, spun him around and drove him backward. Pinned him to the door.

Their tongues battled in a fierce mating that sent shots of scalding need straight to Liev's cock. Chris bit at his lip, sucked on it. He tore at Liev's clothes, seeking the hem of his shirt.

Liev's heart beat harder when Chris's fingers found his flesh. He drove his hips forward, ramming his engorged shaft against the rigid bulge that was Chris's groin. The man moaned, his lips growing more savage. He scraped at Liev's chest. Pinched his nipples. He ground his erection to Liev's, his tongue exploring Liev's mouth with savage greed.

Liev met the ferocity with equal need. He snared a fistful of Chris's hair and pulled, tugging his head back. The man whimpered and drove his cock harder to Liev's groin. Liev lashed his tongue into Chris's open mouth before dragging his lips over Chris's chin, his jaw, down his throat.

"Fuck," Chris groaned, the curse a ragged breath. "Fuck, yes."

Liev captured the curse with his mouth, seeking out and dominating Chris's tongue.

Chris returned the assault, raking one hand down Liev's stomach to his fly as he captured Liev's tongue and sucked.

Raw pleasure sheared through Liev. Hot and tight and absolute. He tugged with demanding pressure on Chris's hair.

Chris responded, rolling his hips, the thick, trapped pole of his erection driving Liev mad with lust. With need.

When the actor's fingers fumbled with Liev's belt buckle, Liev thought he'd pass out. When Chris yanked the buckle free, when he reached for Liev's fly, black swirls of need erupted in Liev's head.

"Fuck," he rasped against Chris's lips.

It was Chris's turn to capture the curse. He drove his tongue into Liev's mouth, as if petrified of breaking contact, of relinquishing the kiss to something as simple as breathing.

Liev gave himself over to his wild hunger. He couldn't fight it anymore. He released Chris's hair and reached for the man's fly, desperate to release Chris's cock. To wrap its length in his fingers.

To feel it in his grip.

To rub its distended head against his own.

To smear its—

A sharp knock detonated on the door right beside Chris's head. "Mr. Reynolds?" a male voice called through the wood. "Is Mr. Huntley okay?"

Liev snapped upright, jerking away from Chris.

"The police are here," the man continued from the other side of the door.

Chris stared up at Liev. His expression was shocked, his lips swollen and red and glistening with Liev's saliva. His nostrils flared. His chest rose and fell with rapid, shallow breath.

"It's safe to come out now," the call came through the door. "The restaurant is on lockdown."

Liev stared back at his boss. His blood roared in his ears.

The climate-controlled air of the office caressed the flesh beneath his navel that his open fly had exposed.

Without a word, he took another step backward. He snared the toggle of his zipper and closed his fly with a single, swift action. He didn't break his stare with Chris. He couldn't.

His gut knotted. His balls throbbed.

Shoving his hand past his waistband, he tucked his shirt back into his jeans. His fingers scraped at his straining erection and a wave of raw pleasure rolled through him.

He ground his teeth, sucking in a sharp breath.

Chris just stared at him. Watched him.

The man on the other side of the door knocked again. "Mr. Reynolds? Is everything okay?"

"Liev?"

Liev squeezed his eyes shut at Chris murmuring his name.

Jesus, what had he done? What the fuck had he done?

"Liev?"

Chris didn't think his heart could slam any harder or faster. He couldn't tear his stare from the Australian. Couldn't breathe. No matter how quickly he tried to suck in air, it couldn't get past his goddamn heart in his goddamn throat. The man's name was barely a rasping whisper as it passed his lips.

Holy fuck, he'd just kissed Liev Reynolds. Why the fuck had he just kissed Liev Reynolds?

You were toked up on adrenaline. The rush of the madness outside, that's all. You were caught up in the insanity and your head just flipped out and you lost touch with reality and control and...and...

Kissed Liev. Because yeah, that's what *all* guys did when they found themselves in a potentially dangerous situation— kiss the guy that helped them through it. Jesus Christ, he'd kissed Liev Reynolds and nothing he could tell himself would deny the fact he'd wanted to. That being pressed against the man's strength and power as Liev had protected him from the frenzied crowd had turned him on so fucking much, made his cock so fucking hard, there had been nothing else to do *but* kiss him. Crush his lips—lips he saw every time he closed his eyes—and plunge his tongue into his mouth and die in the pleasure that instantly consumed him.

He'd surrendered to the urgent, demanding need to taste Liev's lips that had tormented him from the first moment he'd seen him.

And then Liev had kissed him back, and Chris's head had exploded with raw, elemental lust, total, complete rapture. Nothing had mattered any more except that lust, that euphoria. He'd given himself over to every urge and want and longing that filled him. He'd touched the man, flesh to flesh, and was engulfed in new lust and rapture all over again the second Liev's erection pressed to his.

Christ, he didn't think it was possible to experience such absolute, pure pleasure as he had when their cocks mashed against each other.

Even now—heart pounding, blood roaring in his ears, the constant knock on the door behind him telling him reality had crashed back down on him—the urge—no, the *need*—to step back to Liev's body and grind their groins together made his head swim.

What the fuck was happening? And how the fuck did he deal with it?

Liev's mobile phone burst into life in his back pocket. He flinched, grabbing the thing to stare at the screen.

"Mr. Reynolds?" There was more knocking from the other side of the door. Chris ground his teeth, hating whoever was on the other side. Hating him and thanking God for him at the same time.

"Mr. Huntley?"

With a long, ragged breath, Liev stepped back closer to Chris and looked straight into his eyes. Chris couldn't stop his lips parting. Couldn't stop his body aching for contact.

But it didn't come. Instead, Liev's expression grew unreadable. Almost disgusted. "That shouldn't have happened."

The blunt statement sheared into Chris's chest. He didn't answer. How could he when wretched pain, tortured shock and base want ruled him?

Liev placed a hand on Chris's arm. The simple contact sent shards of hot tension through Chris's body, and he swallowed the groan that rose from his chest before the Australian could hear it. Liev's expression grew steely. "Are you ready for me to open this door?"

Chris closed his eyes and swallowed again, grief and confusion warring in his soul. For an insane moment, he wanted nothing more than for Liev to press his lips against his throat, to press his tongue to Chris's flesh where his Adam's apple slid up and down.

No lips touched Chris's throat. Instead, there was just the sound of Liev's ringing cell phone and the waiting silence from outside.

Finally, Chris opened his eyes and, without looking at Liev, stepped away from the door. He needed to regain control. Of himself, of the surreal absurdity of the situation. The only way he could do that was to step away from Liev. To show him—to show the world—he was composed. Relaxed. He crossed to the office desk, rested his butt on the edge and folded his arms. "I'm ready."

His stomach a broiling mess of denied lust and conflicted anger, Liev nodded at his boss and opened the door just as his mobile stopped ringing.

The man who had helped them through the crowd stood

on the threshold, worry eating up his face. "Ah, Mr. Reynolds," he burst out, a concerned smile spreading over his lips. His hair was still disheveled but not as much as it had been before. An attempt had been made to return order. Liev could understand that. He wanted to return order to the madness his life had become.

"Is everything okay?" the man asked, wringing his hands together.

"It is."

"I'm very sorry for what happened. I'm afraid one of our junior waitresses called a friend of hers who happens to be a fan of Mr. Huntley. It seemed to have escalated from there." The man took a tentative step into the room, his worried gaze seeking out Chris. "Please let me assure you, Mr. Huntley, she has been fired."

"No, no." Chris held up a hand and shook his head. "Don't do that." He smiled the boyish smile that had earned him a place at the top of *People Magazine*'s Sexiest Man Alive list two years running. "I'm not hurt. Nothing bad happened. Besides, I remember what I was like the first time I met Bill Murray. I went a bit stupid, I'm afraid." His smile turned to a grin. "I'm pretty certain I ended up slobbering on his feet and promising to fetch him a newspaper."

The man laughed and flicked a still-hesitant glance at Liev.

"I take it you're the owner of the restaurant?" Chris asked, pushing himself from the office desk to cross to the door.

His shoulder brushed Liev's as he passed, and it was all Liev could do not to let out a ragged groan. Fuck, how was he to do his job now he'd tasted Chris's lips? Felt his cock hard against his own?

"I am." The man in the suit held out his hand. "Monty Dwyer. Please accept my apologies a—"

Liev's phone started ringing again.

Muttering an apology, Liev stepped backward, allowing Monty Dwyer to speak to Chris as he took the call.

"Is Mr. Huntley safe?" Bethany's composed voice sounded through the connection.

"He is. Are you?"

"I'm fine. Jeff and I went for a drive around the block. I had to tell him to stay to the left twice."

Liev laughed in spite of himself.

"Did you keep him close?"

Bethany's question sent tight ropes of tension through Liev's chest. "I did."

"Why didn't you answer the phone when I first rang?"

Because I was tongue-fucking our boss against a door.

The confession played through Liev's mind like a wicked taunt. "I was dealing with the situation."

"I want details later."

He snorted at Bethany's calm demand. "Tough. You're not going to get them."

Bethany chuckled. "Yes, I will," she said, and then hung up.

Suppressing a growl, Liev shoved his phone back into his pocket. Chris's P.A. was an enigma. A frustrating, feisty enigma who seemed to have an agenda regarding their boss that Liev couldn't decipher but somehow seemed to be a part of.

Which made her his new favourite woman in the world.

Or his least.

CHAPTER SIX

Chris had only been six when the film, *The Bodyguard* was released. As he grew up and developed a taste for movies, he tended to prefer the violent type pumped full of testosterone, guns and smartasses. Hence, when the Twitter hashtag called *#thebodyguard* took flight he needed to visit IMDb to understand the connection.

Looking at the poster for *The Bodyguard* on the film-database site also clarified the rather impressive images contained in quite a few of the Tweets about him and Liev. The poster for the film had Kevin Costner in his prime carrying a cowering Whitney Houston in his arms. Some clever bastard somewhere in the world had done a rather impressive Photoshop job of replacing Costner's face with a scowling Liev and Whitney's face with Chris's.

He'd be laughing his ass off now at the art if it wasn't for the fact all he could think about was *another* image attached to the incident outside the restaurant. One accredited to a photographer called Holston.

That image made Chris's chest tight and his mouth dry.

Slumped in one of the armchairs on the balcony, a whole eighteen hours after the restaurant debacle, the morning sun warm on his face, he stared at the image on his iPad. It was attached to an article about the "restaurant riot" on TMZ.com, taking up a place of pride on the celebrity-gossip site's front page.

In the image Chris was still sitting in the SUV, just about to climb out of the Audi. He was looking up at Liev who stood glowering at the surrounding crowds. The shot was a little blurred, but not enough to hide from Chris what he knew was there in his eyes.

Desire.

If he needed proof of what he was feeling for Liev Reynolds, it was right there in that image. If the force of their kiss in the office yesterday didn't tell him, the look in his eyes as he gazed up at Liev in the image did.

Open desire.

Thank God, it seemed he was the only one so far to recognize it. Not a single tweet or article had mentioned it yet. The main focus was on how the crowd of mostly screaming women had turned to a frenzied mob and how "the Australian body-guard" had saved him.

That morning, just about every breakfast program had run a clip currently trending on YouTube. It featured slow-motion footage of Liev protecting Chris from the crowd, cut with various bootleg scenes from *Dead Even* to the sounds of Whitney Houston's *I Will Always Love You*.

Once again, Chris would have been laughing at the whole thing, would have jumped right on in and participated in the fun. If not for the fact the truth of the situation was right there in his eyes.

He'd done it before, made fun of himself along with the world. His favourite running gag was the time the rumour had swept through Hollywood that he'd had a penis extension. He'd spent the next twenty-four hours after the rumour surfaced tweeting images of his *new schlong*, images of cucumbers, cacti and rock formations in the Utah desert. When it came to his public image, Chris was happy to play the comedic fool.

He didn't know how to play the fool in this one. No matter how long he looked at the image of Liev standing over him outside the restaurant, protecting him from the crowd, no matter how often he watched the YouTube clip, all he could think about was the kiss that came after.

The kiss…fuck, the kiss.

Throwing his iPad onto the coffee table, he let out a ragged sigh. Since waking two hours ago this morning, he'd taken calls from his agent, his manager, the studio execs, his fellow *Dead Even* stars and numerous Hollywood identities. All asked if he was okay.

He'd given them all the same response. "These Australians are wild. Must be their criminal heritage."

Everyone laughed. Everyone told him they were glad he was okay. A multiple Academy-award winning actor who'd never spoken to him before called from the States to suggest Chris contact the person responsible for the YouTube clip and offer him an editing job on his next film.

Chris had laughed along with them, all the while his gut a churning mess, his heart a hammering tattoo and his mind replaying the kiss over and over and over again.

What would they say if they knew what he was thinking about? What would they say if they knew what he'd done?

Not just that he'd kissed a man—that he'd initiated it. That he'd wanted it. Wanted Liev's tongue in his mouth, his saliva mixing with his. Wanted Liev's body pressed to his. What would his Hollywood colleagues say? The sitcom star about to be crowned the new action blockbuster king kissing a man and wanting so much more.

What would they say if they knew he'd wanted so much more?

If the apologetic, worried owner of the restaurant hadn't

knocked on the door, *more* is exactly what would have taken place. Chris didn't doubt that at all.

Jesus, he'd already started to release Liev's fly. Even now, hours later, he was still rocked by the intoxicating rush of hot blood the sound the lowering zipper had sent through his body. Even now, heady lust and need turned his every breath to a shallow, rapid pant. He'd never ever experienced such raw, potent, concentrated pleasure with a woman as he had in that one savage kiss with Liev. Never.

A low groan tore at his chest and he closed his eyes.

The object of his confused-as-shit desire was currently working out in the gym downstairs, as far away from Chris as he could be without leaving the property.

Neither of them had addressed the kiss.

Bethany had arrived in the restaurant a few minutes after Liev had opened the door to Monty Dwyer and the luncheon interview with the reporter for *Empire* had taken place.

It had gone well. Really well. Chris knew the journalist had been smitten with him. She'd laughed in all the right places, hung on his every word and blushed when he'd flirted with her. But the whole time a part of his mind had been with Liev, who'd spent the duration of the interview outside the restaurant, standing guard at the door.

It had occurred to Chris more than once during the meal the only place he wanted the Australian to be was beside him at the table. It had little to do with Liev's sexy Australian accent and everything to do with the way Chris felt…complete when the man was near him.

Not just safe, but complete.

Which only confused Chris more. He hadn't realized he wasn't whole until then.

The one person he wanted to talk to, his sister, hadn't called, no doubt too busy being a brand new mom. He didn't bear any grudge or malice. Rowan had spent her adult life looking after him. It was about time she focused on her own life now. And it was probably a good thing Aslin hadn't called. Chris didn't know what he'd say if his brother-in-law asked about the crowd at the restaurant. Confess everything? What would the ex-British SAS commando do if Chris told him he'd kissed the man Aslin had assigned to protect him?

Hell, what would Aslin do to Liev?

"I'm sorry to interrupt you, Mr. Huntley." Bethany's calm, efficient voice jerked him out of his ponder and he opened his eyes. His personal assistant stood beside the armchair, her crazy mane of wild red ringlets ablaze in the morning sun. "But you have a press conference for *Dead Even* on the other side of Sydney Harbour in an hour and fifteen minutes."

"I don't want to go," he muttered, closing his eyes again.

"You have to." A shadow fell over his face and he cracked one eye open just enough to see her lean over him and retrieve his empty glass from the table. "Or the people of the world will laugh at you."

Chris pulled a face. "I'm an award-winning sitcom star. Of course they are going to laugh."

"*At* you, Mr. Huntley." Her tone grew reproachful. "Not *with* you. And as clever as that YouTube clip you keep watching over and over *is*, you don't want to be known as the action blockbuster star who went into hiding after being swarmed by fans, do you?"

Chris grunted and wriggled deeper into his seat.

"Do I need to go get Liev? Have him drag you out of that chair and toss you into the shower?"

At Bethany's threat, an image of Liev naked and dripping wet in the shower filled Chris's head. Prickling heat flooded his cheeks. Steely heat sank into his groin. "Liev, Liev. Liev." He scowled. "First-name basis with my bodyguard but you still call me Mr. Huntley. Anyone would think you have something going on with the man."

"He's incredibly good looking, powerful, intelligent, a fire-fighter when he's not protecting VIPs and has that sexy

Australian accent." Bethany cocked an eyebrow. "Who *wouldn't* have a thing for him?"

If it was possible, Chris's cheeks grew hotter. He grunted.

Bethany smiled. "And then there are his lips. Have you really looked at his lips? They are so defined. So sensual. They almost mock the squareness of his jaw and the muscled column of his neck. I can't help but wonder what they would feel like moving over mine. What his tongue would feel like against—"

Chris jolted to his feet. His heart raced. His cock throbbed, well on its way to becoming a goddamn rod in his jeans. "I'm going to have a shower," he muttered, hurrying past Bethany with his head down.

"Good idea," Bethany called behind him. He balled his fists at the laughter in her voice. "I've arranged for Jeff to be waiting for us with the Audi at the Harbour Masters Steps wharf at Circular Quay in an hour. We can't afford to be late or he'll wander off."

Chris stormed toward his bedroom, glaring at his feet as he mounted the stairs. "Wander off, wander off," he grumbled. "Wish I could wander off."

A cold shower didn't help his mood. Soaping up was torture. Every time his hands moved over his groin, tight pleasure speared into him. Every time that tight pleasure speared into him, he instantly thought of Liev. Every time he thought of Liev, his cock and balls grew tighter. It didn't matter how cold the water was, he couldn't stop the erection he'd been fighting all morning from finally standing to painful goddamn attention.

He refused to do anything with it.

He wasn't ready for that. Instead, he ignored it, and all the images his deranged mind presented to him involving Liev's mouth and tongue. Instead, he let the icy water stream over him, eyes closed and tried to recall the pleasure of his last sexual encounter with a woman, a secret moment with one of

Hollywood's leading *serious* actresses after one of those fundraisers just about every celebrity in the town patronized.

He failed in his effort. Dismally. By the time he'd killed the water—fifteen minutes later—he was more frustrated and confused than ever.

Stomping into the bedroom, he saw Bethany had laid clothes out for him on the king-size bed while he'd been showering. Black Calvin Klein jeans, a black Ralph Lauren polo shirt, biker boots and red and black argyle socks.

No boxers or briefs to be seen.

He bit back a growl. His personal assistant was proving to be far more impish than he'd anticipated. If he allowed himself to ponder her behavior, he'd swear she had an agenda.

If that were the case, his sister and brother-in-law would have a meltdown. They'd been quite specific about her role as his P.A. and having an agenda beyond "seeing to Chris's professional needs" wasn't part of that job description. Hell, his sister had gone so far as to suggest to Bethany that she shouldn't fix Chris's meals while in Australia, hinting Chris should cook for himself. What would Rowie say of the super detached, aloof young woman now?

Nothing. Because it was all in his stupid, messed-up head. Bethany was just doing her job. She'd been prickly and efficient from the get-go. Just because every damn thing in the world was making Chris think of Liev Reynolds didn't mean Bethany was a sex-crazed maniac as well.

He snorted, snatching his jeans from the bed and shoving his legs into them. Sex-crazed maniac. Was that what *he* was now?

No answer came. Chris was glad for it. He didn't think he was ready to deal with what it would be.

But if Liev strode into this room and pinned you to the wall, you wouldn't stop him doing whatever he wanted to do to you, would you?

He ignored the thought, yanked his shirt over his head,

raked his fingers through his damp hair and then pulled on his socks and boots. He strode back into the bathroom, cleaned his teeth, smacked Jean Paul Gautier cologne on his cheeks and jaw with brutal slaps, scraped at his hair once more with ungentle fingers and then stormed out of the room.

He really needed to do something about his mood. At this rate, *he'd* be the thorny actor during the interview, not the actor playing the bad guy. All the reporters at the press conference expected his co-star to be reticent and gruff. He was famous for it. Chris Huntley, however, was the funny man who cracked them all up. Unless he did something about his state of mind, he'd snap the head off the first person who asked him what it was like to kiss his leading lady, a question he was asked at every damn interview so far.

Hurrying down the stairs, he grunted. "Kiss *FHM* Magazine's Sexiest Woman Alive?" he muttered. "Fuck, what about what it was like to kiss a—"

He smacked into a solid, unmovable wall.

A warm one.

Strong hands grabbed his biceps, halting his backward stumble. He jerked up his head, his stare locking on Liev's. The man stood on the rung below Chris, his impressive height drawing their eyes level.

Chris's heart smashed its way into his throat. Oh fuck.

"Need to watch where you're going, boss." A fine sheen of perspiration from his workout covered the Australian's body. The muscles of his bare arms and shoulders were so pronounced and powerful it was all Chris could do not to smooth his palms over them.

Chris didn't say a word. Just stared at the man, his heart beating so hard in his throat he couldn't breathe.

Liev's fingers loosened on his arms. Loosened, but didn't slip away.

Chris dropped his stare to Liev's mouth. Bethany was right. His lips were exquisite. And Chris knew *exactly* what they felt like moving over his—like fucking sinful heaven. He wanted to experience that heaven again. All he would need to do was lean forward, a fraction, and he could do that very thing.

Just lean forward…

Liev released Chris's arms and stepped backward onto the next rung down, his expression unreadable. "I'll be ready in ten minutes," he said, nothing in his voice telling Chris he was as charged and aroused as Chris. Nothing. "Sorry. I lost track of time in the gym."

Before Chris could say anything, Liev brushed past him and up the stairs, taking each rise two at a time.

The contact of the man's broad shoulder against Chris's licked through him, a hot sensation that made his breath catch and his gut knot.

He ground his teeth, balled his fists and stomped down the stairs. "Fuck. Fuck, fuck, fuck."

"Is there a problem, Mr. Huntley?"

He snapped his head up at Bethany's question.

She stood at the bottom step, watching him with a worried frown. She'd changed clothes during his shower, replacing the casual jeans and shirt she'd been wearing with a prim and proper linen pantsuit. The emerald green of the material brought out the green in her eyes, highlighted the auburn copper in her strawberry-blonde hair. The tailored cut of the suit emphasized her tiny waist and petite form. In her arms, she held two iPads, a folder he knew contained the approved question list for the reporters along with other information the studio deemed appropriate to share, and the latest editions of the two main newspapers published in Sydney.

At breakfast, Bethany had read each one twice, circling articles of interest she told Chris he should familiarize himself with during the boat trip to the south side of the harbour. "It's very good for the local journalists to see you are aware of what is happening in their city," she'd pointed out, drawing a red line around a small article with the headline *Girl, 8, Saves Koala*. "It makes you less the Hollywood movie star and more human in their eyes."

At the memory of her instruction, a stirring of respect for her insight twisted through his grumpy frustration. His last P.A. hadn't thought to prep him for foreign reporters. All Tilly had tried to do when he was last in Australia was kill his sister.

Bethany studied him, poised and direct and utterly professional. If she *did* have an agenda, there was no sign of it now. "Is there anything I can help you with, Mr. Huntley?"

His cock, still heavy with tension from his stairway collision with Liev, throbbed.

Biting back a curse, he shook his head. "I'm fine, Bethany." He walked past her to the kitchen. "Just on edge about the press conference."

"Do you want me to add the situation at the restaurant to the off-limit questions?"

Chris snorted. There was only one off-limit question on Chris's list—do not ask about his parents' ten-year-old unsolved murder. A group of fans going wild when he arrived at a restaurant hardly counted as something as traumatic as that. Unless Bethany was referring to the *other* restaurant situation, and as far as Chris was aware, she didn't know about that.

Maybe Liev told her? They do seem to have developed a close relationship in the short time they've known each other. Holy shit, maybe everyone knows? Maybe the restaurant owner had a security camera in his office and the kiss is now public knowledge? Holy shit, what—

"Mr. Huntley?" The alarm in Bethany's voice yanked Chris away from the horrifying thought. "Are you okay? You look like you're going to pass out."

He pulled in a sharp breath. "Is there anything new on the gossip sites about me? Anything about what happened at the restaurant?"

Bethany studied him for a second, her eyebrows knitting before she lowered her attention to the top iPad and tapped her fingers against its screen. A few moments later, she returned her focus to Chris again. "No."

He let out a ragged breath and then sucked it in again when Liev appeared behind Bethany, his broad shoulders and wide chest looking impossibly powerful in a crisp white business shirt, his long muscular legs wrapped in tailored ash-grey suit pants, his damp honey-brown hair slicked back from his face.

Chris's chest constricted. His stomach clenched. His groin tightened.

Goddamn it, the guy was fucking hot. How the hell was Chris to concentrate on being funny and witty and entertaining with Liev around?

He stared at the man, the lump in his throat rivaling the one growing in his jeans.

"I think," he said, the words a hoarse rasp, "it will be best if Mr. Reynolds isn't present at the press conference."

Liev's nostrils flared. His spine straightened, an almost imperceptible tension claiming his muscles. His jaw bunched.

Bethany's eyes narrowed. "Because?"

Chris swallowed. "Because I think…" He stopped, his mouth too dry to speak.

Because I wouldn't be able to hide the way he turns me on, goddamn it.

"The focus would become the situation yesterday," Liev said when Chris didn't finish, his stare holding Chris's over Bethany's shoulder. "Not the film. Easier to brush off what happened yesterday as a freak moment if the bodyguard isn't there as a constant reminder."

The statement hit Chris like a swift slap. To Bethany, *what happened yesterday* and *a freak moment* would mean the crowd going mad. To Liev it meant so much more. Chris could see it in the man's eyes. In the tension in his body. Could hear it in the dismissive tone of his voice, in his choice of words. *The bodyguard.* Liev had impersonalized himself to a position, a role. With those two words, he'd reminded Chris what he was. An employee. One who had already pointed out the kiss they'd shared was inappropriate and couldn't happen again.

In one simple statement, Liev Reynolds had summarized it all—a freak moment. It was time for Chris to get a grip on his stupid, confused libido and get on with being what he was—an actor who made viewers around the world laugh with his sharp wit and mischievous grin. A man who made women everywhere swoon with his smoldering good looks.

People Magazine's Sexiest Man Alive twice running and the subject of constant speculation in celebrity magazines and websites as to which famous woman he was sleeping with now, and which one would be next.

In other words, a straight Hollywood sex symbol.

Not a man undone by another man.

He couldn't be that. Ever. His career wouldn't let him.

Even if he wanted to.

And Chris was beginning to fear that was *exactly* what he wanted.

Fuck it.

CHAPTER SEVEN

The press conference went on forever. The award-winning actress cast as his love interest flirted with him for the entire duration, even hinted that their sex scenes in the movie were "intensely real". The tough-guy action star who played the antagonist professed to being jealous of Chris's career, jesting Chris beat him up on set often. More than one reporter congratulated Chris on becoming an uncle.

Chris endured it all. He dropped jokes when needed, flirted right back with Scarlett, suggested the "intensely real" sex scenes were so *intense* the film's director had to call cut over and over to get their attention, and challenged Vin to an arm-wrestle there and then.

The Australian press ate it all up.

They laughed in all the right places, smirked knowingly whenever he and Scarlett spoke to each other, complimented them all on how fantastic and action-packed and believable the film was, and generally made the morning one of the easiest press conferences Chris had attended.

Chris couldn't wait until the damn thing was finished.

He sat in his chair next to his leading lady, all too aware there would be countless stories appearing in the media tomorrow. Articles that would speculate about his on-set affair with the sexy-as-sin actress. Gossip columns dedicated to their "smoldering chemistry" even off screen. He should be joyous, knowing how the talk would be good for his career. Instead, he wondered where Liev was the whole time.

Wondered and hated himself for it.

He had to do something about it. Soon.

Before he cracked.

When the studio's Australian representative asked for one last question from the reporters, Chris couldn't hold back his sigh of relief.

And then the reporter selected to ask that last question did the unthinkable.

"Mr. Huntley." A woman who looked like she'd stepped straight out of a life-size Barbie box rose to her feet. "Do you still feel safe here in Australia after what happened yesterday at the Salted Olive restaurant?"

Chris's breath stuck in his throat.

He stared at the reporter, for a frozen moment lost for words.

Silence hung in the room, the press expectant and hungry.

Out of the corner of his eye, he saw Bethany move.

"Has it tainted your opinion of our country?" the female reporter asked, obviously deciding to ask more questions despite his failure to answer the first. "Have you fired your Australian bodyguard?"

He blinked. He heard the film's heroine shift on her seat beside him. The actor on Chris's other side cleared his throat.

The reporter waited. Everyone waited.

"No," he finally said, leaning forward on his seat to give the woman a relaxed grin. "The last time I was in Australia I was sexually ravaged by an amorous kangaroo." He dropped the reporter a wink. "Once you've been humped by a marsupial, hundreds of screaming fans are a cakewalk."

The room burst out in raucous guffaws.

Chris let out a slow breath. His heart hammered away in his chest a mile a minute. Before he could stop himself, he turned to Bethany, wishing to hell he'd find Liev there with her. But of course, Liev wasn't. He'd stayed outside, out of the reporters' sights, just as he'd said he would.

Chris's heart beat harder. A heavy lump filled his throat. Damn it, he hadn't realized just how quickly he'd grown accustomed to the man being with him every moment of the day until he wasn't.

"All right then." The Australian studio representative walked onto the dais. "That's it for the day. I'd like to thank the stars of *Dead Even* for rocking up for this morning when it's such a beautiful day outside." He turned and smiled at Chris and his fellow cast members. "On behalf of the people of Australia, let me say enjoy the rest of your time here and I hope you have fun at the red-carpet screening tonight."

The gathered reporters and photographers all clapped. Chris grinned at them, rising to his feet. The other two actors did the same. The room erupted in cheers and blinding camera flashes when the stunning actress leant over to Chris and dropped a kiss on his cheek.

Chris laughed, posed some more with his leading lady and then—doing his best to not appear impatient—excused himself.

He had to get away. He needed to see Liev. Even if the Australian wasn't speaking to him, wouldn't even look at him, Chris needed to see him.

Which was stupid, but the way it was.

With a final murmured farewell to his co-stars, he hurried over to Bethany where she stood waiting for him at the side of the dais.

"I need to get out of here."

She handed him a bottle of coconut water. "Yes, you do. You have an appearance at the Royal Sydney Children's Hospital in forty minutes."

Chris raked his hands through his hair. "Where's Reynolds?"

Bethany raised an eyebrow. "Feeling unsafe, Mr. Huntley?"

Without waiting for his answer, she turned and walked toward the door through which his co-stars and their respective entourages were disappearing. Chris swallowed. He'd been one of those actors once upon a time. He'd had an entourage that partied with him, shopped with him, spent his money for him and generally agreed to everything he said. Then his sister had disbanded it and he'd discovered being famous didn't give him the right to a free pass of indulgence. Now he survived with just Bethany, Jeff and, when home in the States, Rowan and Aslin. He'd been completely and utterly content with that.

Was he still as content? He couldn't be, given that Liev Reynolds made him feel complete when he hadn't realized he wasn't whole. Surely?

Letting out a shaky breath, he exited the press-conference room. The media spilled out another door a few metres away. As he walked toward where Bethany waited, he heard his name mentioned often. He had to stop himself from turning to look at every male Australian accent.

He followed Bethany to the elevators being held for the celebrity guests, biting his tongue to stop himself asking again where Liev was.

The trip down to the car-park level with his fellow *Dead Even* cast members seemed to go on for an eternity. He did his best to engage in the conversation with the other actors, discussing the red-carpet event that night, the Australian media versus the American, how cuddly koalas were and what their next film projects were. He felt Bethany's steady scrutiny on him the entire descent. When the elevator finally chimed and the doors slid open, it was all he could do to not sigh with relief.

Saying goodbye to everyone, he walked out of the enclosed, confining space before anyone else could exit.

He stopped dead when his gaze fell upon Liev standing beside the parked Audi a few feet away.

A wave of tortured happiness rolled over Chris. He swallowed, killing the smile wanting to stretch his lips before it could do so. His gut knotted. Never had he been so fucking confused. And it wasn't like he wanted to slam the guy against the SUV and tongue-fuck his mouth. All he wanted to do was walk over to the man and be in his presence. Feel his gaze on his face as he spoke about the press conference. Share with him the surreal experience of being the focus of so many people's unwavering attention. Make a dumb joke about being a celebrity and hear Liev laugh at it.

Christ, all he wanted to do was just *exist* with Liev.

But he couldn't. The Australian had withdrawn from him for professional reasons. They were now, more than ever, famous boss and mute bodyguard.

It fucking sucked.

"I'd heard Australian men could be stubborn." Bethany's voice beside Chris made him jump. He swung his stare to her face, willing his heart to slow down. "But that one..." She nodded at Liev and then shook her head.

As if aware he was the subject of their conversation, Liev turned to the back passenger door and opened it, his focus sliding over the surrounding cars.

"Hurry the fuck up, dude," Jeff called through the open driver's seat window. "The GPS tells me it's going to take me thirty minutes to travel six kilometres, and to be honest, I haven't got a damn clue how long a kilometre is."

Bethany *tsked* once beside Chris, chuckled and gave him a twisted-lip smile. "Ready, Mr. Huntley?"

He nodded, drew in a slow breath and crossed to the Audi. Liev didn't say a word, just continued to scan the surrounding area. Nor did he say anything to Chris for the rest of the day. He did his job well. He made sure Chris wasn't swarmed by enrapt hospital staff and visiting family at the Children's

Hospital. He stayed in the background, his expression friendly if somewhat serious. Chris didn't miss the sneaky smiles and grins he gave the children in their sickbeds as they were led through the hospital by the doctor. Every time Liev bestowed a grin on a giggling, curious child, Chris's chest grew tighter. Every time the Australian winked at one of them, the lump in Chris's throat grew thicker.

Two hours later, Chris was a goddamn emotional wreck. The courage of the sick children tore at his heart. Their open joy at sharing time with a famous actor despite their debilitating—and in some cases—terminal illnesses humbled him. He found himself overwhelmed by their happiness and fighting spirits. He thanked God often for his sister and promised himself he would hug her senseless when he returned to the States.

If it weren't for Liev, he wouldn't have made it. He'd lifted his attention to the man more than once to find him looking at him. Every time their gazes would connect for a moment, just a stolen moment, before Liev looked away.

Every time he did, Chris died a little inside. What made it worse was the way Bethany watched it all. She was smart, smarter than he, Rowie or Aslin had anticipated. If he wasn't careful, his P.A. would suspect something was going on.

What would she do then?

It was only when they were seated in the SUV again, Bethany sitting beside him in the back, Liev in the front with Jeff, that Chris allowed himself to relax. They were returning to the waterfront mansion. Out of the public eye for a few hours before the red-carpet screening of *Dead Even*. He'd send Bethany out with Jeff to find some take-out, maybe Italian or Mexican, and then confront Liev. Make the bastard talk to him. Demand Liev tell him what was going on in his head.

Demand Liev kiss him again. One more time, so Chris could test Liev's theory that the kiss in the restaurant was just a *freak moment.*

It was a sound plan. One Chris was pleased with.

Liev shattered any hope of carrying out the plan however, by announcing he had to leave Chris in Bethany and Jeff's capable hands for a couple of hours a short time after they arrived back at the mansion.

Standing in the middle of the living room, Chris frowned at the man. "Why?"

"My niece has locked herself out of her home. She sent me a text just as we were pulling into the driveway. My brother and his wife are still at work and Caitlin needs to get inside to finish a school assignment that's due tomorrow." Liev dropped his attention to his cell phone, tapped on the screen in a quick series of jabs with his thumb and then lifted the phone to his ear. "I will be back before you leave for the red-car—" He stopped, held up a finger and half-turned away from Chris. "Heya, Turps?" he spoke into the phone, his free hand dragging at his hair. "You on duty? I need to get to Balmain ASAP. Can you get me—excellent, excellent. Yeah, same place. Okay. No worries. I'll be out front. See you in ten."

Shoving his phone into his pocket, he turned back to Chris. "You'll be fine," he said. "Bethany won't open the door to anyone, and Jeff has my permission to punch anyone who tries to climb up the balcony."

It was said in jest. Chris could see that. For some reason however, it angered him. "Gee, anyone would think I'm incapable of protecting myself."

A still calm fell over Liev. He fixed Chris with a steady, unreadable stare. "Isn't that what I'm here for? To protect you?"

Chris ground his teeth. "I *did* punch the shit out of Aslin Rhodes, you know. Twice."

Liev had the nerve to chuckle, the edges of his eyes crinkling with mirth. If Chris weren't so damn irritated he'd revel in the simple fact he'd made Liev laugh. "I saw those punches. It was my first day watching over you from a distance on set. Suffice to say, Rhodes didn't seem hurt."

Cold anger shot through Chris. "So you're saying what? I'm a pussy?"

Liev's nostrils flared. The muscles in his jaw bunched again. "I'm saying, Mr. Huntley, that I would hate anything bad to happen to you. It's my job to protect you, and I need to make certain that when I'm not here to do that, all contingencies are covered. If you want to take that as a slight against your masculinity, I can't stop you."

The anger licking through Chris turned to icy shard of contempt. He took a step closer to Liev, eyes narrow. "Say it. Say you think I'm a pussy. You're a real tough guy, aren't you? A fucking homo who can beat people up. Say you think I'm a pussy who can't look after himself. Go on, I fucking dare you."

Liev stared down at him. He didn't move.

Sour self-disgust boiled in Chris's gut. It coated the back of his throat. His breath grew shallow. His head felt ready to explode. God, he wanted to hit something, hurt something. "Say it," he snarled, leaning closer to Liev, hate and fury and darkness eating at his soul. Devouring him. Destroying him.

Liev didn't say it. He didn't say anything. Instead, he raised his hand, pressed it to the side of Chris's face and brushed his thumb along Chris's bottom lip. "You are not this person, Chris. You're not a homophobic arsehole. You are amazing."

And before Chris could move, before his unhinged mind could register the exquisite warmth of Liev's palm on his cheek, before he could gasp with the sheer rightness of the contact, Liev stepped away from him and walked from the room. Down the stairs. Out of the house.

Chris sucked in a ragged breath. Another. Another. He turned on his heel, searching the room and finding himself alone. Bethany was nowhere to be seen. Neither was Jeff.

He closed his eyes and pulled in another breath, this one not so ragged. The side of his face prickled, his mind telling him exactly where Liev's hand had pressed to his flesh.

"Fuck," he muttered.

Silence greeted the curse.

Opening his eyes, he raked his hands through his hair. Fuck. His stomach rolled.

"I'm going swimming, dude." Jeff's shout shattered the self-loathing and tension paralyzing Chris. He flinched, turning just in time to see Jeff making his way through the living room toward the door that led out to the house's private pool. "You coming?"

Forcing a laugh from his strangled throat, Chris shook his head. "No," he croaked. "I'm going to go work out in the gym for a bit."

Jeff pulled a face without slowing down. "Idiot."

The loud *yeehah* a moment later, followed by a louder splash, told Chris his friend was in the water.

He let out a wobbly laugh and climbed the stairs. He *would* work out. He needed to do something before his next public appearance. If he didn't he may as well tattoo *confused moron* on his forehead.

He was on the fifth step when the sound of footfalls behind him stopped him.

His blood roaring in his ears, he turned.

Liev stood at the bottom of the stairs, looking up at him.

Chris swallowed.

Without a word, the Australian ascended to where Chris stood, coming to a halt on the step below him.

They stared at each other, silent. And then Liev leaned forward and brushed his parted lips over Chris's, a feathering caress of skin on skin. "Amazing," he whispered against Chris's mouth, his palm cupping Chris's jaw with gentle pressure. "Bloody amazing."

And then he was gone. Down the stairs without looking back, the dull thud of the door closing like a gunshot through Chris's chest.

"Idiot," Liev muttered, fixing his stare on the road.

He'd promised himself all last night he wasn't going to touch Chris again. He'd promised himself through his punishing workout in the gym he wasn't even going to look the actor in the eye. The temptation to return to the kiss in the office yesterday was too great. To finish what had started against the door.

Liev wasn't one for denying himself. The day he'd decided to own his bisexuality was also the day he'd decided to follow his gut when it came to desire. Fighting something like that was bloody stupid, especially if the desire was reciprocated. Life was too short to lie to oneself about something as enjoyable as sex and pleasure.

The simple philosophy had worked quite well for him. He'd had some amazing lovers and never regretted any of them.

None of them, however, had been world-famous heterosexual actors.

And none of them had looked at him with such conflicted, tormented confusion after he'd kissed them.

That haunted internal struggle had stayed with Liev throughout the duration of last night. Despite the fact every fibre in his body demanded he storm into Chris's bedroom and pick up right where they'd left off in the office, he'd stayed in his bed, his cock a rigid, aching pole of unfulfilled need, his stare locked on the dark ceiling above him.

He'd left his bedroom at dawn, resolved to treat Chris Huntley like he would a political client who needed guarding —with detached interaction. Guard the body. Be indifferent to the personality.

That resolve had lasted throughout the morning. While Chris was at the press conference, Liev congratulated himself on sticking to his plan. Had told himself he fancied the hot little blonde who seemed to be a part of Scarlett Johansson's entourage. She'd flirted with him and Jeff the whole time they'd waited on the car-park level for the conference to finish. When she'd slipped a small piece of paper into his hand a minute before the lift chimed to tell them the actors had arrived, he'd gladly pocketed it.

But when Chris had exited the lift, all thoughts of the hot little blonde vanished.

He'd fought the undeniable for the rest of the day. Had ignored the warmth spreading through his chest as he watched Chris bring joy to the children in the hospital. Had refused to acknowledge the way he wanted to smile whenever the American did.

He'd battled his mounting desire for the man, right up until they'd bumped into each other on the stairs. The second he'd wrapped his hands around Chris's arms to steady him, all fight had left him.

And then Chris's tortured confusion had erupted in vitriolic anger and Liev had known he was lost to the man. The hurt and self-hate that had shone in Chris's eyes tore at Liev's heart. He'd taken Chris's insults, knowing the man needed to vent them.

He'd taken them and promised himself he wouldn't respond.

All he'd done was try to soothe Chris's tumultuous self-contempt with calm words.

That was all he could allow himself.

All he would allow himself.

He'd left, intent on getting to Caitlin. Seeing his niece would calm his own tormented self-denial.

It was the thought of his niece as he'd stormed away from the house that had led to thoughts of his parents. They'd died in a car accident before he could truly tell them how amazing they were, how much he loved them. Teenage boys didn't tell their folks they loved them, not even bi teenage boys.

Unable to stop himself, his body no longer under his control, he'd turned and reentered the house, doing what he'd sworn for the last twelve hours he wouldn't.

And now here he was, standing on the curb, waiting for Turps to arrive, his lips still tingling from the soft kiss he'd stolen from Chris. It was the last kiss they would share, it had to be, but he needed Chris to understand how amazing he thought Chris was. He *needed* him to know that.

Even as Liev knew stealing the kiss was just as much for himself as it was for Chris.

"Idiot," he muttered again, balling his fist. "You're a stupid bloody idiot, Reynolds."

He was. And something had to be done about it.

The kiss stayed with Chris for the entire walk down the red carpet. He spoke to reporters, signed autographs for screaming fans, posed for pictures with local celebrities. He even accepted a soft toy koala from a wildly giggling young woman who blushed fifty shades of red when he took it from her. He was there on the carpet in body, but his mind was on the kiss. The tender, gentle kiss.

He turned often during the walk down the red carpet, his gaze seeking out Liev who walked a few yards behind. Every time he looked at him, his breath caught.

He'd never seen a man look so goddamn hot in a tux. Liev Reynolds filled out the tailored black suit with such exquisite perfection Chris didn't want to do anything but gaze at him. Devour him with his eyes.

The late afternoon summer sun swathed the carpet in a golden-red glare, and more than once Chris wanted to walk over to Liev and remove the dark Ray-Bans he wore. He wanted to see Liev's eyes. Wanted to see himself reflected in their clear blue depths.

Instead, he schmoozed the crowd, wooed the media, flirted with the ladies and mocked his status as both a sex symbol and action star whenever it was raised. He pretended he was what the world knew him to be, but for the first time since fame had found him, he realized it wasn't enough.

He realized he wanted something more.

By the time the length of plush red carpet ended at the open doors of the IMAX Theatre the squealing cheers of the crowd had grown so loud it was almost deafening. Preparing to enter the theatre, to sit in the dark and stare at a film his movie career hinged on even as he contemplated what that career really meant to him, Chris turned and waved at the ecstatic spectators.

It took a second for his mind to register something falling from the sky toward him—a dark object arcing through the air high over the heads of the people crushing against the velvet-rope barricade in front of him. It took another second before his body began to respond to his mind's command to move.

He frowned, trapped in surreal slow motion. The dark shape fell toward him, growing closer at a phenomenal rate. His brain told him it looked heavy, possibly hard. Told his feet to hurry the fuck up and move.

And then a black-sleeved arm shot out above his head and snatched the dark shape out of the air.

"Got it," Liev muttered, pulling his arm in.

Chris pivoted on his heel, staring into the black lenses of the man's sunglasses.

The crowd burst out in raucous applause. Chris forced a smile to his lips. With every breath he took, Liev's distinct scent filtered into his being.

Black Ray-Bans regarded him for a split second, the tiniest hint of a smile playing with Liev's lips before the Australian turned his attention to the object gripped in his hand. "Bloody hell."

Chris frowned, drawing his head closer to Liev's. Reveling in the stolen moment of being close to the man without fear of rumour or rejection. "What is it?"

Liev chuckled, and for a second his eyes met Chris's over

the thin metal rims of his sunglasses. "Someone really wants you to call them," he said, unraveling what was in his hand.

Chris lowered his gaze to what Liev revealed, a warm softness at his elbow telling him Bethany now stood beside him.

Liev held a cell phone in his hand, a Post-it note stuck to the screen with a phone number written in red pen. Under the cell phone, crumpled but undeniable, was what had wrapped it for its short flight through the air—a pair of black satin panties.

Liev chuckled. "Classy."

"Get those out of here," Bethany instructed, the clipped distaste clear in her voice.

Chris shot her a look.

She pulled a face. "It's gross." Turning from the panties and cell phone in Liev's hand, she moved aside, waving over one of the red-carpet event's security team.

"We love you, Chris!" a chorus of excited female voices cried from the crowd behind him.

"Good thing Liev was here," Bethany said. "Or you'd have skanky panties on your head."

Chris studied her for a second. His heart beat fast, working its way up to his throat. He slid his gaze to Liev. The Australian was watching him with wordless calm. With a nod, he grinned at Bethany. "You're right."

Snaring Liev's hand, Chris swung around and faced the crowd. "My bodyguard, everyone," he shouted, hoisting Liev's arm high in the air. "I couldn't survive without him."

The crowd went wild. Women started chanting *bodyguard, bodyguard*. Camera flashes fired, a maelstrom of detonations that peppered Chris and Liev in white light.

Chris laughed, smirking up at Liev. Liev grinned back, raising his free hand to wave at the squealing, cheering, clapping horde.

And the *whole* time the flashes fired and the crowd cheered, Chris's body thrummed with rising, elemental happiness.

Because his palm was pressed to Liev's palm. Because he was touching him, flesh to flesh.

Right here. In public. For the world to see.

He reveled in that brief moment, loving it. Never wanting it to end.

A soft hand pressed at his shoulder. "It's time to go inside, Mr. Huntley," Bethany whispered in his ear.

He bit back his growl of frustration, shooting Liev a quick look as the man disengaged his hand from Chris's. With a single nod, Liev stepped backward, distancing himself from Chris once more. Returning to his place in the background—where the bodyguard of a celebrity belonged.

Chris's gut rolled. He balled his fist, ground his teeth and strode away through the open theatre doors into the opulent foyer.

He didn't turn around to see if Liev followed him. He knew he wouldn't. Bodyguards did not sit beside the ones they were charged to protect during film screenings. Bodyguards sat a few rows back.

Away.

Exactly where Chris didn't want him to be.

CHAPTER EIGHT

"Tell me all about it. Don't leave out a thing."

Liev chuckled, his niece's excitement evident not just in the joy in her voice and the smile on her young face, but in the way she wriggled on her seat.

"You look like a puppy about to get a treat," he said, flicking the turn indicator to the right. He should be angry at her. He should be giving her an ear-bashing about skipping out of the house without her parents knowing and travelling halfway across Sydney so late at night.

Truth was, he didn't have it in him. He was so happy to see her that the last thing he could be was the responsible adult uncle. So instead, he was being the cool uncle who promised not to tell his uptight brother about Caitlin's misbehaviour. Within reason. He was still driving her back to her home. As much as he loved seeing her, if his brother or sister-in-law walked into her bedroom where she was meant to be sleeping and found her bed empty they would have a heart attack. Liev may not like his estranged brother's attitude toward his sexual choices, but he still loved him. He could only imagine the terror Ian would experience finding his seventeen-year-old daughter missing.

"Tell me, Uncle L." Caitlin smacked his biceps with the back of her hand, impatience cutting the laughter in her voice. "Everything. Who did you meet?"

Negotiating the late-night traffic, Liev gave her a sideward grin. "I meet Burt Newton, Karl Stefanovic, Bill Collins and the Red Wiggle."

Caitlin growled at him. "Seriously? You spent the night at a Hollywood movie opening and the only celebrities you met were Australian ones? Lame television celebrities at that?"

Liev pulled a wounded face. "Hey, nothing lame about Burt Newton, missy. And the Red Wiggle? I remember when you were so happy to see the Red Wiggle you *cried*. Who was I *meant* to meet?"

Caitlin waved her hands about. "Oh I don't know? Maybe the other actors in the movie? Jeez, Uncle L. Did you talk to them? Are they nice? Is Diesel as hot in real life as he is in the movies?"

"Yes, they are nice," Liev answered with a laugh. "And yes, he *is* as hot in real life as he is in the movies."

Caitlin sighed, slumping in the Audi's passenger seat. "I knew he would be. Any chance you could get his autograph for me?"

Liev tossed her a playful scowl. "After the way you laughed at me when I gave you the prime minister's autograph? Hell no. I'm never collecting autographs for you again."

Caitlin's answering snort was so like her father's Liev felt his chest squeeze tight. Damn, he missed his brother. He really did. "Do I have posters of the prime minister on my bedroom walls, Uncle L? No. Posters of hot actors? Yes."

"Ah, see now there's the trouble." Liev made his voice grave. "I haven't seen your bedroom since you were thirteen. You had posters of kittens and ponies and Justin Bieber the last time I saw your bedroom."

His niece let out a sigh. "That sucks. Seriously, Mum and Dad are idiots."

Liev shook his head. "No, they're not. They love you and want what's best for you. At the moment, they don't think I fall into that category."

Her face set in a furious frown. "They're wrong."

Looking to change the subject, Liev let out a loud gasp. "Hey, guess who I *did* get to talk to?"

Caitlin squirmed on the seat, her eyes alight with excitement. "Who?"

"The bloke that was in charge of the on-set porta-loos during filming." He grinned at her. "Maybe I could get *his* autograph if you—"

His niece thumped his biceps with the back of her hand again. "Oh God, gross!"

Laughing, Liev turned his focus back on the road. He hadn't expected to see Caitlin tonight, but he was glad she'd defied her parents.

Half an hour ago, when he had exited the IMAX theater to scope out the surrounding area as *Dead Even's* end credits began to roll, he'd been less than impressed to find her standing a few feet away, waving at him.

Hurrying over to the grinning teenager, he'd put on his best gruff expression only to have his niece burst out laughing and tease him about his tux. He'd struggled to hide his grin as he'd admonished her, told her to stay put and then hurried back into the theater.

Ten minutes later, he'd emerged with the keys to the SUV. Bethany had informed him Chris was traveling to the post-screening party at Russell Crowe's Sydney home with his fellow cast members, and she and Jeff were going for supper at a nearby restaurant.

"Go." Bethany had shooed him away, the smile on her face understanding. "I think you need a break anyways. Jeff and I will grab a taxi back to the house when we're done. Just be ready to collect Mr. Huntley from the party when I call you."

"What about Chris Huntley? Is he as hot?"

Liev's breath caught at Caitlin's sudden question. He gripped the SUV's steering wheel, his gut clenching.

"I meant to ask you this afternoon," Caitlin went on, "but got sidetracked when you were showing me how to break into the house through the window." She nudged his arm with her elbow. "Thanks for that, by the way. It'll come in handy if I ever have to sneak into the house without Mum and Dad knowing."

"Caitlin," he growled.

She laughed. "Kidding. But seriously, is Chris Huntley hot in real life? I still can't believe you get to touch him. I am so jealous."

The answering laugh that fell from Liev's lips was weak. From the corner of his eye, he saw Caitlin frown. "What's up?" she asked.

He shook his head. "Grown-up things. Nothing you need to worry about."

She burst out laughing. "Grown-up things? Seriously? Jesus, Uncle L, what the hell?"

He scowled, turning the car into a quiet street. "Okay, okay. Sorry. But it's still nothing you need to worry about."

He ground his teeth and glared at the road. He'd been doing so well until Caitlin had mentioned Chris's name. He'd spent the movie running through every possible future scenario in his mind, and every one ended with the same result—Chris returning to America, Liev staying in Australia, never seeing each other again. The brief kiss he'd brushed over Chris's lips on the stairs truly *was* the last. It was better for Chris. The tormented self-disgust Liev had heard in the actor's voice when Chris accused Liev of calling him a pussy had ripped at Liev's heart. He didn't want to cause Chris any more pain or grief or anger, and the only way not to was to remove the confusion.

No matter how much he wanted to explore the haunted desire he saw in Chris's mesmerizing blue eyes, he wouldn't.

As it was, he'd had a bloody hard time keeping his cool

when Chris had grabbed his hand on the red carpet and waved it around for the crowd. All he'd wanted to do was haul the man against his chest and kiss him, right there in front of all the screaming fans. Claim Chris's mouth with his own for the world to see.

The moment he'd decided the fantasy had to end—somewhere around the halfway point of the film, as Chris's rogue hero made love to his leading lady's CIA agent in a grimy, dimly-lit hotel room—he'd banished thoughts of Chris from his mind.

And then his niece had gone and asked him if the man was hot.

Was he hot? Fuck, Liev knew he'd never meet hotter again.

"Uncle L?" Caitlin's soft voice scraped at his nerves. "Do you *like* Chris Huntley? Like, *like* like?"

Liev bit back a breath. He tightened his grip on the steering wheel, negotiating a hard left before turning right straight away into his brother's street. "He's my boss, Caitlin," he said, trying like hell to keep his voice calm. "That's it. He's an American actor I'm protecting while he's in Australia. He's going back to the States the day after tomorrow. And besides, he's never dated anyone but women. You know that. You told me who they all were when I first told you I was guarding him."

The prickling weight on the side of his face told him Caitlin was staring at him. He suppressed another frustrated sigh. He'd always been proud of the fact his niece was smart and astute for her age, willing to judge the world without prejudice. Right now, however, he wished she wasn't so perceptive. The last thing he wanted was Caitlin figuring out he was falling in love with Chris Huntley.

His throat squeezed shut, the truth of the situation hitting him hard.

Falling *in love*, damn it. How the hell did he let this happen? He didn't fall in love. He didn't do relationships. He didn't do commitment. He lived for each day. He didn't mess with the status quo. He enjoyed what life had to offer and that was it.

Falling in love with an American movie star who didn't *want* to be sexually attracted to him was dumb.

Dumb, dumb, dumb.

"We're here," he grumbled, pulling the Audi to a halt in front of a large single-story house surrounded by lush gardens. The windows of his brother's house were dark, not a sign evident that Ian and his wife knew their teenage daughter was currently AWOL. Turning to Caitlin, he pointed a finger at her. "In the morning you need to tell them where you were."

She nodded, her expression pensive, but she didn't move.

He raised his eyebrows at her. "What?"

A frown furrowed her young forehead. "Do you remember when I told you the hottest guy at school kept asking me out? Two years ago, when I was only in year ten and he was a senior? And all my friends kept telling me to do it, to go out with him? Do you remember that?"

Liev's pulse thumped hard in his temple. He nodded. "I do."

"Do you remember what you said to me? When I told you I didn't know if I wanted to say yes or not? That I thought he was too hot for me and that I'd only end up getting hurt?"

The grunt that left Liev was choked. "I told you if *any* boy hurt you I'd break them in two."

Caitlin laughed. "You did. You also told me it was impossible for anyone to be too good for me. But more importantly, you told me the worst thing a person could do is reject themselves in fear that someone else will." She frowned. "You told me to think with my mind, to listen to my heart and to be true to myself. I've followed that piece of advice to the letter ever since, and I've never regretted it." She leant forward, as if bestowing a secret on a small child. "Maybe it's time you took your own advice, Uncle L."

Liev couldn't stop his wry chuckle. "Sweetheart, I really wish I could."

She grinned. "So do it. What's the worst that could happen? He could say no?" And before he could argue, she dropped a kiss on his cheek and scrambled out of the car just as the verandah light came to life.

Liev sat behind the wheel, his heart beat fast, his gut knotted. He watched his niece hurry down the footpath leading to the verandah steps, her words—*his* words—replaying in his mind.

Don't reject yourself in fear of someone else doing it.

Was that what he was doing? Was he withdrawing from Chris because he was scared? He knew what scared felt like. Scared was being told when you were only seventeen your parents had died in a car accident. Scared was staring into a burning building and knowing if you didn't run into it, the people inside would die.

Scared wasn't a reaction to a decision. It was a reaction to an event beyond your control, and the only way to deal with that event was to stare it down and refuse to let it beat you.

Surely distancing himself from the American actor was the act of rational thought, not fear. Right?

The front door of his brother's home opened, tearing Liev's thoughts from Chris Huntley.

Ian's tall, lean frame immediately filled the space, and even from this distance Liev could see worry fighting with anger on his face. For a moment, Liev was almost overcome with the urge to lower the driver's side window—dark with privacy tint —to let his brother know it was just him in the car, that Caitlin was fine, safe and not out gallivanting around with someone she shouldn't. Then the harsh fact that, in Ian's opinion, Liev *was* someone Caitlin shouldn't be associating with sank into Liev's gut, and he returned his hand to the wheel.

He watched Caitlin walk up to her father, watched them speak to each other, watched Ian shake his head, his finger, a frown on his face. His shoulders stiffened and then he shook his head again and folded his arms around his daughter, holding her close.

A lump filled Liev's throat and, unable to watch the brother he loved who wanted nothing at all to do with him any longer, he pressed his foot to the accelerator and drove away from the only family he had.

He knew his place in the world, and it wasn't with his brother. And no matter how much he wished otherwise, no matter how sage and profound his niece's teenage advice, his place wasn't with Chris Huntley either.

It seemed he'd lied to his niece all those years ago. Better to reject oneself than to let someone else do it.

It was safer that way.

Three hours into the party, Chris realized he'd had enough. No matter how many times he thought he'd drained his scotch, it was always full when he looked at it. No matter how many times he said no, the little starlet with the silicon boobs, bad weave and broad Australian accent kept trying to put her hand down his pants. No matter how many times he turned around to share something with Liev, the man wasn't there.

He said his farewells to the host, waved off the offer of a driver and, seeing a taxi dropping off new guests through the open front doors, hurried out to it before the starlet could squirm her way through the crowd and try to feel him up again. It seemed like fate was lending him a hand.

The trouble was, now he was *in* the taxi heading away from Russell Crowe's house, he realized he didn't actually know the address of his residence while in Australia.

Added to that, he didn't have a key to get in, nor a way of paying for the taxi even if he did know his destination.

If he hadn't had so many scotches, he'd be feeling goddamn stupid right about now.

Squirming on the seat, he dug his cell from his pocket and dialed Bethany's number.

"Mr. Huntley," she answered on the second ring, voice as poised and efficient as ever. "Shall I send Liev for you now?"

Chris's gut clenched at Liev's name. He slumped on the seat, staring out the window. "I'm in a cab, Bethany," he said. Damn, his head swam. "Heading home."

"Home?" The word was sharp. "To Beverly Hills?"

He laughed, a snorting sound at the back of his throat. "No, the place we're staying in on the water. I know the suburb, Point Piper, but I don't know the—"

The ragged breath coming through the reception was unlike any he'd heard his personal assistant take. "Oh God, you scared me, Mr. Huntley. Please don't do that again."

He chuckled, closing his eyes on his blurring vision. "Sorry." Just how many damn drinks *had* he consumed? Not enough to stop him thinking about Liev, that was for damn sure. Every time he'd heard a deep male voice speaking in an Australian accent his heart had jumped into his throat, his balls had risen up and his pulse had quickened. "I won't do it again."

With a *tsk*, Bethany supplied the address and then waited for him to give it to the cab driver.

"Now," she continued when he'd returned the phone to his ear, "How inebriated are you?"

"I've had a few, but I'm in control of my faculties, if that's what you mean. I don't do fall-down drunk anymore. Rowie would kill me."

She gave a *hmm*. "Do you know how far away you are?"

"No clue."

"Ask, please?"

Chris looked at the driver. "How long until we get there?"

"'Bout fifteen minutes."

"He says—"

"I heard, thank you, Mr. Huntley," Bethany interrupted. "I shall be waiting out the front of the house."

She disconnected. Chris frowned at the phone. For a personal assistant, she really was a bossy little thing. Most actors' P.A.s spent their time sucking up to their bosses. The thing was, Chris realized he didn't mind it. Not at all. It was kind of like having his sister with him even when she wasn't.

Slumping farther down in the seat, he shoved his phone back into his jacket's inside pocket and stared out the window. His thoughts turned to Liev and, too exhausted—or drunk, he wasn't quite sure which—to fight any longer he let them.

He still didn't know what to do about his reaction to the man. If he only got horny looking at the guy, if he only thought of sex—albeit the kind of sex Chris had never had before—it would be easy to believe the whole surreal situation was just a purely physical…thing. The kind of *thing* he could put behind him when he returned to L.A. He could tuck the mind-blowing, explosive passion of the amazing kiss in the restaurant's office into his memory bank and draw on it whenever he needed to emote bone-deep, raw emotion on screen. The trouble was it *wasn't* only a purely physical thing. Tonight on the red carpet proved that. The party he'd just left proved that. The whole time he'd been there, surrounded by fellow performers, entertainers and celebrities, he'd wanted Liev to be there with him. Talking to him, laughing at his jokes, smiling at him, sharing the moment with him. He'd wanted to hear what the Australian thought of the film. He wanted to involve him in conversations, hear what he had to say about things discussed, and it had nothing to do with Liev's accent and everything to do with his dry wit and intelligence.

The plain, simple truth was Chris enjoyed spending time with the man. On every level imaginable.

Which was pretty fucking frustrating considering tomorrow was his last full day in Sydney. He was flying back to L.A. the day after, his plane departing at six in the morning.

Two nights and one day left.

What did he do?

What *should* he do?

"Do I know you?" the taxi driver's amiable voice yanked Chris out of his tormented reverie. "You look familiar."

Chris forced a smile to his lips, meeting the man's puzzled brown eyes in the rearview mirror. "Not sure. Ever been to L.A.?"

The driver laughed. "Nope. Never stepped foot outta Sydney."

"Wow." Chris couldn't hide his surprise. "Really?"

Another laugh filled the taxi's cabin. "No need. Got everything I want here."

The happy contentment of the statement filled Chris's throat with a thick lump. Man, how wonderful would it be to be able to say the same thing—that everything he wanted was right here in Sydney.

Maybe it is?

"You on holiday, or here for work?"

Chris snorted. The guy really didn't know who he was. "Work."

"Ah, that sucks."

A few moments passed in silence. Chris closed his eyes, aware the inebriated lurching in his head was fading.

"Righto, mate," the driver said, and the pull on Chris's churning stomach told him the taxi had come to a halt. "Here we are. That'll be forty-two bucks fifty."

Chris looked at him. "Errr."

Before the driver's frown finished forming, Bethany appeared at his window, tapping on the glass with the back of her knuckles.

"Ah, I see." The driver smirked at Chris. "Little woman been waiting up for you, 'eh? You gonna be in the dog house now?"

Chris pulled a rueful face. "Seems that way."

With a chuckle, the driver lowered his window. "G'day, love."

Bethany leaned forward, bestowed a smile on the man and passed him a credit card. "I hope he hasn't been causing you any grief, sir."

"Not at all. Quiet but friendly. Best fare I've had all night." The driver flicked him a quick look in the mirror. "Hope the night's not too rough on you, mate."

Bethany cocked an eyebrow. "Are you coming in, Rupert?" she asked, using the false name Chris used whenever they were keeping his identity a secret.

He nodded, unbuckled his belt and opened his door. "Thanks," he said, giving the driver a smile.

The man smiled back. "No worries. Enjoy your time in Australia."

Chris swallowed. Enjoy his time in Australia.

If only he knew how to do that?

He walked toward the house, leaving Bethany to pay for the fare. He needed to burn off some tension. Needed to clear his head.

Don't you mean you need to see Liev?

He strode through the door, doing his best to keep his pace steady.

The house was silent, the muted light cast from one of the table lamps in the living room the only sign anyone was awake. Bethany's iPad lay on the sofa beside a collection of papers. A half-empty glass of wine sat on the side table under the lamp, the faintest pink smudge on the rim telling him Bethany was the drinker, not Liev or Jeff.

He looked around, his heart beating fast.

"They're not here."

He jumped at Bethany's soft statement behind him. Swinging around, he watched her walk toward him. "Where are they?"

"Jeff hooked up at the café. Liev had something to deal with."

The lump in Chris's throat grew thicker. Something? Like what?

Bethany's gaze lingered on his face. "He'll be back."

Hot tension flooded through Chris at the empathy in her voice. Jesus, his personal assistant felt sorry for him. And possibly suspected Chris felt more for Liev than he should. Spinning on his heel, he stormed past her, heading for his bedroom. "I'm going for a swim," he threw over his shoulder.

Ten minutes later, his tux a crumpled pile on his bedroom floor, he dived into the cool waters of the mansion's pool.

It cleared the remains of his alcoholic excesses out of his system. He swam from one end to the other, counting each stroke. Ducking under the surface, he spun in the water, planted the balls of his feet against the smooth tile wall and pushed off, swimming back to the other end. Fifty laps later, he pressed his chest to the wall of the pool and rested his folded arms on the side. His heart raced, not from exertion but from turmoil.

Christ, he couldn't stop wanting Liev to be here. He couldn't stop wishing the man would dive into the water and slide his hard body against his.

And at the same time, he couldn't stop imagining nightmarish headlines. *Homosexual Huntley's Career in Free-fall. Funny Fag Fails at Action Career.* And the best of all, *Crowds Quit Queer Chris.*

It seemed his tormented mind was not only vicious but also had a cutting flair for alliteration.

Scraping his hands through his wet hair, he let out a ragged breath and propelled himself up and out of the pool. No matter which way he looked at it, he was—

"Mr. Huntley?"

Chris started at Bethany's calm voice. He spun to his right, his heart thumping hard. He froze when he found his personal assistant smiling at him.

She stood a few feet away, dressed in the skimpiest black bikini he'd ever seen, her gaze fixed on his face. "I think you need my help."

Chris swallowed. His cock, damn near erect thanks to his constant thoughts of Liev, throbbed. "What for?"

She walked toward him, and for a split second the tattoo below her shallow navel caught his attention. His cock throbbed again. For some reason the sight of something rebellious like ink on his poised assistant made his blood rush faster through his veins. And then he jerked his stare back to her face, her crazy mane of wild red ringlets almost hiding her eyes.

A slow smile pulled at her lips. His mind told him they were full and lush lips. Told him the rest of her was lush and beautiful. Told him *this* was what was meant to arouse him. This, not a man with a hard, muscular body, a hard, angular frame and a hard, thick cock.

He was *meant* to be turned on by womanly curves, boobs, curving hips…

So why the hell couldn't he stop thinking of Liev fucking Reynolds?

Bethany stopped a mere foot away, her green eyes reflecting the pale blue light of the swimming pool. "You know what for."

The lump in Chris's throat grew fat. Hot. "Because I want…"

He couldn't say it. Not aloud.

Because I want Liev. God, help me, I want Liev. So fucking—

His personal assistant closed the minute distance between them, slipped her fingers between the waistband of his Speedo and his hips and slid the wet item of clothing down.

His cock sprung free, fresh blood surging through its growing length. The summer night air wrapped around it, a warm caress that made his gut hitch.

"Bethany," he said, his voice a broken croak. "What are you doing?"

"What needs to be done," she whispered.

And before Chris could move, she lowered to her knees, cupped his balls in her hands, closed her lips around the head of his cock and sucked.

CHAPTER NINE

Liev let himself into the harbour-side mansion without a sound. It was almost two a.m. He didn't want to wake anyone up.

After checking to make sure the concertina doors leading out onto the main balcony were locked, he walked into the kitchen. He'd grab a bottle of water from the fridge, check the windows and then head down to the lower floor to do the same there. After that, he'd have a shower in the bathroom attached to the gym, relieve the tension in his body he knew wouldn't ease off until Chris Huntley had left Australia while under the running water—if then—and then head to bed.

Chris's first public appearance later that day was at a wildlife reserve. As conflicted as he was about his feelings for the man, he still needed to be at the peak of his—

A small white sheet of notepaper stuck to the fridge caught his eye.

Need you by the pool. B.

Liev frowned at Bethany's neat, no-nonsense handwriting. By the pool? What the hell did she need from him by the pool? It wasn't like she required sunblock to be rubbed onto her back. Not at this time of night.

What if she's going to test you again? Like she did on the first night? Would you be able to say no tonight? Given how fucking crazy you're going with need for Chris?

Shucking off his tux jacket, he tossed it over the back of a chair and headed for the pool. He didn't have an answer. All he could do was hope to bloody God he didn't find Bethany dressed in sweet fuck all again. He didn't think his strained nerves and taxed control could handle it.

He'd be just as likely to bury himself in her tightness and imagine it was—

He stopped, his heart smashing into his throat with violent force, his stare fixed on the sight of Bethany on her knees, Chris standing before her, his hands fisted in her hair, his cock disappearing into her mouth.

A strangled growl escaped Liev, barely audible over the moans of the two people by the pool.

He stared at them. His blood roared in his ears. The hair at his nape prickled. His flesh flushed, then ran cold.

Beads of water glistened on Chris's body, the pool's blue light dancing in each tiny drop. It highlighted the man's physical perfection, the sculpted strength of his muscles. Liev devoured his naked form, unable to look away.

His gut knotted. An excruciating pressure clamped around his chest. He watched as Chris's head lolled backward, the man's lips parting, his eyes closing. Pleasure etched his face. Pleasure and something else. Something tormented.

A low groan escaped the actor's throat, scraping at Liev's sanity. At Chris's feet, Bethany moaned in reply.

Tight heat lashed at Liev's dick. His balls throbbed, heavy with anguished want. His stare moved to her mouth, his own mouth going dry at the hypnotic sight of Chris's thick, rigid cock thrusting in and out of it.

Fuck, he wanted that cock in his mouth. So fucking much it hurt.

And yet there it was, in Bethany's.

Anger ripped through him, scalding hot and bitter. He snarled, driving his blunt nails into his palms. Tiny crescents of pain cut into his flesh, but still he didn't move. Still he didn't tear his stare from the vision before him.

As much as it hurt him, it turned him on as well.

Fuck, did it turn him on.

He watched Bethany blow Chris and craved the man's flesh on his tongue. Jealousy ate at him, as hot and acrid as his anger, and still he couldn't look away. Still he couldn't turn and leave.

Standing motionless, shrouded by the lush overhanging greenery of the garden, he stared at the erotic act and ached to take Bethany's place.

Fucking *ached* for it. Like he'd never ached for any other thing.

Another groan left Chris, this one louder. His arse cheeks bunched. His back arched. His thrusts into Bethany's mouth increased in speed.

From his place in the darkness, Liev grabbed at his mocking erection and squeezed, willing crippling pain into his groin. None came. Instead, excruciating pleasure scored through him. Twisted and intense and wretched.

Teeth ground, Liev glared at the two lovers, his blood boiling, his balls swelling. He let out an anguished moan when Chris slammed his cock deeper into Bethany's mouth. "Oh, fuck, yes."

Chris's eyes snapped open. He jerked his stare to where Liev stood, his nostrils flaring. At Chris's feet, Bethany withdrew her mouth from his length and turned to study Liev over her shoulder, her expression unreadable.

Liev met Chris's gaze, the American imprisoning him for a heartbeat. Just one.

He had to go. Now.

He spun on his heel.

"Liev."

Chris's plaintive plea stopped him.

He turned back, hiding his pain from Chris behind a bored expression. "Yeah?"

The American stared at him. Naked. Erect. "Don't."

Unable to stop himself, hating his lack of self-control, Liev took him all in. His chest was free of hair, his nipples small and round and beaded. His torso was lean and sculpted, his abs a divine six-pack Liev knew would be heaven to explore with tongue and lips. To chart a journey down to the shallow dip of his navel, to follow the thin trail of honey-blond hair leading from his navel down to his dick.

Unhinged lust surged through Liev at the small bead of pre-come oozing from the tiny slit on the tip of Chris's erection. A groan rumbled in his chest but he denied it. Refused it.

Returning his stare to Chris's face, he crossed his arms. "Don't what?"

He'd always known there'd be a solution to the problematic sexual chemistry between him and the actor. It seemed Chris and Bethany had discovered what that solution was. Unfortunately, Liev hadn't prepared himself for how brutal the solution would be on his state of mind, his soul. Perhaps this was how they did things in the movie world? If that was the case, he didn't want a bar of it.

Chris drew in a slow breath. "Don't go."

Cold contempt cut through Liev's wretched need. "You need me to guard you while you're getting head? Sure. No worries, boss."

"I don't…" Chris sucked in another breath. His chest heaved. "That's not what I want."

A vise compressed Liev's temple. He didn't say a word.

Bethany walked toward him, her hips undulating with each slow step. "I know what he wants, Liev."

Liev narrowed his eyes. "And what's that, love?"

A small smile curled her lips. She reached for the buttons on his shirt. "This."

He didn't move. His over-wrought mind kept him rooted to the spot. When she slipped her hands under the crisp white cotton and slid his shirt from his shoulders, his arms, he couldn't stop his stare sliding to Chris.

"And this." She released his belt, lowered his fly and pushed his tuxedo trousers to the ground.

He didn't stop her.

Nor did he stop her when she inched his boxer briefs down over his hips.

Instead, he stared at Chris. Watched the man watching his flesh, his erection, be revealed to the night.

Instead, he remained a statue. Imprisoned not just by the open desire smoldering in Chris's eyes, but by the foolish hope that what he so desperately ached for was truly about to become a reality.

He watched Chris move toward him. Watched him close the distance between them. Watched him stop but a breath away.

"It's not guarding I need from you, Liev," Chris said, his voice a low murmur. "It's this."

He reached out and wrapped his fingers around Liev's aching cock, dragged his thumb over its distended, weeping head, and the last vestiges of Liev's tenuous control shattered.

His mouth crushed Liev's. There was no holding back. For Chris, holding back, second-guessing, hesitation and confusion no longer existed. He wanted the Australian like no other living soul he'd ever met and was done denying it.

The whole time Bethany's mouth and tongue and teeth had worked his cock, he'd imagined them Liev's. The whole time. Even when he'd tried to accept the reality—that it was his personal assistant giving him head, his female personal assistant

—his body, his mind, his *heart* had rejected it and told him it was Liev.

Liev. And he didn't want it any other way.

He swiped his tongue in Liev's mouth, squeezing and kneading Liev's impressively thick and long erection as he did so. The man groaned into his mouth, meeting the ravenous ferocity of the kiss with equal hunger.

Their teeth clicked. Their lips slid together. Chris pumped Liev's shaft, his grip tight. Strong fingers joined his, the rough callouses telling him they belonged to the man he wanted more than breath. He moaned, capturing Liev's tongue to suck on it with greedy force as he allowed Liev to guide his fist up and down his cock.

To his left, a low sigh caressed the night. Bethany. "Well done, boys. I'll be back."

A part of Chris wanted to pull away from Liev's lips, to thank his assistant for what she'd done before she left. He had no delusions now it had been part of her plan. He'd suspected all along she'd had an agenda. The second Liev had entered the house on that first day, a lifetime ago, she'd begun to bring them together. Why, he didn't know. When he was done losing himself to the absolute perfection of kissing Liev, of fucking Liev with his hand, he'd ask. But not now. Now all he wanted was the Australian.

The man's rigid cock was like steely velvet against his palm. It burned his flesh. He pumped faster, Liev's fingers governing the speed. The pressure.

Chris's head spun. He tore his mouth from the kiss, dragging it over the rough angle of Liev's chin. Tiny bristles rasped at his lips, the sensation flooding his balls with molten delight. Who would have thought a five o'clock shadow could arouse him so fucking much?

But it did. He explored Liev's chin, his jaw, reveling in the friction of stubble under the tip of his tongue. It was so male, so foreign to Chris's senses. With each lick, his cock pulsed and jerked. With each pulse and jerk of his cock, he squeezed Liev's massive length harder.

"Fuck, yes," the Australian groaned. "You have no idea… how much…" He stopped, his breath turning to a ragged gasp, his hips bucking forward as Chris scraped his thumb over the tip of his cock.

The jolting move rammed Liev's hips and thighs to Chris's. Stars of exquisite heat shot through Chris at the delicious contact. He nipped at Liev's chin, sliding his other hand over the man's smooth, warm hip to grab his ass.

Firm muscles bunched under his palm. Another moan vibrated in Liev's chest. Fueled by the raw desire in the sound —and needing to feel their bodies together again—Chris released Liev's rigid length and hauled Liev's hips to his.

Their thighs rubbed. Their cocks slid together. Fresh stars erupted in Chris's head as the warm pressure of Liev's balls pressed to his. He reached for the man's chin, holding it with shaky fingers as he plunged his tongue back into Liev's mouth.

Liev did just what he wanted. He captured Chris's tongue and sucked on it. Hard. Lines of painful pleasure speared through Chris, sinking into the pit of his belly, knotting around his engorged shaft.

Fingers scraped at his shoulders, his scalp. When Liev yanked a fistful of his hair and pulled his head backward, tearing the kiss apart, he protested on a raw moan.

The Australian laved his throat, his Adam's apple with his tongue, all the while rolling his hips faster.

Chris couldn't breathe. The sensations building in him from Liev's cock stroking against his stole any hope of doing anything but surrendering. He raked his fingers over the bunched muscles of Liev's ass again, grinding harder into Liev's thrusts. If anyone had told Chris dry humping a naked man would electrify him more than being inside a woman's tight, wet pussy he would have laughed at them. But he wasn't laughing now. He was moaning and panting and begging for—

Liev stepped backward.

Away from Chris.

Chris snapped his eyes open. He sucked in a sharp breath, staring at the man before him.

Liev's nostrils flared. His chest heaved. The powerful sight —Liev fighting his desire, barely in control—filled Chris's mouth with saliva. Made his knees weak. "I have to know you're sure, Chris," Liev said on a shaky breath. "I can't do this if you're going to hate yourself after. I want you so fucking much I'm in pain standing here, but I'll walk away if you're not sure."

Chris let a small grin play with his lips. "If you walk away, I'm calling the bodyguard guild and having you flogged."

Liev shook his head. "I'm serious, Chris. I need to hear you say it. I need to hear you say you're sure. That you're not just caught in an adrenaline rush. That this isn't just a thing you're trying out for an upcoming role. I need to hear you say you want me. As much as I want you."

"I…"

Chris couldn't pull his stare from Liev. Oh boy, could he say it?

Liev's nostrils flared. "I need to hear it, Huntley. Or I—"

Chris stepped toward him. "I want you, Liev Reynolds." He reached out with his hand, feathering the tips of his fingers over Liev's pecs, across one taut nipple. "I've never been more sure of anything in my life."

Liev's nostrils flared again. "Good. 'Cause I want that thick, hard cock of yours in my mouth now."

He snatched at Chris's wrists, hauled him back to his body and dropped to his knees.

Ungentle fingers wrapped Chris's length. He cried out, liquid need surging into his balls.

"Tell me to suck your cock, Chris." Liev's order was hoarse. Strained.

Chris dropped his head, gazing down at Liev kneeling at

his feet. The man's hot breath fanned over the distended head of Chris's penis like a million licks of warmth.

A shudder rocked through Chris and he pulled in a wobbly breath. "Suck my cock, Liev."

Without preamble or hesitation, Liev closed his lips around the bulbous rim of Chris's cock and sucked.

Concentrated pleasure scorched through Chris's body. He groaned, tangling his fingers in the thick strands of Liev's hair, holding Liev's head to his throbbing organ. The man's mouth was nothing like Bethany's on his flesh. Nothing was like the man's mouth on his flesh. Holy fuck, how could a simple seal of lips around a dick be so exquisite?

Fresh pleasure surged through him as Liev painted the tip of his cock with his tongue.

He bucked his hips forward, wanting to bury his length deeper into the man's talented mouth.

With a pop of releasing suction, Liev flicked him an arrogant look. "Tell me what you want me to do with your cock now, Chris. I've sucked it. Tell me what—"

"Fucking suck it all the way to my balls, goddamn it," Chris ground out, his belly hitching from consuming tension and need. He was trembling. And impatient. Every second Liev's mouth wasn't fucking his dick was torturous. "Please?"

A ravenous hunger flared in Liev's eyes at the plea. He took Chris's cock in his mouth again. Circling its tip with his lips, he cupped the heavy weight of Chris's scrotum in one hand, gripped the root of Chris's shaft with the other and slowly, slowly inched down its length.

Chris barely remained standing for the exquisite duration.

He groaned, the honest sound tearing from his constricted throat.

When he stumbled back a step, Liev released his balls and held him still with a powerful grip, digging his fingers into Chris's ass cheeks. So close to his anus swirls of intense, licentious need filled his vision.

Keeping him still, Liev withdrew up his length, swiping his tongue over the underside of Chris's shaft as he went. He paused at the head, tormented the tiny knot of sensitive nerve-endings beneath the crown with the tip of his tongue and then, faster this time, slid down Chris's cock again. Farther.

Once again, Chris's knees trembled. Once again, Liev dug his fingers into his butt.

A ragged keening sound vibrated in Chris's chest. He slammed his hips forward, driving his dick deeper into Liev's mouth. Deeper. When he felt the head of his organ push against a soft wall, he couldn't control himself anymore.

Liev was deep throating him. Control was futile.

He fisted his hands tighter in the man's hair, punching his hips forward. Over and over. Liev took each wild thrust, the hand on his ass brutal, the hand on his balls the same.

Pleasure and pain melded together. Propelled Chris higher to a mount he ached for even as he willed it away.

Too soon. It was too soon. What if after this Liev decided Chris was not what he wanted after all? What if Chris never got to experience this pure ecstasy again?

Bone-deep trembles began to claim him. He grit his teeth and squeezed his eyes shut. Liev's tongue lapped at the curve of his balls, his teeth scraped at the sides of Chris's length. The painful contact had always disturbed Chris whenever he'd been blown before, but not now. Now he rolled his hips, willing Liev's molars to his flesh.

"Teeth," he burst out. "I want to feel your teeth."

Liev twisted his head, just enough to scrape his molars over Chris's cock again.

"Fuck, yes." Chris slammed his hips forward, ribbons of pleasure unfurling through the pit of his stomach. "That's it. Now suck it. Hard."

Liev's tight mouth slicked up to Chris's cockhead, drawing on Chris's length with punishing suction. He cried out, his orgasm threatening to claim him.

He could feel it, a scalding pressure tingling in his soul. Rushing through him.

"No," he moaned, shaking his head. "Not yet. Not yet. Let me..." He tried to pull away from Liev's masterful mouth. Tried to disengage.

The Australian wouldn't let him. He sank his fingers harder into the muscles of his butt cheeks and plunged down Chris's cock again.

Up. Down.

Up.

Down.

Up. Up. To the tip.

Teeth nipped at the swollen crown before Liev sank down over Chris's throbbing shaft again, all the way down, down, down until he could go no farther.

No farther.

And just when Chris didn't think he could stave off his orgasm any longer, when he knew he was about to come, Liev pressed one finger to Chris's anus and pushed.

Absolute pleasure detonated within in him. He tossed back his head, his spine bowing and cried out Liev's name as his seed spurt from his cock. It pumped into Liev's throat, thick ropes of release pouring from Chris's soul.

Liquid essence that ruptured from his cock and flooded Liev's mouth.

His orgasm seemed never ending. Every time he thought he was on the verge of recovery, Liev would suck a little more on his flesh and his body would shudder again, fresh come spilling from him. He gasped, the sound a panted laugh.

"I-I...I can't..." His lips stretched with a smile even as he shook his head. "I need...oh fuck, that was..."

With a soft pop, Liev released Chris's cock from his mouth. He straightened to his feet and gazed down into Chris's eyes. His naked heat radiated from him, his engorged erection bumping Chris's spent one. "Amazing," he finished Chris's exclamation, a lop-sided smile on his lips. "I told you you were amazing this afternoon."

Chris laughed again, a shaky hiccup unlike any he'd uttered before. "I wasn't talking about me."

Liev cupped his palm to Chris's jaw and, like he had earlier that day, brushed his thumb along Chris's bottom lip. "I was."

He lowered his head to place a lingering kiss on Chris's mouth.

The contact was tender, unlike the savage passion of his blowjob, and Chris hitched in a breath.

"Now," Liev said, "I think you need time to register what just happened. Maybe discuss it with the little minx who works for you."

Chris let out a wobbly laugh. "I think you're right. She has some explaining to do. But later. Much later." He placed his hand on Liev's chest, directly above his heart, loving the way the coarse hairs smattering the man's pecs tickled his palm. "There's something else that needs to be done now."

Liev shook his head. "I'm serious, Chris. What just happened, you need to think about it. Before..." He stopped. Possibly because Chris had smoothed his hand down his torso and was now gripping Liev's thick, rigid cock.

"I've registered it all," Chris said, stepping back to Liev. "And discussion isn't what I need right now." He squeezed Liev's cock in a pulsing beat. "This is. In my mouth."

Liev shook his head. "No. It's too much. Too soon. I don't want to rush—"

"Shut the fuck up, Reynolds." Chris tightened his hold on the man's cock and began to walk backward.

Liev followed, his nostrils flaring as Chris tugged him by the dick to the closest sun lounger.

Maneuvering Liev until the back of his calves pressed the foot of the piece of furniture, Chris wriggled his eyebrows. "It's my turn."

He placed his palm on Liev's chest, placed his lips to the man's parted ones and, with a low chuckle, pushed.

Liev dropped onto the sun lounger. His turgid cock slapped against his belly as he landed on his ass. Chris followed him down, and the last thing Chris saw before he captured Liev's erection in his mouth was Liev's eyes smoldering with a desire and need and hunger Chris knew all too well.

A desire and need and hunger that changed everything.

Everything.

CHAPTER TEN

"Holy fuck."

Liev's elbows collapsed beneath him. His back flattened to the wicker sun lounger, his stare flicked over the stars above him in the black sky.

"Holy…*fuck!*"

Chris plunged his mouth down Liev's cock, fast, hungry and completely unpracticed.

It was singularly the most incredible thing Liev had ever experienced.

He squeezed his eyes shut for a heartbeat, drowning in the sheer pleasure of Chris's inexperience. Head from male partners was a world away from those from female. A man's mouth enclosed a cock differently, the jaw, the palate, all combined to create a distinct blowjob. Liev always enjoyed getting head, no matter the sex of his partner, but *this* head job, from a man who had never given it before was beyond comprehension.

Chris fumbled for his balls. His knuckles collided with Liev's inner thighs, and he flattened his palm against the sensitive globes. He lashed his tongue at the underside of Liev's cock. He gagged once, twice and then a strangled groan vibrated in his throat as he went lower.

Liev hissed, undone for a giddy moment by the American's raw enthusiasm. Oh boy, he was going to come soon. The most artless, unrefined blowjob of his life, and it didn't matter. He was going to come soon and it had nothing to do with Chris's lack of skill and everything to do with his commitment to pleasuring Liev and taking pleasure from him.

Commitment. Not a word Liev had had a taste for until the actor between his legs, owning his cock, had come along. If the concentrated sensation Chris awakened in Liev's body with graceless enthusiasm was anything to judge by, it seemed Liev was ready to give himself over to the concept.

Commitment was about to make him blow his fucking load.

That and Chris's ardent, spirited moans.

He opened his eyes. His ragged pants scratched at his dry throat. Tangling his fists in Chris's hair, he tugged the man's head upward.

The suction on his cock vanished with a pop and he shifted on the sun lounger, inching up a little to focus on Chris's face.

Rejection twisted through the need in Chris's eyes. He fell back, balancing on his heels, his breath escaping him in shallow gasps. "Fuck." He swiped at his lips with the back of his hand. "I suck, don't I?" A humourless bark of a laugh escaped him. "Not in the good way though."

Liev pushed himself into a sitting position and rested his elbows on his knees to smile at the man between his bent legs. "That's not why I stopped you, Chris." He reached out with a steady hand and brushed a lock of stray hair away from Chris's eyes. "I stopped you because I was seconds away from coming."

Chris flicked him a sideways look. "So? Isn't that the point?"

"For God's sake, Mr. Huntley."

Liev swung his head up to look at Bethany where she stood beside the sun lounger, two sweating glasses of ice water in her hands. When had she returned? How much had she seen?

She truly was a sexy woman, a wild thing of sensual beauty underneath the poised exterior she presented. Before Chris came along, he would have seduced that miniscule bikini off her lush, exquisite body in a heartbeat and had his way with her willing flesh.

Before Chris. Now, the sweet bounty Bethany possessed no longer held any appeal for Liev.

It was a profound realization, and a worrying one. One Liev would need to think about later. At this moment in time however, he was torn between the pleasures of Chris's intoxicating, inelegant fellatio and intrigued by Bethany's stern reprimand of their boss.

She frowned down at Chris, placing the glasses on the low table beside the sun lounger. "For someone so smart, I wonder about you sometimes. I've only just arrived, but trust me, he didn't stop you because you're doing a bad job. He stopped you because you rock him to the damn core and he doesn't want to scare the crap out of you with the force of his orgasm."

Liev couldn't stop his gob-smacked grunt. "Bloody hell, woman, are you reading my mind?"

She grinned. "No. I read bodies. And yours was saying loud and clear, holy shit this is so good so good and I'm going to freaking erupt and Chris is going to drown in my—"

Liev held up a hand, his own grin stretching his lips. "Okay, okay. I get your point." His cock throbbed from denied release. He turned his attention to Chris. "And she's correct. That's exactly why I stopped you."

Chris pulled a face. "What if I want to drown in your come?"

Liev chuckled. "How 'bout I buy you some floaties first?"

"Floaties?"

The confusion on Chris's face was endearing. If Liev wasn't doing everything in his power to take it slow, to give the man a chance to catch his breath and consider what was going on, he'd lean forward and kiss the puzzlement right out of him.

But he *was* trying to take it slow. For Chris's sake. He smiled, ignoring the throbbing demands of his impatient erection. "The inflatable arm bands little kids wear when learning to swim," he said.

Chris's lips twitched. "Ah, I'm a little kid, am I?"

Liev shrugged. The fact he was having this conversation stark naked on a piece of furniture outside under the stars with a smugly happy woman watching made the whole thing surreal. And at the same time it was exciting. "Let's just say I don't want to throw you in the deep end yet."

Chris shifted on the end of the sun lounger, moving closer to Liev, smoothing his fingers around the backs of Liev's calves. "Too fucking bad."

He pulled Liev's legs toward him with a swift yank.

Liev lost his balance, his center of gravity disrupted by the abrupt move. Chris wasted no time taking advantage of his displacement. He planted his hands on either side of Liev's hips, rose over his body, ground his groin to Liev's ramrod-stiff cock and captured Liev's lips in a savage kiss.

"Okay, I'm outta here again. Don't forget to keep your fluids up."

Bethany's chuckled instruction scratched at the raw pleasure searing through Liev's mind. He groaned into Chris's mouth, snaring two fistfuls of his hair in a fierce grip. The man returned his groan, rolling his cock up and down Liev's erection.

Hot ropes of fire knotted in his groin. He thrust his hips up into the rough contact, scraping his fingers down Chris's back to grab his arse as he did so. The man's glutes were sublime perfection. Liev could spend a lifetime touching his backside and never tire. What would it be like to run his tongue over it? What would it be like to slide his tongue between the toned, sculpted arse cheeks, over the puckered hole of Chris's anus? Fuck, what would it be like to sink his dick into the exquisite opening?

Fresh heat shot into Liev's balls at the delirious thought. He rammed his fingertips into the bunching muscles, his head spinning.

Chris moaned into his mouth. He lashed his tongue at Liev's teeth, roaming his hands over Liev's ribs, hips, thighs. When his fingers found the hard point of Liev's left nipple and pinched, Liev couldn't stop his wild roar of lust.

"I like making you lose control," Chris panted against the corner of his mouth. "It makes me fucking hot."

Dragging his head over Liev's chin and down the column of his throat, Chris captured the recently pinched nipple with his teeth and sucked.

Shards of wicked pleasure detonated in Liev's core. He bucked, ramming his cock—so hard, so engorged he wondered how there was any blood left in the rest of his body—into Chris's groin.

Chris lashed his nipple with his tongue. Nipped it with his teeth. Liev groaned, balling his fist in Chris's hair again and holding on. Fuck, what finesse the man lacked in oral sex he made up with the way he worked Liev's nipple. With each swipe of his tongue, with each bite of his teeth on the small pebble of flesh, the mounting tension in Liev's body grew.

He wouldn't be able to hold on for much longer. He wouldn't.

Christ, so much for helping Chris find his—

Chris's mouth abandoned Liev's nipple and captured Liev's cock instead.

"Fuck!"

Liev's hips slammed upward.

And then again when Chris grabbed Liev's sac and tugged.

And once more when he thrust a finger between the crevice of Liev's butt cheeks and pushed at Liev's anus.

"Fuck. Oh fuck, Chris!" The words tore from Liev in a choked cry. His balls flooded with impending release. His cock jerked in Chris's mouth. "I'm gonna…"

Chris pressed on Liev's hole again. Harder.

Liev squeezed his eyes shut. Black stars of pleasure burst in his head. The base of his spine sizzled. He came, hard, fast, his seed spurting from his cock.

Toes curled, teeth ground, Liev pulled at the American's hair, fighting to free his dick from Chris's mouth. Fuck, the guy had never given head before. He wasn't ready to swallow Liev's never-ending load. He—

Chris plunged his finger deeper into Liev's anus, stroking Liev's prostate, and Liev lost the ability to think.

Hot waves of pleasure rolled through him, carrying him along until the amazing pressure in his core began to ebb.

To fade.

With steady intent, Chris slowly withdrew his mouth from Liev's dick, inch by inch. By inch.

"Still need those floaties?"

The playful question curled Liev's lips into a grin. Or perhaps it was the sheer contented bliss of his release. Or the fact his inexperienced lover had rocked his fucking world so much words failed him. Whatever the reason, all he could do was shake his head.

"Ha, didn't think so." Chris ran his tongue over Liev's inner thigh and then blew on the moist flesh. A ripple of delight claimed Liev's body and he let out a chuckled sigh.

"Fuck, you have an amazing-looking cock," Chris muttered, his lips drawing closer to Liev's spent length.

Liev laughed, stretching on the sun lounger. "Thanks."

"More than welcome," Chris replied, smoothing a hand over Liev's abs. "Now, I think I need to have a word with my manipulative personal assistant. Do you mind if I call her out here?"

Liev shook his head, too languid with pleasure to do anything else. He wanted to have a word with Bethany as well. Wanted to say thank you.

"Ms. Sloan," Chris called, his knuckles brushing Liev's balls. "Get out here please?"

A few seconds later, Liev heard footsteps on the granite tiles.

"As you wish," she called.

Chris shifted between Liev's thighs. "Ah, *The Princess Bride*. Awesome movie. How come you never quoted movie lines until Liev came along?"

Liev cracked open one eye. Chris knelt on the end of the lounger, casting Bethany a quizzical smile. If it wasn't for the fact Liev's body was still thrumming from the most incredible blowjob of his life, or that Chris's chest rose and fell with shallow, rapid breaths, or that they were both naked and glistening in sweat, Liev could almost believe they were just relaxing by the moonlit pool.

The fact Chris was sporting a semi well on its way to becoming a rather impressive hard-on didn't help.

Or *did*, considering Liev's mouth grew wet at the thought of it sliding over his tongue again. Or in his—

"Until Liev came along, my primary concern was looking after you as professionally as I could." Bethany settled herself into the wicker armchair.

Chris cocked an eyebrow. "And after Liev came along?"

She tented her fingers together and smiled over her unpolished fingernails. "Now my primary concern is making sure you get everything you need."

Chris narrowed his eyes, even as his hands came to rest on Liev's calves. "Liev?"

Bethany nodded. Once.

"How did you know Liev was what I needed?"

Liev's heart thumped a little faster at Chris's total acceptance of Liev as a necessity in his life.

Bethany's laugh was soft, relaxed. And yet, in its lilting note there was something…haunted. "I told you earlier. I read bodies. And both of yours were screaming loud and clear you wanted each other."

Chris's gaze slid to Liev for a second, a tiny, shy smile pulling at the edges of his lips. If it weren't for the itching belief Bethany was sharing something important with them, Liev would have leaned forward and kissed him. Bloody hell, he'd never realized how damn sexy a shy smile could be.

"But," Chris returned his attention to his personal assistant, "I've never had…I've never…" He pulled a face. "Fuck, you know what I'm saying. I've never…for a guy…with a guy before."

Bethany cocked her eyebrow again. "So?"

Liev wanted to chuckle. He recognized Chris's confusion. He'd lived it himself when he was thirteen.

"So how did you know I was into Liev?" Chris shifted between Liev's calves, completely at ease with his nudity. "And why risk your job doing something about it?"

Bethany's smile was soft. "Because I watched my brother deny his homosexuality for too many years. When he committed suicide three years ago because of the resulting depression, I swore I wouldn't let anyone I knew and cared for deny that part of themselves again."

***

Silence stretched for a long moment. Chris stared at his assistant, unsure what to say. Christ, unsure what to *do*.

How could she say something so fucking significant, so goddamn important with such relaxed calm?

"Bloody hell, love."

He swung his stare to Liev, the Australian's muttered response echoing his shock.

Liev frowned at her, his blue eyes serious. "He never came out?"

Bethany shook her head. "Strict parents. Very strict. To be

honest, I don't think I've ever heard Mom use the word sex. She calls it 'naughties'. Neither Adam or I were allowed to date for fear of us being corrupted by the decay of sexual pressure, so you could imagine how they would have reacted to Adam's sexuality."

Chris swallowed. A rational part of his mind told him he needed to do something about still being naked.

Quickly scanning the area, he sought out his discarded Speedo. It was nowhere in sight.

"Here you go, Mr. Huntley."

He jumped at his personal assistant's calm voice, swinging back to find her holding out a towel, a small smile on her lips.

He took it, his mouth dry.

Liev's words were only now beginning to sink into his reeling brain.

Came out.

The words had sounded so matter-of-fact on the Australian's tongue, but as they whispered through Chris's head now, his heart smashed fast in his chest.

Came out. Coming out.

"Are you going to wrap yourself in that, Mr. Huntley? Or sit there looking petrified?"

The gentle, mocking tone in Bethany's voice made him scowl.

"Think you might be needing those floaties now, Chris?"

Chris shot Liev a dark frown. "I thought I was the funny guy in the room?"

Liev's smile was wry. "You are. I'm just the hired muscle. But I've been out of the closet for a long time. I didn't just deflate the floaties, I shredded them."

Chris's heart smashed fast into his dry, tight throat. "Come out of a closet? How the fuck do I come out of a closet when I didn't realized I was *in* one?"

"Is that really what you're worried about?" Bethany asked.

Chris let out a ragged breath, propelling himself off the sun lounger to wrap the towel around his hips. He walked to the pool's edge, glaring at the glistening blue water.

"How *does* one in my line of work do that?" he asked without turning. "Come out? More to the point, is that *really* what I want to do? Reveal it all so soon? Jesus, my cock is only just getting dry from its first blowjob from a man. Isn't it premature to crow about my sexual preference to the masses? Besides all that, I'm heading back to L.A. in a little over twenty-four hours. Come out of the closet? I may not even *need* a closet to hide in when I get home. What if I go back to L.A. and I'm not…what if I don't…fuck, what if I go back to L.A. and I only want to have sex with women? Like I did *before* I came here?"

He stopped and scraped his hands over his face. His gut churned, the heavy itch on the back of his neck telling him Liev and Bethany were watching him. He swiped at his mouth with a shaky hand. The second he left Liev Reynolds in Sydney he may well go back to the person he was before he arrived here—a heterosexual, money-spinning, award-winning, joke-cracking sex symbol about to shoot into the action-star stratosphere. Attracted to sexy, feminine women.

"No one's saying you have to come out of anything," Liev's deep voice rumbled behind him.

He shot Liev a quick look over his shoulder. The man sat on the sun lounger, black boxer briefs once again hugging his hips and groin. When had he put them back on? Did it matter?

"So what?" Chris asked with a shrug. "We fuck. We exchange phone numbers and I leave? Is that it?"

It was Liev's turn to shrug. "It makes sense."

Cold anger shot through Chris. Icy shards of rage sliced at his soul. "It makes sense? Fuck it makes sense. *None* of this makes sense. I rocked up to Australia a guy who fucked women and now I'm a…a…fuck, I don't even know *what* I am anymore and it's because of you and you're okay with never seeing me again? Fuck that. Fuck you."

Liev's chuckle surprised him. The man pushed himself from the sun lounger and strode toward him. "You fucking me is exactly what I have in mind, Chris. And me fucking you. In fact, I'd hazard a guess I've thought little of anything *but* me fucking you and you fucking me, but here we come back to the need for floaties again. Because after just one blowjob, *you're* thinking about telling the world, and *I'm* thinking this man can't wreck his career over just one blowjob."

The churning knot in Chris's gut reached for his heart. "It was *more* than just one blowjob, Reynolds."

The man had the audacity to chuckle again. "Okay, two blowjobs. One a piece."

Chris narrowed his eyes. "That's not what I meant. It wasn't just a blowjob. It was…" He stopped. Swallowed.

Was he just about to say what he thought he was? Before even *trying* to return to his old life?

Sure, he was the first to admit he'd never truly felt fulfilled back then. Honestly, he'd just been going through the motions with a mechanical sense of disconnection for years, but that didn't mean he *was* ready to go on Letterman and tell the world, did it?

Did it?

He had no fucking clue *what* was going to happen when he returned to La-La Land, but surely he had to try?

Bullshit. You know exactly *what is going to happen. Before you go home. You're going to ask Liev to go with you. You knew that the moment you took his amazing, beautiful cock in your hands and sank to your knees in front of him.*

"What was it, Chris?" Liev's gaze roamed his face, his nostrils flaring. "Tell me. Before I do the sane thing and walk away, leaving your career inta—"

Chris shut him up with a kiss.

He didn't hold back. Fuck that. Liev Reynolds had awakened him to an existence he hadn't imagined possible and now didn't want to live without. Holding back with this guy was never going to be an option again. He'd lived his life a lie until Liev had entered it. There wasn't a freaking hope in hell he was letting him walk away, no matter how insane Liev—or the world—considered it.

The world could go fuck itself. The world didn't have to know. It was none of the world's business.

This was between Chris and Liev, and Chris wasn't letting Liev get away. He wasn't.

He thrust his tongue into Liev's mouth, stroking the wet well with feverish lashes. Liev returned the kiss with equal ferocity, grabbing Chris's ass and hauling their hips together. Their cocks rubbed together, the exquisitely painful contact sending a blast of heat through Chris's core. He groaned, snaring a fistful of hair at Liev's nape at the same time as he captured one of Liev's nipples and pinched.

The man bucked, his stiffening shaft grinding harder to Chris's erection. Christ, he'd never recovered so quickly from an orgasm like he had tonight. That told him something. Told him the man tongue-fucking his mouth, mauling his ass cheeks was not just a sexual partner. Liev was *the* sexual partner. The one Chris was meant to be with. The only one.

More than once, Rowan had mentioned her whole body knew the second she saw Aslin that he was the one. She'd also told Chris—usually with a self-deprecating grimace— she'd spent a stupid amount of time fighting that knowledge, sure she knew better than her heart, her body and her soul. She'd told Chris on the day she'd married the British moun- tain of muscle that the minute she *stopped* fighting she'd felt like she was finally seeing the world, like she'd been asleep and was now awake. That everything was beautiful in its clarity.

He'd laughed at her and told her he'd always known she was a corny romantic, even if she could break a man's clavicle with a karate chop.

She'd threatened to break *his* clavicle if he called her corny again, kissed him and told him she hoped one day he found the same clarity.

He'd waved her off, grabbed the closest bridesmaid and spent the rest of the wedding seducing the panties off her—as all good heterosexual, sitcom-star sex symbols are supposed to.

And now here he was, experiencing that moment of clarity Rowie had spoken about with such contented joy.

Clarity. No longer confused. Accepting. No longer fighting against the undeniable.

Fuck, it felt so goddamn right.

He pinched Liev's nipple again, loving the way the man groaned at the pressure, the way his hips thrust forward. His cock pulsed against Chris's. He bit at the fleshy fullness of Liev's bottom lip, sucking the wound better with growing urgency.

Liev dug his fingers harder into Chris's ass cheeks, a shudder vibrating through his hard body. "Fuck a bloody duck, Huntley," he growled, his lips sliding over Chris's parted ones on every word. "I can't believe I'm ready to blow my load again so soon."

With a chuckle, Chris scraped his hand down Liev's torso, shifting just enough to allow his fingers access to the man's engorged cock. He squeezed it, smearing the moisture beading on its tip with the pad of his thumb. "I can't believe you thought you were going to walk away from me."

Liev caught Chris's bottom lip with a quick nip as he rolled his hips, thrusting his shaft upward in Chris's snug grip. "It was an empty bluff."

Chris laughed. He scored a line of kisses along the man's square jaw, up to his ear before closing his lips over Liev's earlobe and giving a little suck. "I'm irresistible, just ask *Vanity Fair*." He flicked his tongue into the shallow well of Liev's ear. "*People Magazine*." He squeezed the throbbing cock in his hand. "Oprah."

In response to his boast, Liev groaned, his head lolling

back. Chris flicked his tongue over the lump of his Adam's apple.

A raw sound escaped Liev, carnal and thick with intention. It was the only warning Chris got.

Liev spun him around in a blur of air and colours. Strong fingers dug into Chris's hips with brutal force, holding him motionless for a split second before Liev's body flattened to Chris's back. The man's massive erection filled the shallow crevice between Chris's ass cheeks, his hands snaring Chris's cock and balls. Fresh heat blasted through Chris. His heart hammered. His breath caught in his throat. Unable to stop himself, he wriggled his ass, wanting to feel that steely length of flesh closer to his untouched entrance.

Fuck, not just wanting to feel it there. Needing it.

Hot lips pressed to Chris's ear, Liev's teeth catching Chris's earlobe. "You have no clue how much I want to sink my dick balls deep into your arse, Chris." He choked Chris's cock in a slow up-and-down stroke, his other hand kneading Chris's scrotum with steady force. "But I'm not taking your floaties off yet."

Chris drove his ass harder to Liev's cock, his chest tight. "Fuck the floaties. I'll let you do CPR on me after."

Liev chuckled, the sound sending new blood into Chris's already aching erection. "I love your bravado, Huntley. And I know the client's wishes are always meant to be followed, but for now, I'm going to guard your body *my* way."

And with that, he twisted Chris to face him once again, brutalized his mouth in a kiss beyond hungry and then stepped backward, out of Chris's arms.

He stared at Chris, his chest heaving, his nostrils flaring. "I'm taking this inside, Bethany." Chris started at his personal assistant's name. Jesus, he'd forgotten she was even here. "You coming?"

Chris swallowed. His gaze jerked to the smiling redhead perched on the wicker armchair beside them. Only a few days ago, he'd blamed her for his body's sexual response to Liev. He'd fancied himself attracted to her. Had entertained the idea of a threesome with her and some nameless flight attendant. And now he knew touching her, being touched by her would be a lie.

He wanted only Liev's flesh on his body, in his body. He wanted only—

"My work here is done." Bethany's calm proclamation stilled Chris's heart. She grinned at him. "I'm going to catch a cab into town. Diesel's personal assistant asked me to meet him for coffee when I was off the clock." Her grin morphed into a playful smirk. "And trust me, I am very much off the clock now." She rose to her feet and walked past them. "See you both for a late breakfast," she tossed over her shoulder as she disappeared into the shadows. "Remember you have a ten a.m. appearance, Mr. Huntley."

Chris returned his stare to Liev. His heart smashed in his ears. His gut knotted. They were alone.

Holy crap, they were alone, and he'd never felt so nervous and yet so ready to be fucked.

He swallowed, aching for the touch of Liev's hands on his body. Craving it.

"What happens now?" he asked, his nerve endings on fire.

Liev's lips curled into a slow smile. "We move to your bedroom. Now."

CHAPTER ELEVEN

Taking it slow was going to be tricky. Bloody tricky. But for Chris's sake—hell, for his *own* sake—that's exactly what Liev needed to do.

He followed Chris into the house and up the stairs to the third floor. It would be easy for him to take the American's hand and walk him to his bedroom, but Liev let Chris lead.

If Chris was to back out, Liev wanted to let him have the chance to do it with dignity, not tug at Liev's hand as he faltered behind.

God, please don't let him back out.

He watched the younger man's back, letting his gaze devour the sculpted muscles and smooth skin.

There was a part of Liev that couldn't believe this was happening. A tiny voice that whispered in his head that Chris Huntley, one of the sexiest men alive, a man of phenomenal success and famous good humour, was not interested in Liev. That tiny voice told Liev he'd been knocked out in a house fire and was lying in a hospital room in a coma. That had to be the only explanation for what was happening now. There wasn't a bloody hope in hell Chris Huntley could be attracted to a simple firefighter-cum-bodyguard whose greatest claim to fame was once stopping a protester from hitting the Prime Minister of Australia with a thrown shoe.

Liev listened to that tiny voice, the thick lump in his throat rivaling the thick heat in his groin, and continued to follow Chris up the stairs.

This wasn't a coma-induced fantasy. This was real. Chris Huntley was sexually attracted to him and, God help him, was leading him to the master bedroom.

A tight spasm claimed Liev's cock at the thought. He ached for what was to come, despite the tiny voice telling him he was deluded.

At the top of the stairs, Chris turned. His startling blue eyes found Liev's and Liev was almost overcome by the unwavering desire and trust in their depths.

Bloody hell, he was *never* going to recover from this. How did a simple man like himself recover from a night of passion with a god like Chris?

Pulling a slow breath through his nose, he drew level with Chris. "There are things I need to get from my bedroom."

Chris's Adam's apple jerked up and down in the strong column of his throat. "Okay."

Unable to stop himself, Liev lifted his hand and cupped Chris's jaw, brushing his thumb over the man's bottom lip. "Remember, you're wearing floaties. I'm not going to shove you under the water. And all you need to do is tell me to stop and I—"

Chris chuckled. "Hurry the fuck up, Reynolds. Before I drag you into my room, throw you on the bed and go all method acting on your ass. I've watched *Brokeback Mountain*. Twice."

The threat tugged a laugh from Liev. He rolled his eyes. "Twice. Then you're an expert."

Before Chris could respond, Liev spun on his heel and entered his own bedroom. In his overnight bag was a pre-lubricated condom. He wasn't yet sure it would be needed, but he wanted to be prepared. In case the unbelievable really did happen.

Do you really think it will tonight? Do you really think, when you press the head of your cock to Chris's arse, he's going to let you penetrate him? Are you that deluded? He'll realize what's about to happen and—

Shutting out the voice hell-bent on destroying his hope, Liev retrieved the square foil packet from his bag. He closed his fist around it. What it represented was almost too surreal to contemplate.

A turbulent wave of disbelief rolled through him. He turned and stared at his reflection in the room's mirror. This was a first for him. He'd never doubted himself prior to having sex before. Had never been nervous prior to fucking before. Sex was just pleasure and pleasure was there to be had. Hell, it wasn't like he'd never had sex with a virgin before either. He'd been more than one man's first. He enjoyed it. Guiding them through the previously unknown experiences of man-on-man sex turned him on just as much as the actual act itself. He'd never been nervous with any of those partners, but holy snapping duck shit, was he nervous now.

Was it Chris's fame? Or something else?

A whisper deep in his soul told him the answer, but he refused to acknowledge it. He didn't do *forever*. He didn't do *love*.

Just like all his previous lovers, Chris Huntley was a passion that had an ending. It was just… Liev swallowed, studying his own face in the glass.

Liev didn't want to think about that ending, because when he did, he saw a new fantasy that was even more unrealistic and painful to contemplate than the fantasy of making love to Chris. A fantasy of being with Chris, beside Chris, in Chris's life for a long time. A fantasy of a *forever* Liev had never ever let himself believe he wanted.

The knot in Liev's gut twisted. His heart thumped.

Falling in love was not part of his plan. "You have to remember that," he muttered.

"Remember what?"

Liev swung to his right to stare at Chris.

The actor smiled at him. "I couldn't wait." He nodded toward the bed beside him. "And I came prepared."

Liev's gaze jerked to where Chris indicated and his cock throbbed at the collection of condoms and a bottle of lube he saw.

"I found them on my bed and thought I'd bring them in here," Chris said, mischievous delight in his voice. "It seems Bethany really *did* have plans for us tonight. Think I'll give her a raise."

Liev returned his attention to Chris, the American's comment making his heart thump faster.

Chris chuckled. "Sure *you* don't need some of those floatie thingies you keep mentioning, Reynolds?"

The jest snapped Liev out of his paralyzed fear. He destroyed the small distance between them and crushed Chris's mouth with his.

He took the man's lips and tongue with impatient urgency, his head swimming as Chris returned the kiss with a ferocity he hadn't expected. He captured Chris's face with his hands, holding his head as he coaxed Chris's tongue into his mouth and sucked.

The man's cock pulsed, its rigid length nudging Liev's groin. Chris moaned, roaming his hands over Liev's back, his backside. When Chris dipped his fingers between Liev's arse cheeks and stroked the puckered hole of his anus, Liev tore his mouth free of the wild kiss and stared down into Chris's gaze. "All you need to do is say stop," he murmured.

Chris shook his head. "Not happening."

As if to prove his words, Chris wrapped a firm hand around Liev's dick, turned toward the bed and, with a deft shove on Liev's chest, deposited him—arse first—onto the soft mattress.

✦

Chris couldn't get enough of the Australian's cock in his mouth. The way it slid over his tongue, the way it filled his mouth. He knelt on the floor between Liev's spread legs, working his mouth up and down the man's amazing shaft.

With every slow ascent up Liev's venous length, he tugged on Liev's balls. With every tug, Liev groaned. The carnal pleasure in the sound fueled Chris's hunger and, rolling his tongue over the tip of Liev's cock, he plunged back down to the root again, sucking the entire duration.

"Fuck." Liev bucked his hips upward. "This is…I'm meant to be…"

Chris drew up Liev's length again, wrapped his hand around the wet pole of flesh and nipped the tip with his teeth.

Liev hissed, his hips driving upward. "Do that again and I'll—"

Chris did it again.

With another hiss, Liev moved. The man was all muscle and strength and before Chris could laugh a retreat, Liev snared him by one wrist and hauled him up onto the bed. Just like that.

The sheer power required to lift Chris off the floor in such a fluid, single move flooded Chris's cock with fresh blood. He would have groaned in appreciation, if it weren't for the man pinning him to his back on the mattress and kissing him senseless. Instead, he tangled his fingers in Liev's hair, wrapped his leg around Liev's hip and ground his erection to Liev's groin.

Their flesh slid against each other. Their balls slapped together. Chris tightened his legs around Liev's hip and bucked upward in a demanding thrust.

Liev moaned into his mouth and thrust back, working one hand between their bodies to capture Chris's cock.

Chris sucked in a sharp breath. Liev held him in a firm fist, arching over Chris to direct the tip of his cock to Liev's.

Head spinning, Chris looked down the length of his body, watching as their pre-come mixed on the ends of their penises. The fluid glistened, a thin thread that joined their bodies together in a way more profound than Chris could fathom.

"Oh boy," he breathed, his mouth going dry.

"It looks amazing, doesn't it?"

He lifted his gaze to Liev's face and nodded, lost for words. *Oh boy* was the best he could do.

"It *feels* amazing," Liev murmured, painting the tip of Chris's cock over his again. "Your flesh, your pre-come on my dick." He grazed his lips over Chris's jaw, his chin, his bottom lip. "So fucking amazing."

Chris lowered his hand to Liev's erection, closed his fingers around its length so Liev could stroke Chris's cockhead over his bulbous one. The slick sensation of wet skin on wet skin tore a shaky whimper from Chris and he closed his eyes, only to open them again when Liev whispered, "You are beautiful. So beautiful."

Chris gazed up at him, his heart racing at the pleasure fogging the man's eyes. "I've been called sexy," he rasped, his throat tight. "Handsome, good-looking. But never beautiful."

Liev's nostrils flared. His grip on Chris's erection loosened. A little. "But you are. You don't like it?"

Chris digested the word. If another man had called him beautiful he would have laughed. Women were beautiful. Artworks were beautiful. A sunset. Chris wasn't beautiful. But when Liev called him beautiful, he felt it. It was an exquisite feeling.

He lifted his hand from Liev's cock and traced his thumb over the man's lips. "I do."

Liev parted his lips and captured Chris's thumb, sucking it into his mouth.

Chris groaned, reveling in the feel of the wet heat enveloping his flesh. Reveling in it even as his body craved other heat. Tighter heat.

His head swam. His cock pulsed. "I want to be inside you, Liev."

The words fell from him in a hoarse rasp.

Liev stilled. He removed Chris's thumb from his mouth. Chris could see the tiny pulse at the base of his neck beating like a frantic moth beneath his skin. "You want me to suck you off? Make you come?"

Chris shook his head. "No. I want to be *inside* you."

Liev's eyes fluttered closed. An unreadable tension crossed his face. His cock jumped, nudging Chris's.

"I want to fuck you," Chris continued, his pulse a roaring tattoo in his ear, his chest tight. "I want to have your muscles surround my cock as I sink into your ass. Let me do that, Liev."

Liev opened his eyes and stared down at Chris, his eyes ablaze with blue desire and undeniable need.

Chris feathered his thumb over Liev's lips once more. "Please? I need to feel you envelop me. Grip me. I need…"

He broke off, unable to vocalize the soul-deep longing inside him.

Without a word, Liev pushed himself off the bed and took a step backward, never breaking eye-contact with Chris.

Chris watched him, his mind whirling.

When Liev moved to the side of the bed and picked up the bottle of lube, Chris's breath hitched in his throat.

Turning to face him, Liev held out the tube of lubrication.

Chris took it, his hands shaking.

Their fingers touched, and it was as if a spark of concentrated energy shot through Chris. Up his arm, across his chest, into his heart. Down into his deepest core.

He straightened from the bed, stood face to face with the man whose very existence had changed his, and bit back a moan of sheer joy when Liev turned to the bed and crawled onto it, his ass thrust backward.

Chris gazed at the offered bounty. Liev's ass was so firm, the muscles honed to powerful perfection. He stepped to the bed, positioning himself between Liev's ankles. With a steady hand, he smoothed his palm over the warm curve, the tiny hairs on the man's flesh a tantalizing caress. Dipping his palm lower, he trailed his fingertips over the heavy globes of Liev's scrotum.

A ragged breath burst from Liev, Chris's caress making his stomach hitch. "Bloody hell, Huntley, you know how to tease a bloke."

The Australian term coupled with Liev's sexy Australian accent sent a jolt of impatient greed into Chris's cock. He skimmed his hand lower and cupped Liev's balls in a gentle hold.

Liev hissed in another breath, his balls shifting against Chris's fingers and palm.

Releasing his prize, Chris brushed his hand back up Liev's ass cheeks, trailing a finger with deliberate intent over his clenching anus.

Another fierce intake of air followed. A tremble claimed Liev's powerful thighs. "You're walking a fine line, Huntley," he grumbled, his gaze locking with Chris's over his shoulder.

The threat sent a thrill of anticipation through Chris's veins, licking over his nerve endings. That Liev didn't move, didn't take command of the situation only heightened his mounting excitement. If he wanted to, Liev Reynolds could render him defenseless and vulnerable to any whim the man desired. Chris didn't doubt that. That Liev didn't intimidate him into submission, didn't dominate him and take advantage of his smaller size, made Chris so fucking hard he could barely think.

Lifting the tube of lube, Chris popped the flip-top lid with his thumb.

And stopped.

"Smear it over my hole, Chris."

Liev's low instruction sent electrical energy into Chris's groin.

"Squeeze a good amount onto my hole, and smear it over me with your fingers."

Chris did, his heart racing. Fuck, his cock was so engorged it was a wonder the flesh hadn't split.

"Christ, that's good," Liev ground out. "Now work it inside me. With how big your dick is, I'm going to need a lot of stretching. That's it. One finger, another…oh fuck, Chris…"

Liev's instruction turned into a groan when Chris pressed a third finger into his opening.

Chris stared at his fingers sinking into Liev's anus, his blood roaring in his ears. He flexed his fingers, his heart slamming harder at the raw groan his actions tore from Liev.

Twisting his wrist a little, he parted his fingers, stretching Liev's entry wider.

"Oh God, Chris." Liev's thighs trembled. "I'm not going to last long."

The confession detonated something purely instinctual in Chris. He pulled his fingers from Liev's ass and, with Liev's protesting groans flaying at his control, snatched a condom packet from the bed. He ripped the foil packaging open with his teeth and then withdrew the slick silicon sheath. Stare locked on Liev, he aligned the reservoir tip over the distended head of his cock and then rolled the condom down over his length.

He didn't want to. He wanted to feel Liev's flesh on his, but knew—this time at least—he had to. There would be many other times to come when their unadorned bodies would enter each other without the artificial barrier. Many. This was only the beginning.

Returning his fingers to Liev's ass, he squeezed fresh lube onto the man's anus and worked his fingers past the tight ring of muscle.

"Inside me, Chris." Liev's voice was hoarse. "Squeeze some in—"

Chris didn't let him finish. He couldn't. The need to sink into Liev's ass was so absolute now he was beyond composure, beyond control.

Grabbing his rigid, silicon-sheathed erection in one strangling hold, he thrust deeper into Liev's ass with his fingers, deeper, deeper, seeking something…something.

"Fuck!" Liev cried out, a shudder rocking him. "Fuck that feels…"

Without waiting for Liev's pleasure to fade, Chris lined the head of his cock up to Liev's clenching hole and pushed. Searing pleasure ignited in his body at the constricting pressure around his girth. He pushed deeper, a tight ring of resistance rolling over the rim of his cockhead.

"Oh fuck, fuck, yes," Liev groaned, pushing back into Chris's penetration. "Oh God, Chris, you feel so fucking—"

Chris grabbed Liev's hips and pulled his ass farther along his cock.

New pleasure detonated within him. He closed his eyes, dangerously close to coming already. Christ, he'd never imagined it would be like this. This was absolute. Liev's ass wasn't just snug around his cock, it sucked at it. Claimed it. Pulsed around it like a greedy mouth.

He ground his teeth, unable to stop his fingers digging into the flesh on Liev's hips as he inched deeper. Fuck, he'd never felt so connected to another living soul before. He thrust a little more, encountering another ring of clenching muscle.

Liev's groan stopped him. He opened his eyes, finding the Australian looking back at him.

Chris gave him a small smile. Nervous self-doubt knotted

in his gut. "Doing okay?" He forced the question to sound far more flippant than it was.

Liev's eyes closed for a second as his lips curled into a slow smile. "You fucking better believe it."

Elated joy surged through Chris. He rolled his hips and withdrew his length until the distended head of his cock stretched the tight ring of Liev's anus.

Liev's hum of appreciation vibrated into Chris's body. He held his position, struggling against the pressure building in his groin, his soul, and then slid his length back into Liev's channel. Deeper this time.

Christ, he was surrounded by hot flesh. Hot, tight flesh. It was perfect. Perfect.

So perfect. So…so…

Liev fisted the duvet, pushing back into the penetration. "Harder."

Chris did as ordered, ready to die in the ensuing pleasure.

It radiated through him, the sucking pressure of Liev's ass propelling him toward a precipice he ached for. With every thrust and withdrawal, he sank deeper into Liev's body, Liev's heat, deeper, deeper until he was buried to the hilt, his balls pressing the heavy globes of Liev's scrotum.

"Holy shit," he choked out the exclamation, his heart wild. "You're all around me, Liev. It feels so…*right.*"

The word burst from him, more true than any he'd ever uttered.

He gazed at Liev's broad back, the clarity of the moment stealing his breath. Right. It was right. It was exquisite and perfect and right.

Embedded in Liev's constricting heat, he bent forward and pressed his belly to Liev's spine, his chest to the man's shoulder blades. "I am where I am meant to be," he murmured into Liev's ear.

"And where I want you to…*holy shit, Chris!*" Liev bucked

at Chris's swift withdrawal of his cock all the way to the rim of its head.

Chris didn't wait for Liev to recover. He plunged in again, slamming back into his lover's ass.

And again.

Shifting on the end of the bed, he planted his right foot on the mattress beside Liev's knee, hooked his fingers harder into Liev's hips and fucked him.

As hard and as deep as he could.

Liev groaned, whimpered, demanded Chris fuck him harder, faster, shoving back into each thrust.

They moved together. There was nothing gentle or tender about it. It was raw, carnal fucking, and Chris couldn't hold on to his release anymore.

His orgasm claimed him, a paroxysm of concentrated pleasure that ignited at the base of his spine and blasted through him. Rhythm deserted him. He threw back his head, his seed erupting into the condom just as Liev's ass clamped around his thrusting cock in an intense grip and Liev roared his name.

CHAPTER TWELVE

Chris had showered with many women in his time. He'd found it the perfect place to get it on without the uncomfortable necessity of snuggling inevitably created by the presence of a bed. Now, standing in the opulent shower cubicle, with five separate shower heads streaming warm water over them, he decided the shower was the perfect place to snuggle as well.

A snort scratched at the back of his throat even as he leaned back closer to Liev's tall, hard body. Jesus, when had the word *snuggling* become a part of his vocabulary?

"Problem?"

He shot Liev a quick look over his shoulder. A more lucid part of his mind told him the man was currently doing an extremely thorough, extremely fine job of washing his balls. "I've just realized I'm a snuggle virgin."

Liev's eyebrows shot up. "A what?"

Reluctant to remove Liev's hands from his sac, Chris wriggled his butt closer to the man's groin. "Snuggle virgin. Snuggling wasn't something I wanted to do before you came along. Fuck, snuggling wasn't even something I *said*, let alone did."

Liev's palm cupped Chris's balls as his other hand

smoothed up Chris's belly. "And now you do want to…" a chuckle vibrated in his chest, "…snuggle?"

Chris rolled his eyes. "Yeah, that's me. Big-time Hollywood action hero and snuggler." He pulled away from Liev a little, twisting in his arms enough to fix him with a steady inspection. "Tell me the truth, *do* guys like us snuggle? Is snuggling allowed?"

Liev's laughter echoed around the bathroom.

Chris frowned. "What?"

"I don't know what's funnier, you saying *snuggle* or the notion there's a list somewhere of what 'guys like us' are allowed to do?"

"You know, I think I liked you more when you weren't mocking me."

Liev chuckled. "Bullshit. You like me more now because we're allowed to snuggle."

"Ah, so we *are* allowed to snuggle? That's acceptable for tough guys like us?"

Liev's gentle grip on Chris's balls grew firmer. His eyes twinkled in the shower's warm light. "Well, maybe for tough guys like me. I'm not sure what the rules are in America."

Chris cocked an eyebrow. His body was telling him just how wonderful it was to have Liev's hard, thick, long cock nestled between the crevice of his ass cheeks. "Perhaps it's a global rule?"

Liev hummed, pressing his hand flat on Chris's belly to pull him back closer into his body. "Perhaps," he murmured, licking at the drops of water beading on Chris's shoulder.

Chris's stomach clenched. He closed his eyes, letting the intimacy of the embrace sink into his soul. With Liev's muscular form pressed to his back, with the front of Liev's thighs rubbing at the back of his, with Liev's powerful arms circling his waist, he could gladly stay here in the shower for the rest of the night, what little of it there was.

Stay in the shower and snuggle.

He grinned. "I think I like the word snuggle."

Liev's lips nibbled at his earlobe. "I think I like it too."

"Reckon I should use it in the next *Dead Even* movie? I'm sure my character would love to suggest to whatever blonde bombshell he's fucking that they should *snuggle*, don't you?"

Liev chuckled, the hand on Chris's belly slowly inching down to Chris's cock, a cock well on its way to being a goddamn straining pole of hot need. "There's your next film title right there. *Dead Even 2: The Snuggler*."

Chris drew in a hitching breath as Liev's fingers wrapped Chris's length. "Tagline: Every man dies. Not every man really snuggles."

Liev nipped at the side of Chris's neck. He slid his fist up Chris's erection with increasing pressure. "One good snuggle deserves another."

Chris wriggled his hips, working Liev's rigid thickness farther between his butt cheeks. "In space, no one can hear you snuggle."

Liev's lips scored a line along Chris's jawline. "It's a sci-fi, is it?"

"Who the fuck knows." Chris chuckled, the sound shaky. Damn it, with the way Liev's hand was working his cock it was damn near impossible to breathe. "What about, Who you gonna snuggle?"

"The best so far," Liev murmured, a second before he turned Chris to face him, lowered to his knees and took Chris's thoroughly erect and ready length in his mouth.

A tsunami of pleasure later, Chris's seed erupted into Liev's sucking mouth. He groaned, the absolute perfection of the moment consuming him. Not just the mastery of Liev's blowjob, but the whole moment. The fact Liev was willing to joke with him about his career. The fact Liev didn't show a hint of jealousy when Chris mentioned on-screen sex. The fact Liev made him completely satisfied with who he was, an actor. A man paid to pretend to be someone else. Who would have thought getting naked with a guy could make Chris feel so content about being someone who made a living playing dress-up?

It was no wonder he was falling in love with the man.

Chris's pulse thumped faster at the thought. Love.

He'd never been in love before. He'd always considered himself unable to experience such a profound emotion, blaming the void in his heart on the horrific murder of his parents before his eyes. He'd grown up watching his sister believe the same thing. When Rowie had fallen in love with Aslin, Chris had never been happier, and at the same time more empty.

And yet here he was, falling in love. There was no other explanation for the sheer and utter contented happiness he felt whenever he thought of Liev, looked at him, heard him, felt him.

It should have scared the shit out of him, but it didn't. Life was too short to deny something so amazing, so precious when it finally fell in your lap.

He smiled, grateful for the tiled wall behind him. His orgasm had been so absolute if it wasn't for the wall, he'd be a puddle of sated rapture on the shower floor.

"Your cock is truly a thing of beauty."

Liev's deep voice stretched Chris's smile wider. "Beauty and snuggling," he murmured. "What every tough guy needs."

"You know, you're not a wuss for having sex with a man."

Chris opened his eyes at the calm reproach in Liev's statement. His heartbeat tripped over itself. "What do you mean?"

The Australian leaned toward him, planting his hands on the wall either side of Chris's head. "I mean, you've commented more than once on your masculinity in the last few minutes, like you're trying to reassure yourself you're still a man."

A heavy lump filled Chris's throat at the observation.

"If it helps, you are." Liev's gaze held his, his eyes intent. "You still have the same level of testosterone in your blood system. Still have a Y chromosome. None of those things changed the second your dick buried in my arse."

Chris swallowed. Or least tried to. The lump in his throat made it damn near impossible. "I didn't…"

Liev's smile stopped his denial. Jesus, was that what he was doing? With all the wiseass jokes about being a tough guy? Trying to convince himself he wasn't a…a…

Fag?

The vile word whispered through Chris's mind like a rotting wind.

"You're scared, Huntley." Liev's gaze didn't leave his face. There was no censure in the man's voice. "You're allowed to be. I've seen it more than once."

Hot jealousy stabbed into Chris's self-contempt at the thought of Liev with other men. Christ, was he truly so insecure in himself he could swing from doubting he was still a man to hating the goddamn notion of Liev being with another one? "How many times?" he asked before he could stop himself. He was pathetic. Pathetic.

Liev shook his head. "How many men I've fucked is not important, Chris. And neither is how many women, but if it helps, not as many as your mind is trying to torment you with right now. I can count them all on both hands." He grinned, a gentle mirth Chris was already growing addicted to. "One for each sex. What's important is how you think and feel about yourself. If you can live with yourself knowing you're attracted to men."

It was Chris's turn to shake his head. "I'm not attracted to men. I'm attracted to you."

A wry chuckle bubbled past Liev's lips. "Perhaps I'm just the first you've acknowledged."

Chris pushed himself from the wall, his nose so close to Liev's they touched briefly. "Nope. The first. Period. And I can live with that because I'm not ashamed of it."

Liev's nostrils flared. "Really? What happens if someone

posts a rumour about your sexuality on Twitter? Have you taken a good look at that image of you and me at the restaurant riot? *I* can see the desire in your eyes. Hell, I can see it in your body. It's only a matter of time before someone else does. What do you do when *E News* or Perez Hilton or some other entertainment gossipmonger is proclaiming to the world you're gay? What do you do then?"

"Tell them to mind their own fucking business."

Liev's answering laugh was a humourless bark. "Yeah, like that's worked for all the celebrities who've tried it before you."

Chris ground his teeth. How could they go from snuggling to this? And in the shower? Jesus, if it weren't so goddamn surreal it'd be hilarious. Perhaps he should tell the writers about it when *Twice Too Many* resumed filming? *Hey, how 'bout we have my character argue about sex in the shower with his latest fuck buddy? Trust me, it'll be a laugh a minute.*

He glared at Liev, his fists bunching. "Let them write and say whatever they want. It doesn't matter to me. Every actor has endured it at some point. Christ, Hugh Jackman's sexuality is questioned every damn day, especially when he's in a damn musical. If the guy who brought Wolverine to life can still live and work with gay rumours, I can too. And you can't get much more of a tough guy than Wolverine, can you? It's Hollywood. It's vicious and nasty and mean spirited when it wants to be."

Liev's gaze never wavered from Chris's eyes. He didn't say a word. He didn't move.

Chris tilted his chin, the warm water streaming over his back and shoulders an incongruous caress on his skin. "What? Not the answer you were expecting?"

An unreadable emotion darkened Liev's eyes, there and gone before Chris could decipher it.

"I don't know what to expect from you, Huntley. From the second you entered my life you've bloody thrown me for a loop."

Chris's heart lurched into his throat. The man wasn't as

unaffected by all this as Chris believed. For some reason, that fact sent a tight ribbon of elated hope into his soul.

"But as for right now?" Liev went on, his voice growing lower. "I don't know whether to shake some sense into you or kiss you senseless."

"I vote the latter," Chris answered.

He captured Liev's lips with his own before the man could move. Flattening their bodies together, he snared two fistfuls of Liev's wet hair and made love to Liev's mouth with his tongue, refusing to let him go.

Liev growled, his rigid cock poking Chris in the belly. Chris reached for it, needing its hot steel in his hand, on his flesh.

Liev groaned, his hips rolling the instant Chris gripped him.

The kiss turned hungry. Wild. Chris surrendered to it, to Liev's domination. When the man yanked open the shower door and pulled Chris from the cubicle, he didn't argue or offer resistance.

When Liev dragged him into the bedroom, he went willingly.

When the man shoved him to his knees at the foot of the bed and bent him face first over it, pressing his chest to the mattress, Chris complied, his breath ragged, his body on fire.

When Liev's hands gripped his ass, spreading his cheeks wide, exposing his anus to the room, Chris could only whimper a hoarse, "yes."

And when Liev's tongue lashed at that puckered ring of muscle, it was all Chris could do not to scream with the intense pleasure shearing through him.

He drove his ass back to Liev's lashing tongue, the sensations of hot, wet flesh on his entrance like pure colours of passion detonating in his soul.

Liev fucked his ass with his tongue, each drilling, flicking thrust pushing Chris higher, closer to the edge of a fall he wanted to take.

Fisting the duvet, he drove his face to the cool silk and begged for more, aching for it.

His whole body was on fire. His head swam with the torment of pleasure. His balls throbbed. His cock—

Liev's fingers wrapped around Chris's erection, a fierce, savage vise that made him cry out.

"Fuck, yes!" He bucked backward, his toes digging at the carpet, seeking traction as he drove his ass into Liev's punishing tongue.

Liev pumped his cock, his hand matching the fevered motion of his mouth. Faster. Faster.

Chris writhed, his world reduced to his ass and his cock and the raw pleasure Liev delivered upon them.

Time ceased to exist. Nothing existed, except Liev.

Liev.

Christ, he wanted Liev in his ass. He wanted the man's thick, massive cock balls deep in his ass. He needed—

Liev tore his mouth from Chris's flesh, replaced it with his thumb and Chris erupted.

His orgasm ripped through him, a scalding explosion of constricting electricity and intense sensations. His come jetted from his cock, splashing the silk of the duvet, slicking Liev's pumping hand. He roared. Fisted the bedding. Gave himself over to the pleasure, the pleasure…

A lifetime later, Liev rested his sweat-slicked body on Chris's back and released Chris's spent shaft. His heart thumped hard against Chris's shoulder blades, a rapid rhythm Chris felt all the way into his soul. "I…" Chris began.

Without a word, Liev straightened to his feet and walked away.

Chris kneeled on the floor, bent over the foot of the bed, unable to move. Behind him, he heard the shower stop. A second later, a warm damp washcloth swiped over the tops of his come-slicked thighs.

Still silent, Liev placed a soft kiss on the base of Chris's spine and then walked back into the bathroom.

The desire to stay motionless welled through Chris. To stay where he was, his used body waiting for Liev to return to it. As satiated as he was, he still wanted more.

He wanted Liev to fill him, stretch him. He wanted to be joined with him, in the same way he'd joined with Liev earlier.

He wanted Liev's cock in his flesh.

At the sound of Liev's footfalls on the carpet, he turned to look at his lover. A sharp sense of disappointed shot through him at the sight of the white towel now wrapped around the man's narrow hips. A tight rope of excitement followed at the sight of Liev's erection tenting the fluffy material.

Repositioning himself against the end of the bed, his bare butt on the floor, Chris rested his elbows on the mattress, not even remotely interested in covering his flaccid cock where it lay against his inner thigh. "Why didn't you take me then?"

"Where? Don't you think it's a bit late for dinner?" Liev shot the watch on his wrist a quick look. "And a bit early for breakfast, given that it's only three forty-nine?"

Chris grunted. "I'm the funny guy in this relationship, remember?"

Liev cocked an eyebrow. "Relationship?"

"Hell, yes." Chris glared. "Relationship. Now quit changing the subject and tell me why you didn't fuck me."

The man's chuckle was low as he closed the distance between them with a few steps. "Floaties, darling. Floaties."

Chris rolled his eyes. "If you mention floaties one more time I'm going to—"

His words died on his tongue when Liev removed the towel from his hips, revealing the most impressive hard-on Chris had ever seen.

"Get on the bed."

Liev's calm command sent a wicked thrill of anticipation into his groin. "Why?"

"Because you need to sleep."

Chris's mouth fell open. He stared up at his lover, lost for words.

Liev laughed. "Bethany will kill me if you're too tired to function properly tomorrow at the wildlife reserve. And Rhodes will kill me if I'm too tired to protect his brother-in-law if more of your fans decide to riot again."

Chris didn't move.

Liev crossed his arms over his massive chest. For a moment, Chris wanted nothing more than to straighten to his feet and capture one of the frustrating man's tiny nipples with his mouth.

A grin played at the edges of Liev's lips. "Trust me, my dick will be just as hard after we've had some shuteye. Harder even." He tossed a nod toward the bed. "For now, we're sleeping."

"Together?"

"How else am I to guard your body if I'm not beside it?"

"Good point."

Rising to his feet, Chris climbed onto the bed and crawled toward the head on all fours. Pausing once, he twisted a look over his shoulder, wriggled his ass in the air and dropped Liev a wink. "Are you sure you don't want to…" He wriggled his butt again.

"Spank your arse? You better believe it, but I'm scared shitless of Bethany. Now hurry the fuck up and get into bed."

Chris crawled farther up the mattress before stopping again. "Do you snore?"

Liev cocked an eyebrow.

Chris grinned. "Just checking."

He adjusted the sheets and stretched out on his side, his blood roaring in his ears as Liev tucked his solid form against the length of Chris's back.

Chris's mind whirled with the reality of the situation. His

heart raced. His soul sang. If he were a poet, he'd spend the night composing sonnets to the man holding him. He'd heard half of Shakespeare's poems were written to the bard's male lover. Lying here now, with Liev's heat and strength enveloping him, Chris could fully understand and appreciate the poet's pre-occupation with his male muse.

Love was a powerful force. One to be reckoned with.

"Now this…" Liev's husky murmur tickled Chris's ear and he twisted in the man's arms, just enough to see his lover's face from the corner of his eye, "…is snuggling."

Chris laughed, one hundred percent convinced there wasn't a hope in hell he was going to fall asleep.

So when he opened his eyes a heartbeat later he was more than surprised at the golden sunshine streaming through the room's floor-to-ceiling glass doors.

He blinked, for a split moment awash in a disorientating fugue, and then a thick, steely pole nudged the crevice of his ass, a thick, muscular arm snaked around his hips and Liev was pressing to his back, his lips grazing Chris's bare shoulder.

"Ready for the deep end, Huntley?"

Chris's heart smashed into his throat. His breath caught. His morning wood throbbed. He turned in Liev's strong arms, his head spinning as their erections clashed and slid against each other.

Serious blue eyes regarded him. Liev's gaze was inscrutable.

"What made you change your mind?" Chris asked, the words a scratchy breath.

Liev's nostrils flared. "I can't fight what I feel for you anymore. It's stupid to do so. And un—"

Chris didn't let him finished. Words weren't important anymore. Nothing was important anymore.

Nothing except this moment. This man and this moment.

Chris slid his tongue into Liev's willing mouth, smoothed his hand over his warm flesh and, with a groan and a whimper, surrendered to it all.

He tried to dispense with foreplay, but Liev would have none of it. Every time Chris begged Liev to fuck him, Liev would rush him toward a precipice of pleasure with his lips, his tongue, his fingers.

The sun slowly charted its morning journey in the sky, throwing shadows over the wall of Chris's bedroom. Chris lost himself over and over again to the raw, concentrated sensations Liev awoke in him. And still he begged for more.

When he didn't think he could survive any longer, when he feared his cock was going to erupt with the mounting pressure of Liev's never-ending stimulation of his body, the man seared his lips with a crushing kiss and climbed from the bed.

Chris's heart—already beating faster than it should—jumped into overdrive. Breath held, he watched Liev walk from the room and then released the air in his lungs in a wobbly sigh when the Australian returned, the bottle of lube in one hand, a condom packet in the other.

Oh God. It's happening. It's happening now…

CHAPTER THIRTEEN

The feverish thought filled Chris's mind. Shifting on the bed, he rested on his elbows, unable to tear his stare from the man moving toward him.

With a small smile, Liev climbed onto the end of the mattress—first one knee and then the other.

Chris swallowed. Every nerve ending in his body fizzed. "D-do you want me to…roll over?"

At Liev's slow shake of the head, a hot spasm claimed Chris's cock.

The man smoothed his hands around Chris's ankles, his gaze holding Chris motionless as he slowly spread Chris's legs apart. "I want to see your face when I enter you, Huntley. I want to see your pleasure as well as feel it."

Chris's pulse beat fast in his neck. His mouth went dry. A low moan of approval vibrated in his chest.

With another small smile, Liev lowered his head to Chris's right leg and charted a path over Chris's flesh with his lips.

"Oh, man…"

The exclamation fell from Chris on a rasping breath. His stomach hitched, the closer Liev's mouth drew to his groin the tighter his cock grew. And grew. A quick glance at the throbbing organ told Chris he'd never been harder or bigger. Christ, at this rate he was going to fucking come the second Liev's fingers brushed his thigh. If not before then.

Returning his stare to Liev, he swallowed.

Before was an extremely distinct possibility. The mere sight of Liev's lips travelling up Chris's leg was like visual Viagra, let alone the silken caress of each kiss on his skin.

"Oh, man," he groaned again. "I don't think I'm going to last long."

Liev chuckled against Chris's knee. His fingers continued their path toward Chris's groin. "It's not a marathon, Chris. And I'm not going to give you a hard time if you come before I do."

Chris's laugh sounded strained, probably because Liev had resumed his journey up Chris's thigh with his lips, the back of his knuckles brushing the heavy swell of Chris's balls.

"A hard time? Isn't that the point?"

For an answer, Liev snared the tube of lube from the bed and popped the lid.

Chris's heart smashed into his throat.

Gazing down at him, Liev squeezed a dollop of the thick, clear liquid onto his fingertips. "Spread your legs wider, Huntley."

Chris did as ordered, the action parting his ass cheeks more.

A low moan rumbled in Liev's chest. His jaw bunched. "Fuck, you have a gorgeous hole. Tight and perfect. Made for fucking." He pressed his lube-coated fingers to Chris's anus and pushed.

Rivers of delicious heat flowed through Chris at the contact. He groaned, driving his heels into the soft mattress and spreading his legs farther. Jesus, he wanted this. So much.

"It's going to hurt, Chris," Liev murmured, his gaze fixed on Chris's entrance. He coated his fingers—three this time— with fresh fluid and returned them to Chris's flesh. "I won't tell you otherwise. When I first push into you it's going to burn like hell, but it's going to feel so fucking good after the pain has stopped." He dipped into Chris's passage, first one finger and then another and finally the third. "I promise."

Chris hissed in a sharp breath, his hips bucking upward. He couldn't stop looking at the man stretching his ass. Liev's warning, his statement, only cemented Chris's desire for him more. "I trust you," he said, the words thick on his tongue. "I want you. You and only you."

Liev's nostrils flared. His eyes fluttered closed. "Fuck me, Chris, hearing you say that…"

He slipped his hands under Chris's thighs and lifted them off the mattress, inching closer until Chris's calves flattened against his chest and his cock pressed to Chris's balls. With deft skill, he snatched the condom packet from beside his knee, tore it open with his teeth and slipped out the slick disc. Wordlessly, he rolled the protective sheath down his length. It took an eternity, each inch covered propelling Chris closer to the edge of insanity. When the condom was finally stretched over his cock, he oozed more lube onto his fingers, Chris's puckered hole and the bulbous head of his shaft.

Lifting his gaze from his handy work, Liev studied Chris. "It's not too late." His voice shook, belying the calm control he projected. "I'll stop now if you tell me to. I don't want to. Fuck, I don't want to, but I will. For you. If you ask—"

"Fuck me, Reynolds." Chris cut him off, reaching for his own straining cock and pumping it once. "Before I come on my damn chest."

Eyes dilating, jaw bunching, Liev smoothed his hands over Chris's hips, under his butt and, without a sound, leaned closer down to Chris's body.

The action aligned the tip of his cock to Chris's lube-sodden entry. Chris rolled his hips, staring up at the amazing man above him.

There was a moment where time stopped, where the world

ceased to spin, and then Liev pushed his hips forward and entered Chris's body. A little.

Intense pleasure speared through Chris, intense pleasure and searing pain. "Jesus," he ground out. "That feels…"

Liev withdrew, removing the stretching pressure of his invasion. "What?" He hovered over Chris, his cock nestled to Chris's burning ass. "Tell me, Huntley. It feels what? I need to know before I—"

"So goddamn good," Chris groaned, squeezing his throbbing erection with a trembling hand. "Do it again."

Liev pushed into him again, deeper this time. "Breathe for me, Chris."

Chris couldn't stop his raw whimper as he released his pent-up breath. "Hell yeah."

Again Liev withdrew, this time pausing at the point his cockhead stretched Chris's ring to its limits before sinking back into Chris's flesh. "Fuck, you're tight, Huntley." His face bunched, beads of sweat trickling down his temples. "Tight and hot and perfect."

Once more, he slid upward, dangling Chris on a razor-wire line of euphoria. The distended edge of his cockhead stroked Chris's prostate. Once more, he groaned Chris's name and declared him tight and hot and perfect. "And mine," he rasped this time. "Mine."

The word stole what little control Chris had left. "Yours," he ground out in agreement, yanking on his own length. "Yours to fuck forever."

Liev opened his eyes. He stared down into Chris's face, his eyes ablaze with longing, his face etched with need, and slammed back into him.

Harder and deeper than before.

"Yes," Chris cried out, pleasure unlike any he could fathom consuming him. This was intimacy, connection. This was giving himself to that person, that one special person and letting that person possess him, own him, complete him…

He couldn't survive it. He never wanted to be without it again.

Never wanted to be without Liev again.

Hot, wet lips grazed a jerky path over his chin, his lips, before Liev drew his hips back, back, back, and once again Chris balanced on the wire, so close to tumbling into the bliss of release.

"Yours," Liev whispered, gaze locked on Chris's face. "God help me, I'm yours whenever you want me."

He sank into Chris again, buried himself to the root, his shaft embedded inside Chris's body.

Chris came.

His seed erupted from his cock, spurting all over his chest, his throat. He thrashed beneath Liev, his orgasm ripping from his core, his bones, his very soul.

And still Liev didn't stop fucking him. Still, the man continued to pound his ass, over and over, each thrust turning Chris's release into something else, something sublime.

Something perfect.

Something pure.

Liev froze for a split second, his shaft buried to the root in Chris's ass. His body thrummed with an inferno Chris felt in his core, and then, with a strangled roar, he threw back his head, drove his fingers into Chris's thighs and came.

His ejaculate burst from his body. Chris could feel it pumping through the turgid length of his cock. The sensation detonated fresh pleasure in Chris's soul and he whimpered Liev's name, over and over again. He took his lover deeper, lost to the desire in Liev's eyes. Lost to the sheer bliss of being with him this way.

When Liev's wild thrusts slowed, Chris allowed his eyes to close. His lover shifted slightly between his legs, enough to let Chris's legs fall from Liev's chest.

The move caused Liev's cock to slip free of Chris's anus and

Chris groaned. The sudden sense of emptiness at the absence of Liev's flesh in his body struck through his heart.

Christ, he truly was gone for the guy. Hook, line and sinker.

Opening his eyes, he couldn't stop the smile spreading over his lips as he gazed up at the Australian still kneeling between his legs.

Liev's chest heaved. Sweat glistened on his forehead, his nose. The fine dark-blond hair on his chest was matted. His abs were an exquisite six-pack defined by exertion. To Chris, he was the epitome of male perfection. Christ, he loved him. It wasn't possible, not after seven days, but he did.

He opened his mouth, the words on his tongue, and closed his mouth again. More than one woman had told him she loved him after sex. He remembered how unsettling the confession always made him feel, and while Liev had used the terms *mine* and *yours* mid-coitus, Chris had no idea if he really meant it.

As much as he wanted to tell the man he was head over fucking heels in love with him, he couldn't. Ignoring the fact he didn't want to make Liev uncomfortable, he really didn't know if that's what guys *did* after sex, albeit amazing, mind-blowing, soul-shattering sex.

This was more than sex, Chris. It was. Tell him. Look at him and tell him what you feel.

Chris opened his mouth again, his stare on Liev's face, and said, "Holy fuck, that was incredible."

The skin around Liev's eyes tightened. His Adam's apple jerked up and down his throat, and then he chuckled, swinging Chris's leg over his body so he could stretch out on the bed beside him. "That's one word for it."

Chris flopped back on the mattress and stared at the ceiling without seeing it. His heart raced. His blood roared in his ears. He couldn't do it. He couldn't say what he wanted to say. What he desperately wanted to say. "Holy fuck," he muttered again, his mouth dry. "Holy fuck."

"I think that about sums it up." At his shoulder, Liev laughed again, the sound relaxed and at ease. Chris wished he felt the same. "Wait, I'm not even remotely religious."

Trying to calm his whirling emotions, Chris rolled his head to the side and gave Liev a contemplative look. "Fiery fuck sounds painful."

Liev pulled a face. "It does."

"And guarded fuck sounds ominous."

Liev snorted. "Disturbing in fact."

Chris returned his gaze to the ceiling. "Holy fuck it is then."

"Holy fuck," Liev echoed.

The urge to turn to the man and tell him he loved him surged through Chris again. Instead, he threaded his hands behind his head and forced a grin to his lips. If Liev could be cool about what they'd just experienced, he could be too. "I'd like to point out," he said, "that the floaties are now well and truly shredded."

"You might be right."

Chris laughed, flicking a look at Liev. "*Might* be right?"

Liev's grin was languid, sated. "There are many other positions, Huntley. When you've tried them all we can talk about the state of your floaties. For example, there's this amazing position called the Anal Drop."

Chris's heart kicked up a notch at the thought of Liev penetrating his body again. If it wasn't for the fact he was so goddamn exhausted and drained, that his cock was currently as limp as an overcooked noodle, that his mind was a turbulent mess of emotional insecurity, he'd flatten Liev to the bed, cover the man's body with his own and demand they try the Anal Drop right that very second.

"And there's also toys." Liev's murmur stroked at his fraying nerves. "The pleasure of a butt plug is not to be—"

The bedroom door opened.

"Far be it for me to be a mood killer," Bethany strode into the room, two steaming mugs in her hand, "but Mr. Huntley is due at the wildlife reserve in less than hour."

With a muttered curse, Liev pushed himself upright, scratched his fingers through his hair and shucked himself to the end of the bed.

Chris stared at him, the cold shock of reality stilling his heart. He'd missed his chance. Their time together here, in this room away from the judging public, was over. The day ahead of them was planned out to the minute, and not one of those minutes allowed Chris to take Liev in his arms, brush his lips over his and tell him what his heart, his mind and his soul knew to be irrevocably true.

How the fuck *did* a guy tell another guy he loved him?

"Mr. Huntley?"

Chris blanched at his personal assistance's poised voice. He jerked his stare to her, fighting the frown wanting to pull at his forehead.

She smiled at him, and if he didn't remember all too clearly the way she'd used her body, her lips as a means to maneuver him and Liev together only a few hours ago, he could almost believe she was just the professionally detached P.A. she presented herself to be. "It's time to get out of bed. Take a shower."

Chris blinked. His head felt like it was spinning.

Bethany's nose crinkled as a smirk that could never be described as professionally detached crossed her face. "And I'm afraid you don't have time to shower with Liev."

At the mention of Liev's name, Chris swung his stare to the Australian.

The man was silent, a still calm claiming his beautiful body. His head rested in his hands, his elbows on his bent knees as he studied the floor. He looked…pensive.

Chris's gut knotted.

Flicking his assistant a quick look, Chris swallowed. "I just need a moment, please, Bethany."

He saw Liev stiffen at his request.

With a small nod, Bethany turned and walked for the door, taking the steaming mugs with her. "Don't do anything stupid," she said over her shoulder. "Either of you. You don't have time for a quickie."

Chris studied Liev's back, unable to miss the way the man's broad muscles flexed at her jest. "What are you thinking?" he asked when they were alone. His heart thumped hard in his ears. He didn't know what the answer was going to be, but for some reason, he was petrified.

The Australian lifted his head from his hands, his shoulders straightening. But he didn't turn to look at Chris. That fact sent cold dismay into Chris's already churning gut. "Was I—"

"No," Liev cut him off before he could ask the bleak question. "You weren't."

Chris swallowed again. "Then tell me what's going on in your head."

A sharp breath left Liev. His shoulders slumped. "I told myself it was just sex. It couldn't be anything *but* just sex."

If it was possible, Chris's heart slammed faster at Liev's murmur. He stayed silent, aching for what he wanted Liev to say.

"It *had* to be just sex," the man continued, still facing the door. "Because if it was more, both of us were going to get hurt."

Chris ground his teeth. "I told you I don't care about what others say."

Liev twisted his torso to finally look at him. "You should. And I should have kept my hands off you. It was my job to be your bodyguard. Nothing else. Fucking you wasn't part of the job description. Nor was fucking up your career."

He propelled himself from the bed and, fists bunched, crossed the room. "With the door closed, I almost forgot the world on the other side. But that world *is* there, waiting for you, the famous movie star. Waiting to live your life with you." He scrubbed at the back of his neck before turning to face Chris. "Please accept my apologies, Mr. Huntley," he said, his stare fixed on a point somewhere above Chris's right shoulder, "for my impropriety and unprofessional conduct. I assure you, it won't happen again in the time I'm still in your service."

And without another word, he turned and walked through the door, leaving Chris alone in the room.

Something tried to tear its way out of Liev's chest.

He hurried to his bedroom, his heart a world of agony, his temples crushing under an invisible vise.

The hurt in Chris's face at his apology had devastated him, but there couldn't be any other way. Liev didn't do commitment. He didn't. And he sure as *shit* didn't lose his bloody heart to a Hollywood star on the verge of fucking up his life over seven amazing days of discovery. He didn't do that either.

Better to rip out his stupid heart and grind it under his heel than do that. Better to save Chris Huntley's career than see it destroyed over a relationship that could never be.

Chris had only just tasted the possibilities of his sexuality. There wasn't a hope in hell Liev would expect him to declare Liev his one and only, even if Liev wanted him to. Which he didn't. Not at all. Because Liev didn't do commitment. He didn't.

Yeah, that's why your heart tore apart when the first words out of Chris's mouth after the most amazing sex of your life weren't I love you. That's why your soul shattered when the words you thought he was going to say, the exact three words you were going to say to him, didn't pass his lips.

Swinging the door shut behind him, Liev crossed to the

bathroom, stepped into the shower and flipped on the cold water.

He needed to get the smell of the man off his body.

Icy needles of water stung his flesh. He closed his eyes, lifted his face to the stream and willed the grief from his soul. Stupid. He was stupid. He'd told himself Huntley was off-limits. He'd told himself to ignore the base lust and chemistry between them.

He'd told himself to stay professional, and like a fucking moron he hadn't listened to a word. He'd thought he could survive it, thought he could lose himself in the glorious, illicit moment and walk away when it was finished. Hell, Chris wouldn't want anyone to know of their tryst. It would be the perfect fantasy—sex with a celebrity, the sexiest man alive, a man lusted after by millions—with no strings attached.

And then he had to go and lose his fucking heart to the man the moment Chris declared he didn't care what the world thought of him.

Stupid. Stupid. Stupid.

Slamming the side of his fist to the cold tile wall, Liev scrunched up his face and willed the aching need inside him away.

No matter how much he wanted to run back to Chris, take him in his arms and apologise for his blunt rejection, he couldn't. Because that was also stupid. And contrary to current behavior, Liev didn't do stupid either.

He killed the shower stream with a quick flick of his wrist, a second before the door to the cubicle swung open.

Chris stood on the other side, long corded legs covered by a pair of faded jeans, the rest of his sublime body bare, his hair wet and slicked back from his face.

Liev's breath caught in his throat. He froze, his stare locked on the man he wanted more than life.

"I wanted you the second I saw you, Reynolds," Chris said, his voice a deep rumble. "I watched you climb off the yacht and stride along the jetty like a goddamn Adonis and I wanted you right then and there. I'd never ever wanted a man before but I wanted you. You were so goddamn powerful, so goddamn confident and relaxed. You oozed sexuality and courage and strength and I wanted you." He jaw bunched. "And now I realize it was all a lie. You're just a coward. More afraid of life than I used to be."

Liev didn't move. He couldn't. The accusation had robbed him of life.

Chris's eyes narrowed. "Yeah, just what I thought. A coward." He shook his head and swung the shower cubicle door shut. By the time Liev shoved it open, the bathroom was empty.

He bit back a choked sob, slumped against the glass door-frame and stared at his feet.

His chest ached. His head roared. He thanked a God he didn't believe in. Chris hated him now, but despite the agony, despite the wretched grief, that was for the best. The man wouldn't throw away his life and career because of Liev now. That was what mattered.

Not Liev's stupid heart.

And definitely not Liev's stupid, ridiculous notion of love.

CHAPTER FOURTEEN

I f Bethany sensed there was a problem, she didn't say anything. But then it was possible she had no idea. Chris had made certain he'd come down the stairs ready for the day's appearance his normal chirpy, flippant self, despite the empty ache in his soul, and Liev had descended from his bedroom in full-blown bodyguard mode, eyes covered by black sunglasses, edgy tension radiating from him.

It helped that Jeff was there. For starters, Chris welcomed the distraction his friend provided. The man had burst into the house five minutes before Liev joined them in the foyer, regaling Chris and Bethany with hilarious descriptions of his nighttime adventures with the hot little blonde he'd met in Kings Cross. For another thing, Liev had never let his guard down when Jeff was around. It wasn't that Liev didn't trust the man. At least, Chris didn't think that was the case. He'd just always presented an image of the consummate menacing bodyguard in Jeff's presence. With Jeff in their company, it was unlikely Bethany could tell Liev wanted nothing to do with Chris. With Jeff around, Bethany would have no clue Chris was dying inside.

Which made for one tormenting drive to the wildlife

reserve. Bethany spent the forty-minute journey drilling Chris on the park's mission to save the endangered Eastern Pygmy Possum, a small nocturnal marsupial on the cusp of extinction thanks to habitat loss and attacks by predators such as domestic cats and dogs. Chris was going to donate a sizeable sum to aid the park's efforts. The donation had been Rowan's idea, decided upon after she'd watched a documentary about the tiny critter on Animal Planet one night when her enormous pregnant belly prevented her sleeping.

Chris had gladly agreed to the donation and appearance, the memory of his last *interaction* with an Australian animal during filming of *Dead Even* still bringing a grin to his face. Of all the events and appearances he'd attended in the country this time, the visit to the wildlife park had been the one he'd looked forward to the most.

Of course, that was before Liev Reynolds had entered his life and torn out his goddamn heart. Listening to Bethany outline what was going to happen and who he was going to meet and greet during the three hours spent at the park, he wondered if the tiny fluff ball could take away his pain as easily as man was taking away the fluff ball's environment.

Unlikely. It was easy to cut down a tree. Not as easy to make a guy love you, want you the way you wanted him.

Glad for the sunglasses he wore, Chris slid his gaze to the back of Liev's head and studied the man where he sat in the front passenger seat.

Was he hurting like Chris was? If so, he was hiding it well.

A sigh welled deep in Chris's chest, but he suppressed it. The day wasn't over. He was flying back to L.A. the next morning and he wasn't stepping a single goddamn foot on the plane until he'd made Liev change his mind about them. He wasn't expecting a marriage proposal. Hell, all he wanted was a promise they'd give each other a chance. The bone-deep hope Liev would consider a long-distance relationship if nothing else sparked within him. If they couldn't be in the same bed every night, they could at least talk to each other every day via Skype or FaceTime. If they couldn't spend months on end together, maybe they could at least be in the same country for a week three or four times a year.

It twisted Chris's gut to think that was the best-case scenario after the soul-deep passion they'd shared only a few hours ago, but if that's all he had to work with, then that's what he was working with.

He would not let the most incredible thing in his life slip away from him over a fucking reputation. Fuck that.

"Are you sure?"

Bethany's sharp question jerked Chris back to the interior of the SUV. He blinked. What the hell had he missed? "Err…"

His personal assistant twisted her lips. "I asked you if you were comfortable with holding one of the pygmy possums for a photo shoot after what happened with the kangaroo last year. I *think* you hummed an agreement." Her attention flicked to the back of Liev's head for a quick second before she frowned at Chris. "Is everything okay, Mr. Huntley?"

Chris couldn't miss the way Liev's shoulders stiffened at the question. Neither, it seemed, did Bethany.

She studied Chris, narrowing her eyes. "You do remember me telling you not to do anything stupid this morning, correct?"

From the front, Jeff laughed. "Huntley is the king of doing stupid things, isn't that right, dude. Remember when you decided to streak through the Beverly Hills Hilton after the *Twice Two Many* season two wrap party? I swear, that was the day your sister decided to…what the *fuck?*"

Jeff's abrupt exclamation filled the Audi's cabin, followed immediately by Liev's growled, "Fucking hell."

Chris strained forward in his seat to peer through the windscreen. Beside him, Bethany let out a ragged breath. "Oh no."

They'd arrived at their destination. The only reason Chris

knew that to be the case was the large sign a few yards away, a kangaroo and a koala smiling at each other above the words *Sydney Wildlife Park and Reserve*. If it weren't for the sign, he'd just as easily believe he'd driven to the gates of some messed-up hell.

Hordes of chanting people crowded the area directly in front of the park, spilling onto the road, shoving against each other. Some smiled and laughed, the signs in their hands shaken with fervor. Signs that read *We Love Chris Huntley, Chris Huntley is Hot, Twice Too Sexy,* and *Marry Me, Chris.* Those people Chris were familiar with. Their kind appeared at every public appearance he made. They were part of his existence.

It was the other kind that made his gut roll now. An angry kind he'd never encountered before. The kind waving placards with *Go Home Yank Pervert* painted on them. The kind brandishing signs that declared *Australia Doesn't Welcome Sickos* and *Protect Our Children.* The kind wielding signs that stated *God Hates Homos.* The kind who announced, with succinct conviction, *Huntley Is A Fag.*

"How..." Beside Chris, Bethany bit her whispered question short.

Jeff pulled the SUV to a halt and shook his head. Chris couldn't miss how white his knuckles were as he gripped the steering wheel. "Huntley is a fag? What the fuck are they talking about?" He shot Chris a frown over his shoulder. "You're not gay."

Chris swallowed. Or at least tried to. The lump that kept filling his throat over the last seven days was back.

Beside Jeff, Liev was a statue of silent tension, studying the madness beyond the car.

"Oh God, no. No, no, no."

Bethany's breathless gasp jerked Chris's attention to his personal assistant. Her head was bowed over her iPad, moving side to side as she stared at the device on her lap.

The headline on the screen caught Chris's attention first. He had to admit, it wasn't anywhere near as creative as the ones he'd imagined a lifetime ago.

Actor and Bodyguard in Poolside Passion

Below the bold black typeface, so large it filled the rest of the iPad's screen, was an image. Blurry, dark and almost indistinct with grain, but recognizable for what it was nonetheless—an image of a very naked Chris lying between the legs of a very naked Liev, Chris's lips closed around Liev's right nipple.

"At least they got my good side," Chris said, his mouth dust.

Bethany jerked her stare up to his face, her skin a sick pallor. "I don't understand…"

Chris nodded at the image, a dull buzz in his ears. "My ass. I've always said it's my good side."

Bethany shook her head, her eyes the size of saucers. "No, I don't understand how they got the image. The pool is…" Her teeth worried her bottom lip as she studied the image again. "I made sure the pool was secluded. Private. I scoped it all out. Even asked the neighbours if I could try and see it from their homes while you were at the party." She lifted her stare to his face again, her cheeks paler still. "I made sure."

"Who took the photo?"

Chris started at Liev's flat question. So did Bethany.

Pulling his stare from his personal assistant, he found Liev's arm extended over the seat, hand open.

"Let me see who took the photo," Liev said without taking his attention from the crowd outside the park.

Chewing on her lip, Bethany placed her iPad on the Australian's flat palm.

Liev took it without another word, his head dipping as he searched for the answer.

"I'm confused, dude." Jeff twisted behind the steering wheel to frown at Chris. "Why do they think you're gay?"

Chris opened his mouth. Closed it again.

Jeff's eyebrows shot up. "Really? You're gay? Holy shit. Since when?"

The lump in Chris's throat grew thicker. His face grew hot. "I…"

Jeff laughed. "Dude, doesn't matter to me at all. These people here though…" he tossed a sideways nod at the protesting crowd, "…seem pissed. How'd they find out about—"

"Holston."

Once again, Chris jumped at Liev's flat growl.

Jeff leaned toward the Australian, no doubt peering at the iPad in Liev's hands. "Ahh, I see." He looked up at Liev, a grin on his lips. "They're some seriously worked thighs you've got there, dude."

Ignoring Jeff, Liev passed the iPad back to Bethany, his stare once more on the crowd. "Carl Holston." Dark contempt cut the familiar name. "Rhodes warned me about him."

Chris looked down at Bethany's lap, noting the image on her iPad's screen was now slightly different, taken a few moments after the first one. The headline was different as well. This one utilized a bad pun along with the words *World Exclusive* to make its derisive point. *Huntley Heads Down Under.*

He laughed, a hollow mirthless sound. "Clever."

The attached image—as blurry and indistinct as the first—showed Chris exploring Liev's navel with his lips. Liev's hands were fisted in Chris's hair, his head thrown back, his eyes closed. Carl Holston was accredited as the photographer.

Chris's blood roared in his ears. Holston was the same photographer who had captured the image of Chris looking up at Liev outside the restaurant. The same photographer who last year had captured images of Rowan and Aslin making out on the back of Aslin's Ducati. Chris had damn near broken his hand punching Aslin in the jaw over those images.

Rowie hasn't seen these yet. Otherwise, she'd be calling you right now.

A tiny beat of relief struggled against his numb shock at the thought. God, what was he going to say when she *did* call?

"I'm sorry, Mr. Huntley," Bethany whispered beside him. "I never meant for this to happen."

He lifted his gaze to her face to give her a warm smile. "Look at the photos, Bethany. The prick must have been miles away, perched in a tree somewhere using a massive zoom lens. Even with the full moon and light from the pool, it's still a dark, fuzzy image. I'm surprised anyone could recognize me with all the grain."

"Look at the next image."

Chris's heart thumped harder at Liev's blunt instruction.

Her hand trembling, Bethany tapped the screen. The next image appeared and she moaned.

This photo was taken only an hour and a half ago. Chris knew the exact time, not because of the bright sunlight in the frame, but because he'd noticed the clock on the chest of drawers beside his bedroom door as Bethany walked through it.

Holston had captured the moment just after Chris had asked his P.A. to leave. He sat in the middle of the bed, amongst the crumpled sheets, obviously naked. Liev was perched on the end, equally bereft of clothing, his head in his hands. A white blur on either side of the image told Chris the paparazzo had taken advantage of the sheer curtains wafting apart on a playful breeze. The man must have been waiting in a boat out in the harbour for the perfect moment.

It seemed Holston had been stalking him since the restaurant. And, knowing the celebrity gossip sites like Chris did, the payoff for the prick would be massive.

"I'm sorry," Bethany whispered again. "So sorry."

Chris shook his head, smiling. "It's not your fault, sweetie. Honest."

"It's not your fault, Bethany." Liev's monotone statement filled the Audi's cabin. "It's mine."

Liev studied the crowd, a crowd he couldn't help but notice was growing more frenzied by the second. And brave. The chanting people were drawing closer to the Audi, as if sensing their prey nearby. He didn't turn back to Chris or Bethany. He didn't dare. Not when he was consumed by black rage and self-contempt.

If he'd done his job the way he was meant to, none of this would be happening. None of it.

"What do you want me to do?" Concern laced Jeff's voice.

Liev shook his head. "It's too volatile. Not safe. I'm surprised the cops aren't here yet." The path of one particular protester drew his attention and his gut knotted. The man was swinging a placard with the slogan *Go Home American Poof* painted over a printed image of Chris's face. Grinding his teeth, Liev shot Jeff a quick look. "Turn around. Chris isn't getting out here. Bethany can—"

"Wait a minute," Chris burst out from the back seat. "I'm not running away. I run away, they win."

"Mr. Huntley," Bethany spoke, the distress in her voice clear. "I think Liev is right. This is not—"

"Something I'm running away from," Chris cut her off. "I've got no reason to run. I've done nothing wrong."

Liev ground his teeth and, unable to stop himself, he finally twisted in his seat to glare at the actor. "You may think that, but they don't."

"Why? Because some low-life pap photographed us fucking?" Chris grinned at him. Grinned. If Liev wasn't so aware of the unruly mob but a few meters away he could believe Chris was just shooting the breeze. "Nothing wrong with that. In fact, I remember quite clearly the words *amazing* and *incredible* being uttered after the deed. Oh, and we *both* agreed holy was the only term appropriate for how *amazing* and *incredible* it was. So their signs about God hating homos is misinformed, wouldn't you say? At least let me explain to them how much we *homos* love God, okay?"

Cold anger knotted through Liev's hot rage. "That's enough, Chris."

Chris laughed, an infuriatingly relaxed sound. "No it's not." He slipped his fingers under the door handle and dropped a wink at Liev. "Not even close, lover. Watch this."

Before Liev could say a word, Chris opened the door and stepped out of the Audi. The crowd of fans and protestors erupted into squeals and shrieks at the appearance of their target. They ran at him, a single frenzied horde.

"Oh no," Bethany moaned from the back seat.

"Shit." Liev scrambled to release his belt buckle. "Shit, shit, shit."

"Fuck," Jeff echoed the sentiment.

Liev yanked open his door just as Chris walked past the nose of the SUV, heading for the crowd. The screams assaulted his ears, as did the shrill ring of his mobile phone bursting into life. Snatching the communication device from his hip pocket, he tossed it to Jeff without looking at the screen. "Deal with whoever it is," he ordered over his shoulder as he hurried after Chris.

Above the noise of the crowd, the sounds of sirens wailed. Liev wanted to curse. The situation was volatile and dangerous, more so than the restaurant riot had been. At least at the restaurant there hadn't been people after Chris with hate and contempt in their narrow-minded heads. If Liev had kept his fucking dick in his pants, if he'd been professional about the job, none of this would be happening. But no, he'd not only had sex with the client, he'd done it outside. Outside. What the fuck had he been thinking? He'd been so consumed by his desire and need for Chris he'd forgotten the first rule of being a bodyguard—never, ever let the client be exposed.

Thanks to Liev, Chris *had* been exposed. On every imaginable level.

"Huntley," he called, lengthening his stride to catch up with the American. "Stop."

Chris didn't.

Nor did the swarming crowd. In fact, at the sight of Liev, the squeals and shrieks and chants grew louder.

"We love you, Liev!" someone shouted.

"Poofta!" someone else shouted in reply. "Fucking fag."

Liev ground his teeth, snaring Chris's forearm in a tight grip. "Huntley."

Chris turned and gave him a wide grin, his backward steps a springy skip. "Trust me, lover."

He spun back to the crowd, held up his hand and waved. "Heya, guys. You all here to see me play with a furry little thing?"

Chris's fans squealed and giggled. Those there because of the images hurled abuse, waving their insulting placards and signs.

Chris laughed, still walking toward the wildlife reserve's entry. Liev stepped up beside him, arms out, protecting him from any attack or threat forthcoming. "Of course, I'm not talking about this guy here." Chris whacked the back of his hand against Liev's chest in a playful slap. "There's nothing little about him."

A large proportion of the crowd laughed.

Chris dropped Liev a sideways wink. "As you probably all saw in the photos, am I right?"

People chanted Chris's name, Liev's name. The laughing adoration coming from the fans grew louder. So loud it almost drowned out the insults of the shouting bigots.

A kerfuffle to Liev's left drew his harried glance. He bit back a growl. The press had found them.

"Chris, Chris," the reporter from the country's leading current affairs program cried into a microphone. "How are you feeling about this invasion of your privacy? Are you officially declaring your homosexuality?"

Chris smiled, continuing to walk for the park's front door. "The photographer captured my good side. Can't complain about that."

Another reporter, this one from the second-highest rating breakfast program, shoved a mic at Chris. "Are you gay, Mr. Huntley?"

Liev swiped the microphone away from Chris's face, keeping his expression neutral. He'd done a piss-weak job of being professional up until now. It was time he did what he was being paid to do.

"How long have you and Mr. Huntley been lovers, Mr. Reynolds?" The reporter thrust the mic toward Liev, almost stumbling over his feet as Liev and Chris kept walking.

"You heard of love at first sight?" Chris gave the tripping man a quick grin.

The surrounding crowd of fans cheered and laughed. The protestors hurled fresh insults. Above it all, the approaching police sirens wailed, closer by the second.

"So it's love?" Another reporter poked an iPhone forward, swinging it back and forth between Chris and Liev. "Care to comment, Mr. Reynolds?"

"You once worked as a bodyguard for the prime minister," the first reporter on the scene shot at Liev. "Stopped a shoe from hitting her."

Chris cocked an eyebrow at Liev. "Who throws a shoe?" he asked in his best Austin Powers impersonation. "Really?"

The unexpected urge to chuckle rolled through Liev. Bloody bastard. Quoting movie lines at him during a situation most politicians and sane people would run screaming from.

"Are you returning to America with him?" someone from the crowd shouted.

"Mr. Huntley, you've never been linked to gay rumours before." A new reporter shoved her way in front of Chris and

Liev, hurrying before them in awkward sideways strides. "Was it just research for a movie role?"

"Was what?" Chris asked her with a smirk.

The woman's cheeks flooded brilliant vermillion. Her lips parted but nothing came out. Around them, signs declaring Chris would burn in hell bounced and waved.

Chris laughed, drawing to a halt. "Listen…" he smiled at the people held back by Liev's extended arm before lifting his attention to those behind them, "…I'm not embarrassed by those photos. For two reasons. One, I've got a goddamn amazing butt, wouldn't you say? The world deserves to see more of it, especially from that angle." He had to wait for the legion of his fans and admirers to quiet down at the bold statement. "And two…" he slid Liev a glance, the corners of his lips curling into a smile Liev felt in the centre of his soul, "…an explanation isn't necessary when I've done nothing wrong."

"Faggot!" someone screamed from the back of the crowd.

"Random citizen!" Chris shouted back before grinning at the closest reporter. "Hmm, was I too rough on him? Too insulting?"

The deafening cry of a cop car prevented the reporter responding. Which, as far as Liev was concerned, was a good thing.

The next person to shout an insult at Chris was about to see what a six foot three bi-sexual firefighting bodyguard looked like when angry.

He'd reached the end of his control.

Bi-sexual? Huh. You're kidding, right? You know bloody well you're never going to look at another living soul again after Chris, man or woman.

The thought punched into Liev. Hard. The truth of it stole his breath.

His pulse thrummed in his ears and his heart smashed in his chest.

Shit, what the fuck did he do now?

CHAPTER FIFTEEN

His sister rang him three times during the three hours he was at the wildlife park. The first time Bethany took the call, her murmurs impossible to hear over the crowd as he entered the main building from the street.

The cops had arrived just in time to clear the anti-gay protestors. Whoever had organized the turnout hadn't wanted to stay around when the authorities appeared. By the time the first police car pulled to a halt next to the crowd, those with placards declaring Chris the spawn of the devil and other slurs of the ilk had blended into the mass of Chris's fans ecstatic to see their idol, the signs discarded on the ground.

Liev had stood guard, watching the sea of chanting, squealing people, his black sunglasses hiding whatever he was thinking from Chris and the questioning journalists.

He'd refused to make any further comments or answer any more questions. The last words Chris had heard him utter before the manager of the park arrived and the impromptu press conference came to an end was, "I'm just the bodyguard."

Those four words played with Chris's sanity for the next three hours. Enough that he found it damn impossible to focus on the baby pygmy possum an animal keeper handed to him the second he walked into the reserve.

The second call from his sister had come while he was talking to the manager of the park, the park's resident veterinarian and a politician who seemed to know Liev well given how often she called him by his first name while talking to Chris. Chris had rejected the call, not because he didn't want to talk to Rowan, but because he wasn't ready to have a discussion with her about what she no doubt had finally discovered back in L.A. He wasn't ashamed. He just wasn't prepared to talk about Liev while standing in a wildlife park holding a baby marsupial in his hands, especially when Liev was nowhere to be seen.

Whatever plan of attack the Australian had for dealing with the media frenzy and protestors outside, it involved being as far from Chris as possible once inside the park. That absence *also* played with Chris's sanity.

The third time Rowan called—two hours and forty-five minutes into his appearance at the park—he'd been signing autographs for the staff, surreptitiously searching for a man who wasn't anywhere to be seen. Bethany had cocked an eyebrow at him, her face a silent question. He'd shaken his head and returned to the pieces of paper offered to him. Better to keep up the façade of the flippant, friendly celebrity and pretend his goddamn heart wasn't a pummeled lump of aching uncertainty.

He'd signed autographs, cracked jokes, posed for photos and petted lots of marsupials and other critters before doing what he'd come to do—pledge a massive amount of money to the park.

The whole time he'd wondered about Liev's response to the media furor and what it meant for the man's future.

His own future, he was surprised to realize, he didn't give a flying fuck about. All he wanted to do was find Liev, thread his fingers through the stubborn man's fingers and tell him it was going to be okay.

When Bethany told the manager the visit was finished, Chris's heart had jumped into rapid flight. Finally, he'd be able to talk to Reynolds.

Liev, however, had other plans.

There were no signs of fans or protestors by the time Chris and Bethany exited the park. Jeff waited by the Audi a few yards from the main entrance, chatting with four police officers. Two squad cars were parked beside the SUV.

"Where's Mr. Reynolds?" Bethany asked as she and Chris walked toward Jeff.

An uncharacteristic grimace pulled at Jeff's face. "He's arranged for you to have a police escort for the rest of the day. Apparently someone on the force owes him a favour."

"He's gone?" Bethany's shock cut through the numb disbelief creeping over him.

Jeff nodded. "Said it was better for Chris."

The world grew cold. Heavy. Chris swallowed. The prickling stares of the cops made him want to squirm. Or maybe it was the emptiness in his soul.

"Mr. Huntley?"

He blinked at Bethany's soft voice.

"No sweat." He chuckled, the laugh sounding brittle and forced. "I couldn't be in better hands than these fine officers', correct?" He crossed to the cops and shook their hands with a grin.

All four nodded and professed their enjoyment of his work.

He thanked them with a smile, slapped them on the back with friendly ease and then climbed into the back of the Audi. He needed to get home.

Home? Which one? Here in Sydney? Back in L.A.? Or wherever the hell Liev is now?

An hour later, with the cops driving away from the

harbour-side mansion, Chris stood in the living room and stared at the television.

The image of him and Liev beside the pool had gone viral.

It was everywhere. News channels were running stories on it, gossip shows were drooling over it, comedians were riffing on it. Speculation was rife whether Chris was gay or bi. There was an opinion by some commentators the whole thing was just a hoax to garner media attention for *Dead Even*'s international release. Those people wouldn't believe *the* Chris Huntley, the sexiest man alive twice running and renown Casanova was really homosexual.

With every flick of the remote control, with every change of channel, Chris witnessed his very life dissected and analysed more than ever before. He'd thought it grueling when his parents' murder became fodder for the media. He'd thought it harrowing when the media learned of the attempts on Rowan's life by his ex-personal assistant. That was nothing compared to this.

Nothing.

The phones never stopped ringing.

His cell phone, Bethany's, Jeff's, the mansion's landline. If it was a means of communication, it made a noise. He half-expected a flock of carrier pigeons to land on the main balcony, all with tiny cameras strapped to their heads and a list of questions to be answered wrapped around one leg.

Have you always been gay?

Do you still have sex with women?

Will your character come out on Twice Too Many?

Are you going to host the Tony Awards?

Do you like Barbara Streisand?

"I'm going to have to start answering some of them, Mr. Huntley."

Tearing his stare from the television, on which a still image of Liev protecting Australia's prime minister from a thrown shoe now filled half the screen, he let out a ragged breath. "Tell them to call my manager. Or my agent. No doubt the two of them will have already concocted a game plan by now."

Bethany nodded and raised the ringing cell in her hand—his, he noticed—to her ear. "Bethany Sloan speaking," she said, watching him.

He had to admit, she looked shell-shocked.

Chris felt sorry for her. For the six months she'd been his assistant, the most controversial thing she'd had to contend with was the time he'd decided he wanted a Big Mac for lunch and was photographed ordering at the drive-through, resulting in PETA calling for a boycott of *Twice Too Many* and *Dead Even*. After that, Bethany had been stalked by PETA spies desperate to prove Chris was not only a carnivore but possibly tortured small animals for fun in his spare time.

That kind of attention had not prepared her for this.

Hell, *he* wasn't prepared for this, and he'd spent the last five years of his life in the public eye.

So why wasn't he freaking out now? And how did he convince Liev not to either?

"Mr. Huntley?"

He turned away from the television. "What is it, Bethany?"

His personal assistant held his cell phone out to him. "It's your agent."

Chris pulled a face.

Bethany didn't move.

Letting out a muttered curse, Chris took his cell from her hand and pressed it to his ear. "Leonard."

"This is why I told you it was fucking stupid to go to Australia without your manager," the most gravelly voice in Hollywood barked through the connection.

"I'm a big boy, Leonard. I can travel on planes and go to the bathroom all by myself now."

"It's not the planes or the bathrooms I'm worried about, funny guy," his agent grumbled back. "Bartowski would've at least made you keep your dick in your pants."

Chris dropped into the nearest armchair and killed the television with a stab of his thumb on the remote. "Oh, you're worried about my dick, Leonard? You shouldn't be."

"I am," Leonard shot back. Chris could almost see the man chewing on the stub of a cigarette like it was a raw leg bone. Leonard Braff was a ruthless, heartless predator. It was one of the reasons the man was so good at his job. "Now, want me to tell you why *you* should be worried about your dick as well?"

"Why?"

"Because I've just had a call from the studio suits. They're wanting to renegotiate your contract for the sequel to *Dead Even*."

Chris's gut clenched. He gripped his phone tighter. "Why?"

"Because their action star is fucking another man." Leonard's concrete-on-glass voice grew hoarse. "And the suits don't like that."

"So what you're telling me is my sexual choices are dictated to me now by the studio execs?"

"They are if you're going to keep making those *choices* out in public where any prick with a zoom lens can photograph it. Fuck, Chris, you know what the paparazzi are like in Australia. They're almost as bad as the lot here in the States."

A dull buzz thrummed in Chris's head. His eyes throbbed. His throat felt thick. He scraped a hand through his hair, all too aware Bethany still stood beside him. Bethany, not Liev. "And what do the suits want?" he asked, already knowing he didn't want to hear the answer.

"They want you to make a public statement that your... *dalliances* with the bodyguard was research for an upcoming film. They want you to declare your heterosexuality as loud as possible and to be seen in public every day with a woman until *Dead Even* finishes its cinema run. They've sent me a list of preferable candidates. They've suggested a sex tape with one of the candidates leaked onto the net would be a good idea as well."

The throbbing in Chris's eyes moved to the rest of his head. He scrunched up his face, each word his agent said cutting him deep. "And if I don't?" he asked.

There was a long pause on the other end of the connection before Leonard finally said, "Do you really want to commit career suicide so young, Chris?"

There was no hidden meaning in the threat. Chris's action-film career was over if he didn't declare himself straight.

He swallowed, the lump in his throat thick and hot and bitter.

Beside him, Bethany's phone began to ring in her hand. He flicked her a look, an invisible blanket of suffocating wool wrapped around him.

"It's your sister," Bethany mouthed, reading her iPhone's screen.

Chris's head buzzed some more. The hair on his nape pricked. "I've got to go, Leonard," he said into his cell.

He ended the call before his agent could finish shouting a protest.

Taking Bethany's offered cell, he raised it to his ear and watched his assistant walk from the room. "Rowie?"

"Heya, squirt." His sister's warm voice tickled his sanity. "Is there something you want to tell me?"

"You've seen the images, I take it?"

She laughed at his stupid question. A faint gurgle through the connection told him his sister was holding his new baby niece. "Hard to miss. I don't know what it's like in Australia, but it's impossible to escape it over here. Glad to see they got your good side."

"See?" Chris gave a weak chuckle. "That's what I said."

"So tell me, how long have you been showing your good side to guys?"

The question was calm. He wished he could see her face. He truly had no idea what Rowan was thinking. Was she disgusted? He didn't think she would be, but he didn't really know. She'd never expressed any distaste for homosexuality, but then it wasn't something they'd discussed often. "Not long," he answered, studying the ceiling. "Twelve hours or so."

"Okay, wasn't the answer I was expecting."

He snorted. "It wasn't?"

"No, I'd psyched myself to give you a lecture on not trusting me enough to tell me your sexual preferences. You've taken my thunder away."

Chris frowned. "So you're not upset?"

"Upset?" He could hear the shock in her question. "Why would I be upset? Aslin is pissed at Liev for being unprofessional, but me? Chris, I don't care if you're gay or straight. You're still my brother."

A tingling pressure rolled up Chris's spine and over his scalp. He dragged a hand through his hair. Jesus, he wished Rowan was here with him. He'd never needed his sister as much as he did now. "I don't know if I'm gay. Maybe I'm bi?"

"Bi?"

He shrugged, which given Rowan was on the other side of the world was a stupid thing to do. "I've slept with my fair share of women, sis."

"True. Do you want to sleep with more?"

The tingling weight creeping over his head turned into a hot vise around his temples. He closed his eyes. The answer to the question twisted a knot around his heart. "No. Not anymore. I honestly can't see myself with anyone else but Liev."

Silence followed his flat statement. He wondered what Rowan was doing? Chewing on her bottom lip most likely. It was her favourite expression when thinking about something important, and the bombshell dropped upon her definitely fell into the important category.

"So this is you now?" she finally asked, her voice soft.

"I think this has been me forever, Rowie," he answered, his chest tight. "I just didn't know it until I met Reynolds. I've never felt connected to any of the women I've dated, no matter how perfect for me they seemed to be, even back in high school before the fame and the money. Remember how often you gave me a hard time for not taking any of them seriously? For being a prick about casting them off just when it was obvious they'd become serious about me?"

"I do."

"I used to think that was just the way I was. I used to laugh at the idea of explosive passion and soul-deep fulfillment. Thought it was just some bullshit created by poets and propagated by song writers, chick-flick writers and Mills and Boon."

"Oh, Chris," Rowan murmured.

He opened his eyes and studied the ceiling again. "And then when I saw that you'd found it with Aslin…" He petered out, not sure how to tell his sister how jealous he'd been.

"And now you feel all this? Explosive passion and soul-deep fulfillment? With Liev Reynolds?"

A wave of tormented happiness ebbed over Chris. He smiled, picturing the Australian who'd forever changed him. "For the first time in my life, I feel alive, sis. Truly alive. If I can borrow from Tom Cruise for a moment, I feel complete when I'm with him. Not just when we're having sex, but just being with him. Being in his company. I feel happy and content and safe and me. One hundred percent me. I haven't felt any of those things since Mom and Dad were killed, Rowie. None of them."

"Why do you sound so sad then, Chris? Are you worried about your career?"

He let out a ragged breath. His career. Television's highest-paid sitcom star, a movie star in the making, a sex symbol. "I'm not. As far as I'm concerned Hollywood is just going to have to deal with the fact the tough guy on the screen kicking ass and taking names is sleeping with his male lover when the credits roll. Fuck it. Hollywood loves to talk about how liberal it is. I'm going to make them put their money where their collective mouths are. If Neil Patrick Harris can be openly gay, so can I.

It's about time Hollywood embraced a homosexual leading man, not just a secondary character in a television show. If the studio suits don't like that, they're going to have a fight on their hands." He smiled, picturing Rowan chewing on her lip in L.A. "I'm good at fighting when I need to. My sister taught me how to do it."

Rowan's answering laugh was warm. "I'm glad I've had a positive influence on your life, squirt. Now tell me why I'm still hearing pain in your voice."

Chris swallowed. "Because Reynolds is being a stubborn pain in the ass and won't even be in the same room with me."

"Why not?"

The steely edge in Rowan's voice made him smile. She'd protected him for over ten years, and now it seemed she was prepared to protect his heart. "Because as far as I can tell, he thinks I'm better off without him in my life."

"What are you going to do about that?"

Chris laughed. "Show him he's wrong. There's another thing you taught me over the years, sis. Just as important as picking my fights."

"And what's that, squirt?"

"You taught me never ever to give…"

The rest of the statement died in Chris's throat when Bethany walked into the room. With Liev walking beside her.

"Chris?" Rowan said.

Chris stared at the man, unable to breathe. Unable to move.

"Chris?" his sister repeated.

Without a word, he held out his cell phone to Bethany.

"Hi, Mrs. Hemsworth-Rhodes. It's Bethany." He heard her say the words, but her voice was soft. Distant. Fading.

He pushed himself to his feet, his focus locked on Liev.

The Australian walked deeper into the living room, his hands in his hip pockets, his jaw bunched.

Chris's pulse beat in his neck, a wild tattoo of nervous

excitement. He swallowed, his throat rougher than sandpaper. "Thanks for the police escort."

The man didn't say a word.

Chris licked his lips. He watched Liev draw closer. Christ, he was gorgeous. And here. Right here in the room with him. "It came in handy when Jeff received a text the Audi's brakes had been cut and we couldn't drive less than eighty miles an hour."

Liev didn't react.

"Yeah, that was lame," Chris said, his gut knotting. "Sorry. I'm still recovering from the attempted alien invasion. Good thing the cops were there to stop it. And I think I saw Will Smith as well."

A foot away, Liev stopped. His gaze held Chris prisoner.

"Okay." A scratchy laugh hiccupped its way past Chris's lips. "Will didn't actually make an appearance, but there was this suspicious looking BMW that kept following us. And Jeff has no clue what the speed limit actually is in the country and I think the cops were just trying to keep up with him."

Fuck, he was babbling.

Liev's nostrils flared. His chest rose and fell with slow, steady breaths.

The urge to close the distance between them welled through Chris. He shifted his feet, aching to smooth his hands over Liev's chest, snare a fistful of the man's hair and tug his face down so he could kiss him senseless. Instead, Chris pulled a deep breath, squared his shoulders and said, "I want you to come back with me to L.A. tomorrow."

Liev lifted his eyebrows.

"I know it's insane," Chris went on before the man could say anything, "but I'm not fucking about. I don't know if it's love, it fucking *feels* like love, who knows? I've never been in love, but I'm goddamn sure I'm in love with you and I know you've changed *everything* in my world. Everything. And I don't want to leave Australia without you. I want you to come back to L.A. with me and see if what *this* is…" he waved a finger back and forth between them, his stare locked on Liev's face, "…really *is* what I think it is. I want you with me, not as my bodyguard, but as my lover, my partner. I can give you whatever you want, Reynolds, whatever you want. You won't want for anything. You won't even need to work. Geez, that sounds like I want to make you a kept man. I don't, I just…fuck, I'm doing a fucking piss-poor job of this." His chest constricted and he scraped his fingers over his scalp, his heart slamming in his throat. "I fucking… Man, why won't you say anything? How can you be standing here so fucking calm when I'm… when I'm…*fuck*, I just…I just…"

"Take a breath, Huntley."

Liev's deep voice flayed Chris's senses. He scrunched up his face, tugged at his hair and pulled in one long, slow breath.

Holding it for a count of ten, he let it out just as slowly and then opened his eyes. "I want you, Reynolds. Not just for sex, but for everything. Come back to L.A. with me. Please?"

The muscles in Liev's jaw knotted. His Adam's apple jerked up and down the smooth column of his throat. Without a word, he took the final step separating them, cupped Chris's face in his strong hands and lowered his head.

His lips brushed Chris's. It couldn't be called a kiss. It was too reverent, too tender. It filled Chris's soul with contentment and joy.

And then it was over.

Liev stepped away from him, one step, just one, and shook his head. "You don't want to destroy your career over someone who doesn't do commitment, Huntley."

An invisible fist punched into Chris's gut. His blood roared in his ears. He stared into Liev's eyes, refusing to believe what he was hearing.

Liev raised his hand and traced his thumb over Chris's bottom lip. "I will always remember this." His jaw bunched again. His breath left him in a hitching groan and then he turned and walked away. He stopped at the top of the stairs to turn back to Chris. "I checked your schedule. You don't need me for your remaining time in Australia. I've arranged a police escort to the airport for you tomorrow morning and the airline will meet you at the arrival gates with a security team to keep the crowds at bay before you board your flight." He bent sideways at the waist and collected his overnight bag from the floor. "Goodbye, Mr. Huntley. Good luck with your future movies."

He turned and descended the stairs to the foyer without looking back, the sound of the door closing telling Chris he was gone.

Gone.

And it didn't matter how long Chris stood there waiting for him to come back, to say he'd changed his mind. He didn't.

He didn't, goddamn it.

He didn't.

CHAPTER SIXTEEN

Two weeks of self-exile didn't help Liev at all.

He worked out in his home gym, jogged the streets in the early hours of the morning before the sun broke the eastern horizon, punched the shit out of the punching bag hanging in his garage, and spent every damn hour of the day punishing himself for his lack of self-control.

It didn't work. Every bloody time he closed his eyes he saw Chris bloody Huntley.

He refused to answer the phone or door. He'd rung his captain at the station house the day Chris flew out of Australia and told the man he was taking a month off. He had time accrued and needed to take it. The man didn't ask why. The whole bloody world probably knew why. Any body-guarding work lined up he cancelled. Politicians didn't need a celebrity guarding them, and that's what he currently was—a celebrity, famous for being caught *deflowering* Chris Huntley.

It was that headline that sent him into hiding. The morning Chris left the country, Liev had opened his morning newspaper to read the headline *Bi-sexual Australian Bodyguard Deflowers American Actor.*

He'd folded the paper, placed it on the table, collected his iPod from the cupboard, stuck the earbuds in his ears and hit play. AC/DC had blasted his ear canal louder than was medically sound.

He'd walked down into the garage, hung the heavy punching bag on its hook and begun punishing himself.

Self-disgust churned in his gut every bloody minute. Disgust at hiding from the world, disgust at destroying Chris Huntley's life. Every minute of every day, he berated himself for what he'd done, for what he was doing. Every minute of every day, he wished he could take it all back. Go back in time to the moment Aslin Rhodes had called him from the States and asked him if he'd act as Chris's bodyguard while the actor was in Australia promoting his film.

And every time he wished he could change history, acrid self-contempt flooded him because he knew he wouldn't even if he could. The seven days he'd existed in Chris's world were the most incredible, wonderful, amazing days of his life. Nothing could ever come close to the night he spent in Chris's arms, in his bed. He'd never felt so whole.

If it was possible, he hated the man for ruining him for any future sexual partners even as he knew there would never be a second when he didn't love Chris for giving him those few seconds and minutes and days of sheer paradise.

Of course, just to add to the fun of his existence now, whenever he *thought* of future sexual partners, his gut rolled as if his body rejected the notion of someone else apart from Chris penetrating him.

He wasn't surprised. He knew for a fact his heart and his soul would reject anyone else entering his body for the rest of his life.

Fuck a bloody duck, he was a waste of space.

A pathetic, gutless waste of space.

Slamming his fist into the punching bag, he focused on the burning pain radiating through his overworked muscles, the searing heat in his raw knuckles.

Inside his ears, Eddie Vedder and Pearl Jam growled and sang, pummeling at the constant thought of Chris. At this rate, Liev reckoned he'd be insane by Friday. Two and a half weeks after experiencing absolute happiness in Chris's arms and he would be ready to be admitted to the nuthouse. It was kind of fitting, really. A bloke like him would have to be insane to do what he'd done—destroy another man's life because he was horny.

It was always more than sex, Reynolds. And you know it.

The wretched thought tore at what was left of his control and, a roar ripping at his throat, he smashed his bleeding fist into the bag one last time before stumbling away from it.

This was no good. None of this was working.

He needed…

Chris.

Grinding his teeth on the tormenting name, he snatched his towel from where it hung on the bench-press weights and stormed from the garage, slamming the door shut behind him.

He'd go for a run. Maybe a few hundred miles of pounding the pavement would—

Movement to his right snapped him around, his fists raised.

"Jesus, Caitlin," he burst out, yanking the buds out of his ears at the sight of his niece climbing through his living room window. "What the hell are you doing? You're lucky I didn't hurt you before I realized it was you."

Caitlin glared up at him, struggling to disengage herself from the curtains and the venetian blinds as she planted the foot inside his house on the floor. "If you'd answer your fucking phone I wouldn't be needing to put my life at risk, would I?"

Stunned disbelief shot through Liev. He scowled, hurrying over to his niece to help her escape the soft furnishing. "Since when do you use language like that?"

Brushing her hands on her thighs, she shot him a look he

could only describe as scathing. "Since you became a fucking moron."

He narrowed his eyes and jabbed a finger at her. "Okay, that's enough, girlie girl. What are you doing here?"

With a grunt and a huff at her fringe hanging over her eyes, Caitlin shoved her right hand into the back pocket of her shorts and withdrew an iPhone cased in a candy-pink shell. "There's someone who wants to talk to you. Someone who gave up trying to get you on *your* phone and decided to do it via *my* phone."

She thrust the smartphone out toward him, glare firmly in place. Liev had never seen her so angry. Or so like her father. If it weren't for the fact her anger was directed at him, he'd give her a hard time about it.

"Hurry up," she snapped. "I didn't just break my bloody thumb wriggling open your window for you to just stare at my phone, did I?"

Biting back his chuckle, Liev took her phone from her fingers and raised it to his ear. "Hello?" He had no idea who would be calling him on Caitlin's phone, but if it was someone from the media he was tearing them a new one for coming at him through his teenage niece. And then he'd track them down and tear them a new one in person. No one put Caitlin in this kind of situation without paying the—

"What the fuck do you think you're doing, Reynolds?"

Liev's gut dropped into his balls at the sound of Aslin Rhodes's thunderstorm voice.

"How many sodding years have we been mates, and this is what you do?"

Liev squeezed his eyes shut, his grip on Caitlin's phone growing tighter. In the fortnight since he'd withdrawn from the world, there were two people he wanted to talk to more than anything, even as he hoped neither would ever want to talk to him again. Chris and Rhodes. Now it seemed one of them had done the unforgivable and got at him through Caitlin. Trouble was, not only was Rhodes in the States, Liev knew he couldn't tear the Brit anything, let alone a new arsehole. He deserved Rhodes's rage just as much as he deserved the man's contempt. He'd not only destroyed Rhodes's trust in him, he'd made him look like a bloody fool.

Hot guilt lashed at him, churning his sickened gut. Caitlin was correct. He was a fucking moron.

Scrubbing his free hand at the back of his neck, he stared at his feet. "I'm sorry, Rhodes," he muttered. "Jesus, mate, you have no idea how much I'm—"

"Going to regret what you've done?" Rhodes cut him off. "Sodding oath you are. I've got a brand new baby in my house and instead of spending my waking moments enjoying every precious second with her, all I'm seeing is my sodding brother-in-law moping around the place grumbling about being empty and incomplete and having his heart ripped out of his chest."

Liev shook his head, the lump in his throat choking him. "I'm sorry, mate. I really am. I know I fucked up and I…wait, what did you say?"

"Chris is grumping about our home," Aslin growled through the phone, "*our* home, Reynolds, not his, constantly sulking about being rejected by the love of his life. If you don't get your arse to L.A. ASAP and deal with the situation *I'm* going to have to deal with it myself, and trust me, Liev, you don't want that. It's not that I don't like having my brother-in-law in my house, it's just all the moping is beginning to sodding grate. I'm a tired, angry, fed-up Pom at this point in time, Reynolds. You know me well enough to know what that means."

Liev frowned, unsure he'd heard what his friend had said correctly. "Back up for a sec, Rhodes. Are you telling me you're not pissed I slept with Chris, you're pissed he's in your home—"

"Why the hell would I be pissed you slept with my brother-in-law? You're both grown men and I like you enough to know family get-togethers wouldn't be a living hell to experience. I'm pissed because you're too gutless to accept what seems to me to be something pretty special, and I'm the one dealing with the fall-out because Rowan has her hands full looking after our baby girl. By the way, Rowan says if you don't stop breaking her brother's heart she's going to kick your balls so far up into your *ass*, you'll need a mining team to find them again. Her words, Reynolds, not mine."

Liev blinked.

"And Liev?" Aslin's voice was calm and laced with an emotion that might be mirth. Or menace. "I know you don't *do* commitment, but I also know you're not stupid or a coward. Or am I wrong?"

Before Liev could answer, Bethany's voice sounded over the connection. "I've sent you an email," she said, her American accent jarring so soon after Aslin's British one. It seemed to Liev the whole world was furious with him at the moment. "Your niece has it opened already."

The phone clicked in his ear, the connection terminated. Liev jerked the thing from his ear and swung around, his gaze falling on Caitlin standing behind him.

She grinned at him, holding out his open laptop. "See? I'm not the only one who thinks you're being a moron."

A scowl fell over Liev's face. He ground his teeth, his glare sliding to the white screen of his laptop.

"Read the damn thing, Uncle L." Caitlin shoved the computer at him. "Or I'm going to call you a wuss for the rest of your life."

His head thrumming, his lips tingling, Liev lifted his laptop from his niece's hands, lowered himself into the closest armchair and balanced his computer on his sweat-slicked knees. He stared at the screen, the subject heading of Bethany's email simple. *Watch this.*

He placed his fingers on the track pad and, feeling like he

was engulfed in cotton wool, double clicked on the only content of Bethany's message—a hyper link to a YouTube clip.

It was one of those late-night talk shows the Americans loved so much. The host had a shock of orange-red hair and an infectious smirk. He sat behind a wooden desk, grinning at the man sitting on a sofa beside him.

Liev's heart slammed into his throat.

"Now tell me about this Australian," the talk show host said, fixing Chris with a pinning look. "This…what's his name, Liev Reynolds? Sounds like Liev Schrieber and Ryan Reynolds got together and made a bodyguard." A superimposed image of Liev wearing a tux at the Australian *Dead Even* red carpet event appeared on the screen. "Oh my God," the host proclaimed. "He *looks* like they did too. Damn, that's an impressive looking man right there, isn't it?"

The audience cheered and clapped and whooped. On the sofa Chris laughed. "Impressive is one word I'd use, Conan."

The host leaned forward on his desk. "One word? What's another?"

"Perfect," Chris answered, his smile utterly relaxed. "Funny. Powerful." He paused. "Sexy as all hell."

"Wait a minute," the host held up his hand. Liev's gut knotted. "Wait a minute. That's seven words."

The audience laughed. So did Chris. "True though."

"So, impressive, perfect, funny, powerful and sexy as hell? Anything else you want to tell us? Hairy ass? A tattoo? Birthmark shaped like a kangaroo? I couldn't really tell from the photos."

There was more laughter from the audience. Chris chuckled, shifting on the sofa to lean closer to the host. "None of those. But I will tell you, he's got the best ass on the planet. Better than mine, in fact."

The host whistled. "So is it love?"

Chris laughed. "Conan, Liev Reynolds is the man who

made me realize who I really am. And I really like who I really am. If that's not love, I don't know what is."

The host turned to the camera. "Yeah!" he said, pumping his fist. "I'm really, really a fan of love." Turning back to Chris, he held out his hand. "Thank you for coming on tonight, Chris. And congrats again, not only on *Dead Even* breaking box-office records but on the announcement of the sequel. Thanks for sharing that news here."

The clip ended.

Liev stared at the screen.

Without a word, Caitlin leaned over his shoulder and clicked on the top link on the right of the page.

Another clip opened, this one of a different talk show. The host sat behind a desk, Chris sat on a sofa, smiling at the audience as the host rattled off a list of records *Dead Even* had broken since its international release—fastest film to break one billion dollars in the US, fastest film to break one billion in Europe, fastest film to break one billion in the UK. Highest-grossing action film in U.S. history. Highest-grossing film of the decade.

"Which makes you a very successful guy," the host pointed out.

Chris nodded. "It would seem so."

The host straightened his note cards on the desk with a sharp rap. "So, this guy from Australia, what's his name? Burt Reynolds?"

Chris laughed along with the audience. To Liev, he'd never appeared more relaxed or gorgeous. "Liev Reynolds, Dave."

"Ah, that's right." The host adjusted his glasses. "He's a big scary guy, isn't he? How did you meet?"

Liev's heart thumped faster at the cheeky grin that stretched Chris's lips. "He was selected by my brother-in-law to be the perfect bodyguard."

"And was he?"

Chris wriggled his eyebrows. "You've seen the photos, Dave. You tell me."

The audience erupted. The drummer beat out a riff.

The host waved his hand, smiling. "Seriously, Chris," he said, his blue eyes intent behind his glasses. "Are you worried about being so open about this? There aren't that many action heroes willing to discuss their gay sex life. Do you fear your career will suffer?"

Chris sat back on the sofa and rested his arms along the cushions. "There should be more of us, Dave. There's nothing to be ashamed about. Who I want to be intimate with, who I *chose* to be intimate with is neither offensive nor significant to what I do for a living. Someone I know very well told me just because I'm gay doesn't mean I've less testosterone in my system. It just means I've got different taste."

The audience applauded. The lump in Liev's throat grew thicker. He stared at his laptop's screen, drinking in the sight of the man who'd shaken his world.

"Wise words." The host tapped his index cards on the table again. "Who said them?"

Chris's smile sent Liev's heart racing. "Liev Reynolds."

The host looked into the camera as an image of Liev from the current fire-fighters charity calendar flashed onto the screen. "And I'm not going to argue with him. Have you seen the size of this guy's arms? I think he's got testosterone to spare."

The clip ended on the audience's cheers. Before Liev could contemplate what he'd just watched, Caitlin started another.

A different show, a different host, but showing the same thing—Chris talking openly about his sexuality, the host congratulating him on the phenomenal success of his film and its announced sequel, the audience showing their adoration for Chris through their cheers and applause.

Liev didn't know what to do. Or say. He watched each one Caitlin opened, guilt twisting through amazement.

When he didn't think he could take any more in, when his gut couldn't get any tighter or his chest any heavier, Caitlin clicked on a clip called *Chris Huntley Announcement on Leno*.

It was a short clip. No more than a minute. Chris stood beside the talk-show host, looking sexier than ever in a pair of faded blue jeans, an open-neck white shirt and a five o'clock shadow on his jaw Liev knew would feel like heaven against his lips.

"Ladies and gentlemen," the famous host waved his hands about in the familiar way he did, "before we finish for the night, Chris has got something to tell us. Chris?"

Chris turned to the camera and grinned. "I've just been named *People Magazine*'s Sexiest Man Alive again. For the third time."

The crowd went wild. Chris burst out laughing. And the clip ended.

Liev stared at the frozen image of Chris. Just stared at it.

"Uncle L?"

At his niece's soft—and worried—voice, he jolted to his feet and ran for the bathroom.

"Uncle L?" Caitlin shouted from his living room. "What are you doing? You're not throwing up, are you?"

"Get my credit card out of my wallet," he shouted back, grabbing the hem of his sweat-drenched shirt and yanking it over his head as he toed off his running shoes. "I need you to buy me a ticket for the first flight to L.A. you can while I have a shower. The first flight."

"You don't have to do that, Uncle L." Caitlin's voice floated back to him just as he reached into the shower cubicle to flick on the water.

Suppressing a grunt, Liev turned and hurried back out to the living room. "Yes, I…"

He froze.

"No, you don't," Chris said.

Liev stared at the man standing in the middle of his living room.

Chris looked just as gorgeous, just as stunning, just as sexy as he had on Leno. The stubble on his jaw was longer, his hair messier, his shirt—white cotton—was crumpled.

Liev swallowed. Chris Huntley was here. In his bloody living room.

Movement from the corner of his eye caught his attention. Aslin leant against the wall, his arms crossed. Bethany stood beside him, iPad pressed to her breasts.

With a chuckle, Chris's brother-in-law pushed himself from the wall and jabbed a finger at Liev. "Get your sodding act together, Reynolds, so I can get back to my wife and my daughter. Hear me?"

Before Liev's brain could make his mouth open, Aslin snared Caitlin by the elbow and dragged her from the room, a grinning Bethany in tow. "Hurry the hell up and kiss him, Reynolds," Aslin called. "And say you're sorry."

"Sorry is a good start," Chris murmured.

Liev swung his stare back to Chris. His breath caught in his throat. A throat well on its way to trying to asphyxiate him.

The actor smiled, shoving his hands into the back pocket of his jeans. "I thought you Australians were meant to be brave."

His voice caressed Liev's senses. Made his head spin. "We *are* brave. Just not that smart, it seems."

Chris laughed.

The sound flooded Liev with euphoric pleasure. And still he couldn't move. Couldn't take that step to close the distance between them. "Not smart like you," he said, the words a rasping breath.

Chris shook his head, his smile loose. "Nah, I'm the funny guy in this relationship, remember?"

Liev swallowed. "There's a relationship?"

"I didn't just fly halfway around the world to tell you you're a moron, did I?" A frown dipped at his eyebrows. "Maybe I'm not as smart as you think I am?"

Liev's snort echoed around the living room. "Bullshit, Huntley. I just spent the last half hour watching you on YouTube."

Chris smirked. "I know. I was standing outside waiting for you to finish. Just in case you were wondering, your niece really has a flair for the dramatics. When I called her, she told me she knew exactly what to do to make you see the light."

Liev's chest ached. "I didn't need to see the light. I saw *you*," he said, unable to stop his gaze roaming Chris's face. Hell, he'd seen it every night in his dreams since he'd walked away from the man. He'd seen it every time he'd closed his bloody eyes, and never once was it as breathtaking as it was now. In reality. "I saw how comfortable you were talking about us, about who you are. What you are. I saw the hosts eating out of your hands and the audience hanging off your every word." He shook his head, his pulse pounding in his neck. "That wasn't just you being funny, that was you being honest and smart. They loved it. They loved you."

Chris stood motionless. His gaze found Liev's and held it. "I don't want *everyone* to love me, Reynolds. I just want—"

Before he could finish, Liev crossed the room and crushed Chris's lips with his.

How could he not? The man he loved was here in his living room even after he'd behaved like a fucking idiot and sent him away.

Chris fisted his hands in Liev's hair. The crisp cotton of his shirt stroked Liev's bare chest. Liev's nipples pinched hard. A heavy spasm claimed his cock.

From the other room, on another planet, a jubilant and thoroughly teenage *whoohoo* filled the air. "Way to go, Uncle L," Caitlin called.

With a chuckle, and far more reluctance than he imagined

possible, Liev broke away from the kiss and stared down into Chris's face. "Fuck, I'm sorry, Chris. I was an idiot."

Chris cocked an eyebrow, smoothing his hands from Liev's hair down over his shoulders to his bare chest. "Yes, you were. But I won't hold it against you."

Liev sucked in a sharp breath. Christ, if his niece wasn't in the other room right now... He dragged his thumb over Chris's bottom lip. "You know, I'm never letting anyone else guard your body but me, right?"

Chris leaned forward and brushed his lips over Liev's. "Wouldn't have it any other way, Mr. Costner."

The quip sent joy radiating through Liev's soul. "Mr. Costner?"

Chris grinned. "Mr. Costner. You know..." He threw back his head and burst into the theme song from *The Bodyguard*, his voice ludicrously off key and pitch.

Liev laughed, holding the man who had changed everything for him closer, and then, incapable of holding off anymore, kissed Chris silent.

The man may be bloody funny and as sexy as all hell, but he couldn't sing for shit.

THANK YOU

If you enjoyed **Guarded Desires**, you can continue following the adventures of Nick Blackthorne and his old band members in the *Heart of Fame* series, available now.

Sign-up for Lexxie Couper's newsletter, the Lexxicon to receive a free copy of her (erotic) paranormal short story, **The Cavern**, plus never miss out on exciting announcements and giveaways!

ABOUT LEXXIE COUPER

Lexxie writes fun-with-feels romances. She lives with a manic rescue dog, a self-absorbed rescue cat, a very patient husband not rescued from anything, and two strong-willed teenage daughters who will one day rule the world.

Lexxie lives by two simple rules – measure your success not by how much money you have, but by how often you laugh, and always try everything at least once. As a consequence, she's laughed her way through many an eyebrow raising adventure. You can find details of her writing at www.LexxieCouper.com

steady *beat*

LEXXIE COUPER

FIRST CHAPTER PREVIEW: STEADY BEAT

HEART OF FAME, BOOK FOUR

He never missed a beat…until she taught him a whole new rhythm.

Steady Beat
(*Heart of Fame*, Book Four)
Available In Digital and Print

"How the hell do you replace Nick fucking Blackthorne?"

The surly question dragged Noah Holden's contemplative gaze from the nearby waitress in snug black hot pants holding his attention. He blinked, turning to face the man slouched in the chair opposite him. Sitting here with the four remaining members of what was once the hottest rock band in the world, Noah let his confusion show. "Why are we talking about Nick?"

Samuel—the lead guitarist—scowled. "You too busy checking out the broad in the tight duds to follow the conversation, Holden? Levi's writing the score for the sequel to *Dead Even* and the director is on the lookout for something different for the closing credit soundtrack. Jax suggested we get the band back together for it and maybe record an album as well, just for shits and giggles." Samuel tossed the two men sitting either side of Noah an exasperated glare. "And *I* just pointed out finding someone to replace Nick was fucking impossible."

"Not impossible." The man to Noah's left—Jaxon Campbell—leant forward with a grin, snaring Samuel's beer from in front of the guitarist and taking a swig. Letting out a satisfied, "ahh," he wiped away the thin line of foam on his top lip and turned to Noah. "Just bloody tricky, is all."

Noah snorted. Jax reveled in taunting Samuel. The keyboardist thrived in seeing just how far he could push the man before Samuel lost it. It made for a turbulent relationship—but holy hell, it also made for an amazing dynamic on stage and in the recording studio. The two men loved each other like brothers—and antagonized each other the same way.

Plucking Samuel's beer from Jax's grip, Noah returned the sweating bottle to its rightful owner and tossed the man on his right a curious look. "So you're thinking we can do this, Levi? Find someone to sing lead and hit the studio?"

Levi Levistan's broad shoulders rose and fell. "Why not? We've spent the last six years fucking about, and none of us are truly happy. And I know the director is keen for us to record the track. *If* we can find someone to replace Nick, that is." He shrugged again. "It worked for Alice in Chains. And Genesis."

"Genesis?" Noah shook his head. "If we're using Genesis as an example, *I* should become lead singer, and we all know I can't sing lead for shit. Backup vocals, sure. The odd solo line when Nick worked the stage, but lead, nope. Not if we want to keep our dignity intact."

Levi rolled his eyes and shoved a hank of dirty-blond hair from his eyes. "I'm not saying *you* should sing, Holden. I'm saying we go looking for new talent. Inject something different into the band. Surely we've had enough interaction with the music world to know what's out there?" He tossed a peanut at Samuel. "You've been touring with the Boss this last year. You must have scoped out his talent. What are his backup singers like?"

"All girls," Samuel answered. He threw the peanut back at Levi. It stuck in the bass player's hair, dangling by his temple like an oversized bead for a brief moment before Levi snared it in his long-fingered hand. "Besides, what are we going to call ourselves? We can't be Blackthorne without a Blackthorne in the band, can we? And we've only ever performed under that name."

Jax waved a hand. "Semantics."

Samuel cocked an eyebrow. "You want to call us Semantics? Really?"

Levi threw the peanut back at him. "Fucker."

Samuel grinned, his blue eyes dancing with sardonic mirth. "I'm only repeating what Jax over there is suggesting."

Noah chuckled. A wave of warmth swelled through him. It *had* been a long time since the band was altogether in one place, and he'd missed the sense of familiar mateship. They'd gone their separate ways the night of Nick's swan-song performance in Sydney over six years ago, only coming together as a group again for his wedding a year after that.

Samuel had toured with various solo performers, filling in whenever a guitarist who knew how to wring out a note was needed. Jaxon had written a tell-all biography that had stayed on the *New York Times* Best Seller list for three years and ended the persistent rumours about his sexuality once and for all. Levi had become Hollywood's latest musical darling, writing more than one award-winning soundtrack for equally award-winning films that somehow always involved an extreme level of angst and violence. And Noah…

Noah drew a slow breath, the warmth in his chest cooling. He let his gaze on his scotch shift out of focus. Well, Noah had had his heart ripped out. Figuratively speaking, of course. Eight years with the love of his life and she'd up and left him for their dog walker. Their dog walker, for fuck's sake. If it weren't so bloody painful, he'd be laughing himself silly right now.

"Oi!"

Something small and hard struck Noah on the nose and he blinked himself out of the bleak memory.

"Focus, Holden."

Drawing his attention to Samuel sitting opposite him, he frowned at the word. "I *am* focused. Levi's brought this opportunity to us, Jax's keen to give it a try and you're…what? Scared?"

Samuel scowled. "Blow me, Holden."

Noah shook his head, his smile pulling at his lips. "Samuel," he leant forward to rest his elbows on the table between them, "I think it's a bloody brilliant idea. *If* we can find the right man to fill Nick's shoes. If we can't, I'm not interested."

Levi slapped him on the back. "There you go! The drummer boy here makes three."

Samuel slumped low in his seat, his fingers plucking at invisible strings on the table, an unconscious action Noah knew only occurred when Samuel was seriously weighing up options.

"C'mon, Gibson." Jax threw another peanut at the lead guitarist, a cajoling grin on his surfer-tanned face. "It'll be fun. The money is freaking easy. No live shows, an air-conditioned recording studio, we get to see a movie before the rest of the population, and who knows, you may even add an Oscar to that embarrassingly large award collection you've got. This *is* a Nigel McQueen film after all, and Chris Huntley can't fart without being handed one gong or another at the moment. And Levi's been making a shitload of money writing music for Hollywood. With him bringing this opportunity to us, you could buy your own island."

Samuel slid his gaze to Noah. Of the four of them, Noah and Samuel were the closest. They'd been with Nick the longest, the first to join him after he signed his first recording contract. Samuel and Noah's names were on the back of every album Nick had released, from his first at the age of twenty-one to his last at thirty-seven. "So you really think this is a good idea, Holden?" he asked. "Re-forming? Finding a replacement for Nick? Pulling a Linkin Park and writing a song for a movie?"

Noah fixed him with an unwavering look, turning the questions over and over in his mind. Did he think it was a good idea? When Nick retired, Noah had removed himself from public life and focused on a sedentary existence with Heather. As focused as Noah could be, that was. All his life he'd struggled to keep his attention fixed on one thing. His parents had bought him a drum kit when he was eight in an effort to find him some kind of outlet for his almost manic energy. The trouble was, even now Noah had difficulty locking his attention on anything that wasn't music, that wasn't the beat. Hand-built yachts were never finished. Memoirs never completed. The interior of the house he'd shared with Heather for seven years never moved beyond three-quarters painted. The home theatre he'd begun to build had never had its first screening. Even their dog hadn't manage to snare his constant attention—hence the dog walker. Heather's last words to Noah as she left their partially painted home, with Maxie the mutt in tow, were four letters: A D H and D.

Playing for Nick Blackthorne had been the one true focus of Noah's life. The only time he'd felt truly centred. Calm. Which, for a drummer, was bloody ironic. But was that focus due to the magic and talent of Nick himself, or was it music in general? Did Noah want to risk the hideous discovery it wasn't the beat that had kept him sane, but the influence of a man no longer performing?

"Well?" Samuel asked, uncertainty clear in his blue eyes. "Do you?"

Noah drew a slow breath, his stare locked on the guitarist's. "I do."

"All right!" Levi shouted, drawing more than one curious glance from the bar's patrons. "It'll all up to you now, Samuel."

From the corner of Noah's eye, he noticed the cute waitress in the sexy hot pants cleaning the table beside them. She had bloody gorgeous legs. They went all the way up to her—

"Anyone spoken to Nick about this?" Samuel's question pulled Noah back to his fellow band members. The faint whiff of delicate perfume tickling his nose told him the waitress was still there.

Levi pulled a face. Jax rubbed at the back of his neck, his expression sheepish. "Err, nope."

Samuel rolled his eyes. "You don't think he'd like to know?"

With a snort, Noah dug into his hip pocket and withdrew his mobile phone. "What's the time in Australia, Levi?"

"Five p.m.," the bass guitarist provided. "Tomorrow."

"Still freaks me out how quick you are with shit like that, Levistan," Jax muttered.

Grinning, Noah scrolled through his contacts until he reached Nick's number. He lifted his attention to the men sitting around him. "Now, we're sure about this?" He focused on Samuel. "About finding a replacement for Nick for a new album?"

Jax and Levi turned their stares on the lead guitarist.

Samuel studied Noah. On stage and in interviews, Samuel had played the bad-boy brooding guitarist to Noah's slightly unhinged, manic drummer. The truth was, Samuel was more grounded and contemplative than the rest of them. Making a decision like this quickly wasn't part of his nature.

Noah raised an eyebrow at his friend, thumb paused over the call key. "Strings?"

With a grunt, Samuel threw up his hands and dropped back in his seat. "Fuck it. I'm in."

Noah hit dial. The phone rang three times. No one uttered a sound. Three sets of eyes watched him.

Halfway through the fourth ring, Nick answered. "Holden, you bloody bastard. How goes it, mate? To what do I owe the honour?"

Noah laughed, the sound of Nick's voice at once calming and exciting. "G'day, Nick. Doing well. You?"

"Not bad. Currently watching Lauren waddling around the kitchen making dinner. Pregnant women are bloody sexy, mate. Never knew that before now. How's Heather?"

Noah's gut clenched. He balled his free hand in a fist, glad it was resting on the top of his thigh under the table where his bandmates couldn't see it. "No more, I'm afraid. She finally got jack of me three months ago. We haven't gone public with it yet."

"Ah, fuck." Regret cut through Nick's curse. "I'm sorry, Noah. Shit, you should have called me. You okay?"

Noah drew a slow breath. "Yeah. Thinking of getting a cat. Or a fish."

Nick laughed, but Noah didn't miss the sorrow in the sound. Even in his wild groupie days, Nick had always believed in a happy-ever-after. No one in the band had realized how much until he'd found Lauren again and retired. He'd spent many a night when they were still touring in a drunken haze telling Noah how Noah had it all with Heather and to never fuck it up.

Despite all those inebriated words of advice and guidance however, Noah *had* fucked it up. Big time. By being—

"Where are you?" Nick's question yanked Noah back to the conversation. "In Australia? Wanna come spend the week with me and Lauren? We've got plenty of room, what with Josh living in Sydney and Aslin happily entrenched in L.A."

Noah chuckled. There was a part of him that wanted nothing more than to crash at Nick's house to lick his wounds. However, Noah doubted he could survive a day watching the man who'd once made women scream with lust the world over dote over the love of his life. "Thanks, mate, but I'm in New York," he answered, pulling a face at Jax who was waving his hand at him. No doubt in an effort to hurry him up. Behind the keyboard player, Miss Hot Pants took an order from two very gropey men in business suits. "With the guys."

"Really?" Delight filled Nick's voice. "Tell 'em I said g'day. What are they all up to?"

"Well, that's the reason for the call. Nigel McQueen wants us to record the end-credit title for Chris Huntley's next film, the sequel to *Dead Even*, and we're thinking of saying yes. On the proviso we can find someone to fill your bloody big shoes." He paused, picturing Nick's face. "What do you think?"

"Hell, yeah." Enthusiasm flooded the answer. "Go for it."

Noah's stomach tightened. "You sure?"

Nick laughed. "Holden, I'm not going to lie and say I don't miss performing at all. I do. And I miss performing with you guys a shitload. But I love my life now even more. I'm one hundred percent okay with you going for it. Replace me. Make fucking amazing music. Win awards. Lots of awards. Break chart records. Got a name for the new band yet?"

"Synergy."

The name fell from Noah's lips before he knew it was in his head. He blinked. A hot prickle razed over the back of his head.

"It's a good name," Nick said, the smile in his voice clear. "Helluva lot better than Blackthorne, that's for sure. Not quite so egocentric."

Noah laughed. "Yeah, you could say that."

Opposite him, Samuel frowned. "*Well?*" he mouthed.

Noah tried to think about what the other guys had heard. At this point, they'd still be in the dark.

"Synergy?" Jax muttered beside him. "What the fuck is he talking about?"

Samuel shrugged.

"If it's a band name," Levi commented, popping a shelled peanut into his mouth, "it's a truck load better than Semantics."

Jax tossed a coaster at him, the square piece of cardboard flinging past Noah's face like a ninja star. "Fuck you, Levi."

Nick's laughter slipped through the connection. "And on that note, Holden, I'm leaving you to deal with them. There's a plate of toasted-cheese sandwiches waiting for me and my stomach is growling. Say g'day to the guys for me."

"Shall do, mate." For some reason, Noah let his stare wander to the waitress in the hot pants, now cleaning a table to his right. Her hair was the colour of lush sable. Her creamy skin seemed to almost glow in the bar's muted lights. She was nothing like Heather, who was a sun-bronzed Californian-blonde bombshell.

The waitress straightened, and Noah's heart slammed into his throat as her brilliant-blue eyes met his. Christ, she was beautiful.

"Oh, and Noah?"

"Yeah?"

"Look after your heart, okay?"

"I will," he said into the phone, holding the woman's stare for a heartbeat. And then she turned away, moving to the next table to smile at the three men dressed like Wall Street wannabes giving her their orders.

He disconnected, his head fuzzy. He'd never seen eyes so blue. Deep and clear and direct. Like she'd pinned his soul with just one glance. Damn, maybe he needed to order another drink? Why hadn't she taken their orders in the first place? Had she been here when he first arrived? Could he convince the guys to move tables? Could he—

"Earth to Holden." A sharp clicking noise sounded near his ear. "Earth to Holden. What did he say?"

Noah blinked, shaking the haze from his head. He frowned

at the three men staring at him. "What did who say? Did you guys see the—"

"Nick," Samuel burst out, almost throwing himself forward. He fixed Noah with an unwavering focus. "What did Nick say?"

Noah shifted on his seat enough to shove his iPhone back into his hip pocket. His gaze flicked toward the waitress again, almost of its own free will. Her ponytail hung over her shoulder, long and straight and thick. If he pressed his face to it, what would it smell like?

Returning his attention to his fellow musicians, he settled himself once again in his seat. "Before I tell you, has anyone thought to talk to Roger about this?"

All three men blinked.

Noah snorted. He may have ADHD, but at least he kept his business head on his shoulders when needed. It seemed none of the others had thought to contact their ex-manager.

Jax opened his mouth and shut it again. Levi fidgeted in his chair. Roger Daltry hadn't exactly gotten along with any of them in their touring days. He had been a very good manager, had refused to take any of their shit and kept them on task when their wild parties had threatened to undo them, but he'd never hidden his dislike for their lifestyle. It didn't surprise Noah at all no one had thought to call him.

With a wry chuckle, he waved a hand at them. "Don't worry about it, I'll call him tomorrow."

Levi straightened a little. "So Nick said he didn't mind?"

Noah nodded. "He told us to go—"

A pair of perfect breasts swung directly in front of his face, encased in snug red satin. He sat back, his gaze jerking up to find a platinum-blonde woman smiling down at him. "Sorry," she said, barely moving her boob away from his face. "I was just reaching for some coasters."

He frowned.

Behind the woman, Jax laughed.

"You're Nick Blackthorne's band." The blonde drew herself upright, a deliberately slow shift in position designed to highlight just how incredible her body and boobs were. Noah couldn't help but notice Samuel was taking great interest. "Where's Nick right now? Is he with you?"

"Blackthorne's in Australia," Samuel answered. He turned a sultry scowl on the blonde. "With his wife."

The woman leant forward and plucked a peanut from the bowl in the middle of the table, affording Samuel a generous view of her more-than-generous cleavage. "So what's his band doing here?"

Noah bit back a low chuckle at Jax's grin. "Partying," the keyboardist answered. "Wanna join us?"

The blonde traced her fingers over Noah's shoulder, her blue eyes gleaming with open hunger as she moved her gaze over all four of them. "I'd love to."

Noah's gut clenched. He'd participated in more than one gangbang with a groupie since the band had come together almost two decades ago. Heather had been the last. He'd woken up beside her the next morning—the rest of the band long gone—and never slept with another woman again.

Taking in the blonde's lush breasts, tiny waist and long legs, he wondered if a group fuck was exactly what he needed to find his centre once more.

Or maybe it was performing with the band?

Or maybe nothing will help. Maybe you need to mainline Valium or Ritalin or some such shit until you're a comatose—

"Give us a sec, love," he said to the woman, killing the bleak thought. "We've got something to finish first."

Samuel grunted and Jax chuckled. Levi snared a handful of peanuts, his expression ambiguous.

The blonde pursed her glossed lips, her gaze roaming Noah's face. "Don't take too long, 'kay? I promise I'll blow your world." She lowered her lips to his ear, her breath warm on his flesh. "I have no inhibitions. I'll let you do whatever you want to me."

Across the table, Jax groaned.

She flicked her hot tongue at Noah's ear and then straightened. Her hips swayed with provocative rhythm as she walked away.

"I don't know if you plan on tapping that, Holden, but I sure as shit do."

Noah rolled his eyes at Jax's enthusiastic declaration. "I don't doubt it, mate."

"Me too," Samuel added. He shifted on his seat, his stare tracking the blonde's path to the bar. "Three or four times, in fact. But Holden's right. We need to decide if we're doing this Synergy thing."

Noah cocked an eyebrow at him. Samuel snorted in return, the side of his mouth pulling in a small smile. "It's a good name. Two or more forces interacting in such a way their combined effect is greater than the sum of their individual effort. Suits us."

A peanut struck Samuel in the temple. "Thank you, Mr. Dictionary," Jax laughed.

Samuel glowered, although Noah couldn't miss the fact his smile grew. "Shut the fuck up, Jax." He turned back to Noah. "So, what did Nick say?"

Noah slid his gaze to the waitress in the hot pants a few feet away before returning it to his fellow band members. He pulled a deep, slow breath and then leant forward, retrieved his scotch from the table and held it aloft. "Gentlemen, let's find ourselves a new front man."

"To Synergy," Levi murmured, tapping his beer to Noah's glass, his smile relaxed.

Jax grinned, his glass meeting Noah's and Levi's above the table. "To rocking out with our cocks out."

Samuel laughed, clinking his bourbon against their glasses. "Hell yeah."

Noah smiled. He felt calmer already. More focused. Being a rock star truly was the best job in the world.

###

Being a waitress was the worst job in the world.

Okay, that wasn't true. There were worst jobs. Pepper Kerrigan knew that. Inspector of the incoming pipes at a sewage plant would be worse. Cleaning up the horse poo at those medieval dinner shows would be worse. Handing out flyers for discount pork products at a vegan convention would be the pits. But what she was doing right now, waitressing at a bar in New York, was pretty depressing. Especially given she'd dreamed of so much more.

Of course, dreaming was easy. Almost as easy as failing. And Pepper had made a career out of failing. If she was good at one thing, it was failing. At least that's what her mother told her. Right up until the time Lulu Kerrigan walked out on her family, leaving Pepper to be raised by her dad. Who, according to her mom, wasn't good for anything either except "writing shit about shit".

Pepper *was* good at more than failing. She knew that. For one, she had a knack for organizing. But failing was easier. And when you grew up being told you were a failure by your mom, you reached a point where you just accepted that was the case. When you were chronically shy like Pepper was, failure was a lovely safety blanket. One you could wrap yourself up nice and tight in. It had driven Pepper's extrovert mother crazy. Turned her resentful. Or maybe the resentment had come from the fact Pepper got the *shit* her dad wrote about and could talk for hours on end about it. But only to Paul Kerrigan. Whenever someone else was around, Pepper clammed up. Withdrew.

Failed.

Lulu Kerrigan's parting advice to her sixteen-year-old daughter was to aim low. "'Cause honey, you're never going to hit high."

So here Pepper was, working tables in a noisy New York

bar where the customers didn't pay much attention to her unless it was to feel her up. All in all, not the future she'd imagined for herself as a young girl.

But her head was still crammed full of the *shit* her dad wrote about, and her heart ached with a dream she wanted more than anything, and since Nick Blackthorne's old band entered the place, the tickle of a plan had begun to form in her soul.

Her soul refused to believe she was a failure, and right now it was telling her to do something she'd never, ever done before.

Be courageous.

She watched the man with the choppy brown hair holding his half-empty scotch high. Noah Holden was the best drummer in the world. This was an indisputable fact. Music magazines and websites proclaimed it often. Her father had mentioned the fact more than once in more than one article on Nick Blackthorne and his band. Her dad had sat her down when she was twelve and made her listen to Holden's various solos and fills, commenting often how the Australian had a way with ghost notes, time twists and technically demanding grooves. What her dad had never mentioned was how goddamn sexy the drummer was.

Pepper studied his profile even as she wiped a recently vacated table clean, the generous tip deposited safely in her apron's pocket. No one on the planet could ever say Noah Holden was ugly, but holy smack, in person he was gorgeous.

His shoulders were broad and exquisitely muscled, no doubt from years of playing the drums. His honey-brown hair spiked up around his head in a sexy mess Pepper knew a lot of men paid a fortune to emulate. She'd worked as a receptionist in an exclusive men's-only hair saloon for a while, and more than one wannabe had come in with an image of Noah Holden clutched in their optimistic hands.

Ice-blue eyes twinkled with an energy almost too charged for one man. Thick black lashes framed their electrifying depths, longer than a man's lashes had any right being. When he'd looked at her earlier, when their eyes had connected across the room, her knees had almost buckled beneath her and she'd needed to swallow her gasp before it could escape her.

But it was his lips her stare kept falling to. They were friendly. Welcoming. His smile said, "Let's do it." Pepper didn't know what *it* was, but there was no dismissal in his smile. It made her heart beat faster. And her soul whisper with encouraged possibilities.

It helped that she'd overheard what the band was discussing.

A new singer.

They were looking for a new singer. Someone to replace Nick Blackthorne.

Pepper's father would scoff at that idea. In fact, Pepper suspected the entire music-loving world would scoff at that idea. But she didn't.

Because of the whisper in her soul and the dream in her heart.

She'd managed an indie grunge-rock band for a while, and even as she'd organized their gig schedule, recording sessions and media appearances, she'd itched to do something else with them. Something they'd all laughed at when she'd asked.

Taking her time cleaning down the table, she watched Nick Blackthorne's band—one of the most successful on the planet —complete their toast.

Her chest grew tight.

She didn't think she'd have much time to act. The blonde woman who'd so blatantly offered herself to them earlier was now watching them like a hawk, predatory lust turning her blue eyes hard. Aggressive.

Calculating groupie eyes, Pepper's dad had called them. The eyes of a woman who planned to score herself a famous fuck, maybe even a famous offspring to snare a famous paternity payment.

The blonde wasn't the only one though. The moment word had gotten out Nick Blackthorne's band was in Rupert's Bar, it had begun filling with women poured into tight dresses. Women who watched the four men like leopards waiting for the optimal time to attack.

The blonde had been but the first to make a move.

Pepper heard more than one competitor call the woman a skanky bitch. Pepper wanted to point out just how revealing the speaker's neckline was, and how high the hemline of her dress.

She didn't, of course. That would mean opening her mouth and drawing attention to herself. She didn't do that.

And yet, she was running out of time to do that very thing.

What if the band left before she found the courage to put her plan into play?

What if—

Samuel Gibson and Jaxon Campbell stood.

As did Levi Levistan.

Pepper's stomach dropped. "Oh no," she whispered.

Like a blur in skin-tight red satin, the blonde moved from the bar, pressing her voluptuous curves to Samuel's side. The lead guitarist smoothed his long-fingered hand over the woman's ass as words Pepper couldn't hear moved his lips. Jaxon threw a handful of bills onto the table, his smile wide, and then, with a wink at Noah, the three turned and walked away, the blonde flattened so close to Samuel's side Pepper wondered how she managed to walk.

Movement from the corner of Pepper's eye caught her attention. She froze, watching as two women dressed in body-hugging black leather damn near slithered over to the remaining band members. One woman stroked her hands up Noah's muscular arm. The other trailed her fingers over Levi's hip, skimming the sizeable bulge of his groin with black-polished nails.

Pepper's heart smashed into her throat. She stared at the spectacle, cursing herself.

She'd failed. Again.

All she'd needed to do was speak to the band before they left. Easy, especially when the table they sat at was next to her section. But no, she'd held back, taken too long. And now, Noah and Levi were—

The women in black leather walked away from the drummer and keyboard player, disappointed scowls on their immaculately made-up, sultry faces.

Pepper's breath caught.

She snapped her stare back to the musicians.

Noah rose to his feet, offering his hand to Levi.

They shook hands and then hugged. Levi slapped Noah on the back with a solid thump before leaving the table, dark sunglasses covering his eyes as he made his way toward the exit.

At least, Pepper assumed he was heading for the exit. She couldn't tear her stare from Noah Holden.

He'd always been her favourite of the band. While her friends had creamed their panties over Nick or Samuel, she'd imagined what it would be like to meet the drummer. To stand close to him and feel his manic energy radiate from him as he awoke the throb in her very core. He was almost forty, eleven years older than her, but that didn't make him any less sexy. Yet it wasn't the desire to sleep with him that made her stomach knot and her mouth dry now. It was…

No pressure, no diamonds, chickpea.

Her father's words whispered at the edges of her self-doubt.

She studied the drummer, the plan in her soul fed by the dream in her heart. A dream she'd held since the very first time she'd ever watched Nick Blackthorne perform live, ten years ago.

Driving her nails into her palms, Pepper drew a deep, slow breath, counted to ten and crossed to the lone member of the band.

"Hi, Mr. Holden," she said, holding out her hand. God, she hoped it wasn't sweaty.

Arctic-ice-blue eyes swung up to her, and for a split second Pepper almost turned and fled.

Almost.

And then Noah Holden smiled, that let's-do-it smile that gave her hope, and Pepper lowered herself into the chair beside him, resting her elbows on her knees and giving him her own smile back. "I have a proposition for you."

ALSO BY LEXXIE COUPER...

The Always Series

Unconditional
Unforgettable
Undeniable

The Outback Skies Series

Bound to You
Breathless for You
Burn for You
Bare for You
Better with You

The Heart of Fame Series

Love's Rhythm
Muscle for Hire
Guarded Desires
Steady Beat
Lead Me On
Blame it on the Bass
Getting Played
Blackthorne

www.ingramcontent.com/pod-product-compliance
Lightning Source LLC
Chambersburg PA
CBHW032009050726